WILD SCOTTISH CHARM

THE ENCHANTED HIGHLANDS
BOOK EIGHT

TRICIA O'MALLEY

LOVEWRITE PUBLISHING

"When the roots are deep, there is no reason to fear the wind."- African Proverb

GLOSSARY OF SCOTTISH WORDS/SLANG

- Bloody – a word used to add emphasis; expletive
- Bonnie – pretty
- Hen – woman, female
- "It's a dreich day" – cold; damp; miserable
- Lorry – work truck
- Luch - Celtic version of Luke
- Och – used to express many emotions, typically surprise, regret, or disbelief
- Scran – food
- Shoogly – unsteady; wobbly
- Tatties – potatoes
- Tetchy – crabby, cranky, moody
- Tea – in Scotland, having tea is often used to refer to the dinnertime meal
- Wee – small, little
- Wheesht (haud your wheesht) – be quiet, hush, shut up

CHAPTER ONE

Faelan

I was no stranger to new towns.

I had unpacked my things in more villages than I cared to count—most of them quaint, remote, and filled with locals who squinted at outsiders as if deciding whether they were worthy of their trust. But Loren Brae was different. Already, I'd been welcomed, and was even on my way to making a few new friends, which made me wonder just what, exactly, was going on in this town.

For one, the last vet had fled.

People in Loren Brae didn't talk about it directly, but I'd overheard enough murmurs while ordering a blackberry scone from the bakery that morning to piece together the general story. Dr. MacAllister had barely handed the keys off to me before he'd disappeared. Not just from the practice, but from the town as well. No warning, no goodbyes.

And the way people talked about it—with uneasy glances and hushed voices—told me it wasn't because of an overdue tax bill or scandalous affair.

Something strange had sent him running.

Which was why I was standing outside the empty clinic, a simple stone building tucked on the shores of Loch Mirren, wondering what I'd gotten myself into. It wasn't in my nature to borrow trouble, instead I typically ran from it as much as I could. But I'd barely had one day with the prior vet to go over any outstanding files and patients before he'd hightailed it from town. Unease prickled, and I glanced behind me at the loch, where the waves tumbled across the surface, tipping over into white caps.

It had been a week since Dr. MacAllister's departure, and I'd hit the ground running. The office itself was no more in order than the day I'd stepped through the door, thinking I'd have time for an easy transition as I was introduced to the people of Loren Brae. Instead, I'd been left with a stack of files, no receptionist or assistant, and a flood of patients coming through my door.

Today I'd come downstairs early, hoping to get a handle on the medicine inventory so I could place an order if needed. It seemed the only way to get this office into shape was if I did it myself while the clinic was closed. The practice had come with a small flat above, with a separate entrance, and I'd been grateful for the package deal. This was my first time officially owning my own practice, and for the thousandth time, I hoped I hadn't made a mistake in moving to Loren Brae.

"All right, then," I muttered, fishing the keys from my

pocket and pushing the door open. "Let's get your life sorted."

The scent of old wood, herbs, and just a whisper of something sharp and metallic greeted me. The place was cozy—a reception desk covered in stray dog hairs, a small exam room with an oak table, a surgery and recovery room, and a large storage closet filled with supplies.

And curled up on the counter, watching me with unsettling intelligence, was a fox.

I frowned. "Now how did you get in here?"

The fox's ears twitched, its golden eyes locking on mine. Then, with an almost lazy motion, it lifted its head and let out a soft chuff—less a warning, more a cry for help.

A chill ran up my spine. It wasn't the first time a creature had looked at me like that.

I set my bag down and stepped closer. "You're hurt, aren't you?"

The fox shifted slightly, and that's when I saw its front leg, tucked awkwardly beneath its body. I didn't need an exam to tell it was broken.

But I could mend it.

I glanced at the front window, making sure no one was watching from the street. Being a newcomer in a small town meant all eyes were on you, and I'd learned long ago to try to fly under the radar as much as possible.

I leaned forward, reaching out a hand, slow and steady. "I won't hurt you."

The fox didn't move at first. Then, as if sensing the truth in my words, it exhaled—a small, weary sigh—and let me touch its injured leg.

I brushed my fingers over the break, a breath catching in

my throat as the fox's pain flickered through me. Magick unfurled beneath my fingertips, warm and soft, a golden thread through the air.

Bones whispered their alignment, sinew stitched itself back together, and beneath it all, the fox's heartbeat slowed, its pain easing. I exhaled, and the world settled.

The fox stretched its leg, testing the weight. Then, just to be dramatic, it hopped onto the reception desk and flopped down, tail flicking over the paperwork like it owned the place.

I winced. "Sure, go ahead, make yourself at home."

The fox yawned, utterly unbothered, and I just shook my head as I found a bowl to fill with water and slid it in front of him on the desk. After he drank, he lifted his head and met my eyes.

Understanding passed between us.

"I see you, Faelan."

My eyebrows winged up as I studied the fox, tilting my head. Eriska, my mother, who'd insisted I call her by her first name as witchy women should, had always told me my familiar would find me. But none had yet joined me, even though Eriska had foreshadowed it would happen one day in a town most powerful.

It seemed Loren Brae had its own secrets, just like I did.

"And I see you, wee one. Do you have a name?" I asked, happiness lighting me up. I'd finally found my familiar.

"Gloam."

"Gloam. As in the gloaming?" I tilted my head to study his eyes—the color of whisky in firelight—and to examine his golden russet coat for any further injuries. The gloaming was a time of day in Scotland when the day shifted to night

4

and gilded light brushed across the land. The fox resembled this light, and I could picture him shimmering through the twilight as he slipped through the forest.

"Aye. It's nice to finally meet you, Faelan."

"Och, so you *are* mine." I lifted a hand and waited until Gloam bobbed his head once, before reaching over to scratch behind his ears. "I must say, Gloam, you're an exceptionally handsome fellow."

"I know."

Gloam's eyes slitted closed, and his mouth opened in a smile as I continued to scratch. I chuckled at his words. I could hear him perfectly in my mind, as though I had my Sony Earbuds in, and his voice sounded like he was permanently amused.

"Cocky as a wee dug with two tails, are ye now?" I laughed as Gloam opened his mouth and made a soft huffing sound, like he was chuckling at me, and I ran my hands over his sides. "Is there any other place you're sore, my wee friend? I'm worried for you."

"It's just my leg. A trap."

"Oh no." I sighed. He'd been lucky with just the broken bone then. Traps could also rip through ligaments or tear flesh, so I was pleased he'd only snuck away with a break. Nevertheless, I wanted to keep him close for monitoring. Today was Sunday, and I hadn't planned to open the clinic today, because I needed at least one day to actually settle into my flat upstairs, as well as make some sense of the office. Still, being interrupted by an emergency call wasn't uncommon, and it would seem odd to anyone stopping by to spot a fox on my desk. "That's such a shame, Gloam. That must have been quite scary. I'm glad you managed to get yourself here for help. Listen, I had planned to organize down here, but I'm worried someone may see you. Want to come upstairs with me and I'll unpack a bit and you can have a wee rest while I do so? I just want to make sure you're in tip-top shape before you go back outside."

"I'm quite tired. I could use the rest."

"I don't blame you. We'll get you sorted out." I scooped him up, and he burrowed into my arms, resting his head on my shoulder. For a moment, I just held him, shocked at the realization of just how much I needed a hug. Likely from a human, but this one still filled me with an overwhelming sense of comfort. His fur was so soft, it was like cuddling a real-life stuffed animal. Some of the tension I'd carried with me since moving here eased as I locked up and headed to the flat. Nudging the door open with my shoulder, I carried Gloam inside my new home. *Our* new home, I supposed, if the fox wanted to stay here with me. From what I knew about familiars, they liked to choose their domain.

The flat wasn't much, a simple one-bedroom, with the main door opening to a galley kitchen and lounge area and a second door that led to a bedroom with an en suite bathroom. But it had a cozy couch, and two large windows that overlooked the stunning waters of Loch Mirren. Already I could see myself curled up by those windows, watching the light play across the water, while reading my favorite romantasy novels with candles lit. I didn't need much, as I was used to moving, but still I liked to make each new spot my home in my own way. I paused as I realized that this time, my stay would be different. I owned the place and could decorate how I wished. The thought intrigued me, as I'd been so good about not acquiring anything that I couldn't pack up and easily leave with. Looking around, I realized just how sparse it was in here.

The apartment had come furnished with a simple loveseat, a small table with two chairs, a bed, and a chest of drawers. Both rooms had small closets, as well, but I'd yet to do much digging. Now, I carried Gloam to the couch and settled him gently on the soft cushions.

"How's that? Comfy?"

"Aye, that'll do me just fine."

"That's grand then. I'll just try to make sense of my life here, while you rest. Then we can have ourselves a wee chat, all right?"

Gloam just closed his eyes, and I took that as agreement. I had about a million questions for my wee familiar, but since I had no idea just how long he'd been injured, it was more important that he rest for now and regain his strength. Humming softly to myself, I crossed the room and put the kettle on and then moved to the first box in the middle of the floor.

Pausing, I brought a hand to my heart and took a deep breath, and then another. Focusing on a spot outside the window, I forced Gloam's pain from my body and exhaled a smokey dark cloud that writhed in the air before disappearing out the window. Healing always taxed me, though I'd grown strong with it over the years, but I always needed to expel the pain I took in. I'd need to gulp about a pot of my rejuvenating tea before I'd feel normal again.

Picking up the scissors, I slit the tape on the top box. Two suitcases and four boxes. The entirety of my personal and professional belongings. At least it made it easy to move on, as I'd done over a dozen times in the last seven years. I'd forced myself to be sentimental over very few things in my life, and as I slit the first box open, my gaze moved to one of those items.

A framed photo of me and my mother, Eriska, taken about ten years ago. We sat on the grass, a field of wild-flowers haloing our heads, a picnic spread before us. It had been a rare day of sunshine and laughter, neither of us talking of tomorrows, both knowing fate was unavoidable. She'd always been destined to leave me, as it was written in the stars. Or so she'd told me again and again, preparing me for the day she'd known was coming since she'd had a vision when I was just four years old.

It would have been easier if it had been an illness to take her, as maybe I would have been able to help—to do some-thing, *anything* at all—but instead it had been a patch of black ice and an elderly driver that had ended her life. And even though she'd prepared me for it, promising me our time together was short, her absence took up more space than her presence had.

The kettle clicked off, shaking me from my despon-dency, and I stood with the picture in hand. Moving across the room, I put the frame on the windowsill, where I could see it and speak to her when I looked out over the loch.

Gloam shifted, letting out a soft laughing sound in his sleep, and I pressed my lips together. I'd never had a pet before, though I'd taken in plenty of strays and nursed them back to health. I'd never wanted to get too attached, since I'd always known that the things you loved got taken from you.

It made moving on easier.

And letting go almost impossible.

A sharp hammering of knocks startled me, and Gloam popped awake with a startled yip. A doorbell rang somewhere in the flat, connected to the vet's office below, and I moved to the window to peer down at the front door of the clinic.

A man stood there, cradling a dog, his shirt covered in blood, his face ravaged with grief.

So much for my day off.

"Stay here. This might take a while."

"Be well, Faelan of the flowers."

I paused at the door, shooting a surprised glance over my shoulder at Gloam. How had he known my mother used to call me that? Still, I had no time to delve deeper, as I raced down the stairs to the panicked man pacing out front.

One look at his face, and I knew we didn't have much time.

Or maybe it was already too late.

CHAPTER TWO

FAELAN

"What happened?" I was already unlocking the door and pushing inside, the man at my heels.

"Car hit him. Faint but steady pulse, wound on his hind quarters near his femoral artery."

At his clipped words, I glanced over my shoulder, and even though his eyes held worlds of pain, his movements and words were efficient.

He must have medical training.

In most emergency situations, my clients would be in full panic, unable to respond clearly or in hysterics, and even though I could tell this man was emotionally invested in the dog hanging limply in his arms, he was holding it together. Which I appreciated, seeing I didn't have an assistant to run interference with a distraught pet owner. Even as he laid his dog down on the table, I was reaching for my stethoscope to confirm his words about the pulse. Shifting through the soft fur at the dog's chest, I was relieved to find it was still alive.

"Name?"

"Luch. Oh, sorry. Shite. Not me. His name is Oban." The man cleared his throat even as he continued to maintain pressure on the wound on Oban's hindquarters. "Oban is where I found him."

I slid a hand under Oban's gums to find them leaning more to gray-blue than pink, and I knew I had very little time to help. Needing a distraction for Luch, I tapped his hands.

"Have you had any medical training, Luch?" I winced when Luch removed his hands and I saw the rip in Oban's flesh.

"Aye." The word held enough grief to let me know he understood just how close we were to losing Oban. Determination fired. I had a soft spot for those in the medical profession, knowing how difficult it was to care for humans and animals, day in and day out, often with little thanks for the long hours and emotional toll.

"Great. There's a storeroom at the back of the clinic. Let's get Oban on an IV to provide some pain relief." I was still inventorying the supplies and hoped we had enough of what we needed. *Or enough to keep Luch busy until I healed as much of Oban as I could without causing suspicion.* "See if there's any methadone or medetomidine. Bandages. Saline. If you can gather that, I'll get this cleaned up and take a closer look," I said, praying he'd take enough time to start my healing and do what I could before he came back.

I was proud of my gift, but it wasn't something I could

openly share with others. My mother had dragged me out of more than one town in the middle of the night, with no chance to say goodbye to any friends I'd managed to make. By the time I was a teenager, I'd given up trying to meet new people and instead had buried my head in books, filling my time with making friends with animals. They never judged me. It was the honor of my life to be able to help them in my profession.

The minute Luch left the room, I closed my eyes and pulled the pain from Oban straight into me, without even taking the time to ground myself. There was no time. I found his life cord, his soul balancing precariously on the edge between here and the afterlife, and I reached for it gently, winding it around my finger as I would a ribbon, and tugged him delicately back from the veil. On the way, I knit a broken femur back together and closed enough of the rip in his skin to stem the flow of blood.

The wound had missed the femoral artery by a hair's width, and I steadied my breath as I took Oban's pain. Luckily, I couldn't find any internal bleeding, and he must have been running at a fast pace when the car caught the corner of his body.

"I've got most of it," Luch called from the storage room, "but I can't find a suture kit."

"I've got one here." Blinking back to the room, I shuddered in a breath, and then another, knowing I'd pay for taking Oban's pain and not releasing it. I'd do it later, but not before it left its mark. Usually in large unsightly bruises of some sort, but I didn't mind. Not if it meant I could save another life.

Oban shifted on the table when Luch bounded back in,

his arms full of supplies, which he promptly dropped on the table when Oban tried to get up.

"Hey, buddy. No, just lie there." Luch's eyes met mine when Oban let out a soft whimper, full of pain.

"Let's get the pain meds in him and start sedation so I can stitch this up."

"Do we need to sedate him?" Luch asked, hooking up the saline IV bag. He clearly knew what he was doing, so I took his question seriously.

"I wouldn't typically suture a patient with this type of injury while awake, largely because I don't enjoy getting bitten. Do you know if he'll stay still? Can you restrain him?"

"I can. I'd like to avoid sedation if possible." Luch crouched at Oban's head, and the dog opened his eyes and gingerly swiped his tongue across Luch's cheek. "Hey, bud. I need you to do me a favor."

Luch's voice dropped, and I cleaned the wound area while he murmured to Oban. He was a Scottish Terrier, a traditional black "Scottie" dog, which were known to be fiercely loyal. Grateful to see that my healing had done most of the work and there wouldn't be much need for suturing, I threaded a needle and waited.

"Go ahead." I snuck a quick glance at Luch to see him holding Oban's head and then I moved quickly. There was no point in drawing this out longer. Oban was slowly healing. Working fast, I stitched the deeper layer with a dissolvable suture, before quickly closing the rip in the skin. Oban had been lucky the car hadn't nicked his artery, or he might not have made it here in time.

"There, done." Stepping back, I let out a shaky breath. I

hadn't yet eaten today, and the pain of Oban's wounds roiled around inside me, making me slightly dizzy. Two healings in a day with little rest and no food were pushing me into the danger zone.

"What about internal bleeding? X-rays? His back leg was broken." Oban writhed on the table, shaking his head from Luch's grip, and rolled to his feet. Straightening, Luch put a hand to Oban's side to steady him, the other still holding the unused saline drip. "What the ..."

"He must have just been in shock." It was a line I'd used many times to explain away the unexplainable. Surprisingly it worked well enough. Until it didn't, that is, and then I'd be packing my bags and be on my way. But not this time. No, I was determined to stick this one out. I'd heard enough about Loren Brae to know they had some sort of magickal trouble going on here, which meant nobody would have time to look too closely at the vet who had a high success rate with healing animals in need.

"That's not possible. His leg was broken. I'm certain of it."

Only then did I really look at Luch. I'd noticed him, of course, objectively as a human holding a dog in need, but now I took the time to genuinely assess him.

He was big.

Big in the way of men who took up space in the room, like all the air molecules shifted and rearranged around him as though they needed to make space for his presence. An undercurrent of ... something ... rippled down my spine and I shifted on my feet, unsure if I should inch closer to the door or not. There was nothing outward to suggest he was dangerous, aside from his broad shoulders and thick arms, but there was something about his tawny green eyes, just glinting to gold, that seemed to see too clearly.

I didn't like it.

I didn't like it at all.

I hadn't even unpacked my bags yet, but I wasn't going to let this man, whose dog I'd just saved, cast suspicion on my healing methods.

"When animals are in shock, or unconscious, their bodies hang limp. Clearly Oban means a lot to you, and you were panicked. I'm a doctor, Luch. I know what I'm doing. Now, you're welcome to take him home as he'll rest easier in a comfortable space he knows. Monitor his water intake and feed him in small bits to start. If he still seems to be in pain or exceptionally lethargic tomorrow, bring him back in. That'll be fifty quid for the sutures." I just named a quick price since I had no idea what the last vet had used as a pricing structure.

Luch looked from me to where Oban sat on the table, his eyes halfway open as he rested from his recovery. The dog would sleep for ten hours and then hopefully be right as rain.

"Oh, and don't let him lick the sutures. Do you have something you can use as a protective collar? I didn't see any when I looked through the storage, but I'm still getting myself sorted here."

Luch ran a hand through his hair, so dark it was almost midnight black, his expression unreadable. He had the looks of a warrior of olden ages, broad shoulders, a sharply angled jaw, and a fierce countenance that made me want to usher him out of the door as fast as I could.

"What happened to the last vet?" Luch stroked Oban's ears, ignoring my attempt to get him on his way.

I'm not going to be able to stay upright for much longer.

I began to clean up, hoping he'd take the hint to leave, as a wave of exhaustion made my arms tremble. Moving to the sink, I stripped my gloves off and tossed them in the bin and then washed my hands vigorously.

"Och, I can't really say. He was in a rush to go, and though I'd planned to take over in a few months, he moved the date up. I'm making it work, but I haven't had the transition time I'd hoped. Hit the ground running as soon as I got here." I glanced over my shoulder as I dried my hands. Luch still just stood there, petting Oban, and I leaned back against the sink, towel in hands.

"That's a bit odd, don't you think?"

"Don't know. Didn't know the man all that well." I needed Luch to move on. "Right. Oban's looking well enough, and I think it's best you get him home now. He'll be needing a good long rest after his adventure today. Today's my day off, and I dearly need to use this time to unpack and get my things sorted."

"Right. Sorry about that. We'll just be off then." Luch reached in his back pocket and pulled out his wallet, counting out fifty pounds, before he handed it over to me.

A spark leapt between our hands when we touched.

Bloody hell. What was that?

Luch stared down at our joined hands and then raised his eyes slowly to mine. I swallowed, nerves kicking low in my stomach, as my entire body prickled with awareness. Be it lust or danger, I couldn't quite tell, but either way, how he looked at me seemed to foreshadow an ominous outcome.

"What did you say your name was?" Luch asked, still holding my hand. I pulled it back, breaking contact, and I would have stepped away had my back not been to the sink. Instead, I raised my chin ever so slightly, a challenge.

"I didn't. But my name is Dr. Faelan Fletcher." I emphasized the word "doctor." Not only had I worked hard for my credentials, but I found the title often put overbearing men in their place. I didn't add any pleasantries about it being nice to meet him. Because I wasn't entirely sure that it was.

Oban made a soft sound, a huff of sorts, and Luch snapped to attention, turning to pick up his dog. Even though I found this man to be highly intimidating, my heart still softened just the tiniest bit. There was just something about a strong man cradling a dog that made my insides go warm and gooey. It certainly didn't hurt when said strong man was also wickedly handsome with a face straight out of a warrior movie. Not that I was paying much attention, because I was fairly certain I'd collapse into a chair if Luch didn't leave my clinic immediately.

"The practice is closed today. But if Oban runs into any trouble, or if you have any questions, feel free to contact me." Leaving the exam room, I walked to the waiting room where I'd put a box with my cards on the front desk. Since I moved on to new towns so often, it only had my email and phone number as contact information, and no clinic name or address. I handed Luch a card and then paused to pat Oban's head. The dog wriggled in Luch's arms, lunging forward, and I laughed as he licked my face effusively.

"You're very welcome, good sir." I knew he was thanking me. My patients always knew when I used my power to heal them, something I never took for granted. *Such an amazing gift, even though I could never openly share it.* Animals were far more in tune with the magickal world than humans ever were. And I definitely found them easier to connect with than humans, which was a bonus given my "line of work" so to speak.

"Och, I should be thanking you as well." For the first time, Luch's hard expression dropped, and when he looked down at Oban, a smile wreathed his face.

It was a lightning flash in stormy clouds, lighting his entire face, and my breath caught.

Aye, this man could be dangerous in more ways than one.

"Nae bother. Happy to help." *Please leave. Please just go.* For some reason, the more Luch lingered, the more uneasy I became. "Hope your day goes better, Luch."

"It's Dr. Carmichael, actually." Luch held my gaze over Oban's head. "*Dr.* Luch Carmichael. I'm really impressed with your work here today, Dr. Fletcher. I know how hard it can be to treat accident wounds. It's a miracle, really, that Oban wasn't more injured. Isn't it?"

Bloody hell, the man was a doctor. I knew he'd had some medical training, but this was my worst nightmare.

"I can't say. I didn't see the accident. How was it he got hit by the car again?"

My shot hit home. Luch winced, and his brows drew together as he looked back down at Oban.

"I didn't close the gate. It's my fault my wee pal got hurt."

"It's a tough lesson, but you're certainly lucky it wasn't

worse." *Please leave.* The pain from healing Oban roiled around inside me, and I needed my tea, some food, and a nap ... *now.*

"Give him lots of love today," I said, letting out a shaky sigh of relief when Luch finally left the practice. Quickly locking the door, I moved past where Luch stood in front of the practice and was almost around the building to the stairs to my flat when his words followed me.

"I'll be certain to do so. Thanks for all your ... *work*, Dr. Fletcher."

Bloody hell. Was I just super sensitive because of my exhaustion or had Dr. Luch Carmichael been far more astute than I imagined?

CHAPTER THREE

LUCH

As promised, Oban crashed as soon as I got him home, curling up in his comfy bed and letting out the cutest wee dog snores a pup could emit. I'd conducted my own examination once we'd gotten home, but he truly seemed no worse for wear other than the stitches in his side. It was a miracle, that was for sure, and one that had me on edge.

Now I stood at my front window, a fire crackling in the grate for wee Oban, even though I typically ran hot. Rain sleeted outside, the forest surrounding my house shrouded in murky light, the waters of Loch Mirren choppy. The sharply edged waves reflected my mood, as did the rain, and I cracked the window open to let in a cool breeze. Scents of the forest came with it, the moss creeping up old trees, damp earth, a tinge of salt from the waters of the loch.

She'd smelt like spring.

A soft spring rain, to be exact. After the first flowers had bloomed, and a gentle mist of rain caressed their petals, releasing their scent into the dewy morning air.

Dr. Faelan Fletcher was an enigma. She was tall, taller than most women I knew, and it hadn't taken much for her to meet my eyes in challenge. And challenge me she had. The woman was hiding something, of that I was sure ... but what?

Her eyes were a contradiction. Much like the words she was saying didn't quite match her actions, they shifted between slate gray and brilliant blue, seemingly unable to decide which direction they wanted to go.

Would the color deepen when she was aroused?

Annoyed at the thought, I shifted away from the window and went to my kitchen to make another cup of tea. There was no reason I should be thinking of the sexy veterinarian like that. And yet, I'd just thought of her as sexy. Again.

Because, *bloody hell*, but she was. Soulful eyes just hinting at sadness, thick auburn hair bundled messily on her head, and soft curves shifting under her loose jumper. She'd known, instantly, when I'd suspected something was amiss, her shoulders straightening.

Leave it alone, Luch.

She'd healed Oban, hadn't she? What did it matter how?

I knew why it mattered, but right now, I couldn't go there.

Wincing again as I replayed the accident in my head, I swore softly under my breath as I flicked the kettle on. Oban was typically really good about staying close to me and usually I closed the gate that lined my expansive property line. It was an old gate, just a worn wooden door hinged to a stone wall that had likely bordered my land for a century or more, but still I always made a point to latch it. Mainly to keep any stray dogs out.

But today I'd been distracted. It had been a long shift at the hospital, I'd lost a patient, and I'd carried that melancholy home with me. I'd been checking my phone when I'd come through the gate, and seeing I'd missed a few phone calls from my father, I must have forgotten to close it.

I never particularly enjoyed seeing a missed call from my father.

But several?

That usually signaled bad news.

I hadn't even had a chance to call him back yet. A bounding rabbit had caught Oban's attention and the subsequent chase, squealing of tires, and trip to the vet meant I'd forgotten the missed calls entirely. Sighing, I scrubbed a hand over my face and opened my fridge to examine the contents. I still hadn't slept and could feel the energy seeping from me as I pulled out a leftover box of pizza. It would do, for now, and after a nap I'd grill up fish and vegetables for my dinner.

My phone rang again and seeing my father's name, I sighed, before swiping it open.

"I'm sorry. I just got off shift and then Oban was hurt. I wasn't ignoring your calls." I crammed a bite of pizza in my mouth and picked up the kettle to pour more water in my mug.

"I was wondering why I hadn't heard from you. What

happened with Oban? Is he all right?" My father's voice, strong and sure, took on a concerned note.

"Aye, he's fine. He got out of the gate and a car hit him. But the new vet fixed him right up. He's resting now."

"Such a shame." My father made a tsking noise with his mouth. I stilled, waiting for what was next. "Maybe it's best you come home now."

"Maybe it's best you come home now." Home. Scalloway. Where I'd grown from a wee bairn to a man, but it was past tense now.

"We've talked about this." I'd moved to Loren Brae over a year ago, had built a reputation in A&E and frankly, this place suited me nicely. It was quiet. It didn't hold on to my past with a vise-like grip. It felt ... like me. And yet, my father used any problem—any hint of disruption—to try and persuade me to return to Scalloway.

"I don't see why this has to be an issue. Your mum misses you."

I winced. He loved playing the "Mum" card.

"I'll visit soon." I wasn't going to start an argument, but now that I knew my father had only called to talk me into returning home, I needed to distract him. Dr. Faelan Fletcher popped into my mind again, and I believed using her as a diversion wasn't too inappropriate. *Because I have a feeling about how she treated Oban, or rather, why my pup is alive and well.* "Say, Dad, question for you. I remember you told me that after I was born you went after those healers. Whatever ended up happening with that?"

Silence greeted me. I knew I was picking at a scab, and my father would resent me for it, but I'd lived under the guilt of my birth for years now, and nothing would change that.

"Those chancers? No, never did find them." Frustration laced my father's voice.

"There was a family of them, though, right? Still in the area?" My father was also a doctor, though he specialized in cardiology, while I thrived in the A&E. He'd been mid surgery when my mum had gone into labor and had arrived home late. *Too late.* It was one of the reasons I so rarely brought the healer up, but I thought broaching the topic today was necessary. *Sorry, Dad.*

"I only know of the one that hurt your mother. I think we were too overwhelmed with everything to investigate further at the time, and then when we could focus on finding them, they'd vanished. But if you're asking about my take on healers in general? I don't think one can dismiss the power of the mind, as there's been enough studies on the placebo effect to prove it to be a viable alternative." My father's voice lowered, and I heard a door closing behind him. "However, you bloody well know how I feel. They can all burn, as far as I'm concerned." *For what they did to your mother.* His voice trailed off, and I heard him take a sip of his drink through the phone. There was no need for him to repeat the words I'd heard so many times before.

"But is it possible? To heal with magick? And be used for good?" I dropped a fresh tea bag in my mug and leaned against the counter, my eyes going to where Oban snoozed by the fire.

"I'm not remotely objective in this. As far as I'm concerned, science is the answer for healing. We've seen firsthand just how horribly wrong it can go."

"And you haven't come across any since ... then? Nothing at the hospital? Healers, that is?"

"Why are you asking? Have you met a healer?"

My father was incredibly astute. He hadn't risen to the top of his field by sheer determination alone. At the same time, I wasn't sure I wanted Faelan to land on my father's radar. Or anyone's really. There was something about her that made me want to protect her just as much as I wanted to learn all her secrets.

"Not really. Just curious. The nurses were reading a book about it at work."

"Hmm." My father paused. "Son, as much as I hate to say it, if you do run into someone with such abilities, you have a responsibility."

"I know." I pressed my lips together. The rain intensified, mirroring my mood, and Oban shifted, lifting his head at the noise. "That's Oban awake. I'll be off then."

"Give him our love. And, son, think about what I said. You shouldn't be alone out there. It's not right."

"Give Mum a hug from me. Gotta run." I hung up before he got started on his favorite topic again and crossed the room to where Oban blinked wearily up at me.

"Hey, pal." I dropped to the floor and ran my hands over his fur, scratching his ears lightly. Turning his head, he licked my palm with his sandpaper-like tongue. "I'm sorry. I'm so *so* sorry. It's a bloody eejit, I am, that's the truth of it. I know better than to leave that gate open."

"*It's not your fault,*" Oban said, his voice rough and scratchy after the day he'd had. "*I knew better than to chase after that damn rabbit.*"

25

I breathed a sigh of relief at hearing his voice in my head.

"You scared me."

"She healed me." Oban turned his head and sniffed at his sutures, but didn't lick. He was a smart dog, and my best pal. I'd been lucky to find him.

"I thought as much." Worry kicked through me at the confirmation from Oban that Faelan was a healer.

"She'll be in pain now. She took it in."

I'd heard tell of it, through the years, healers bringing the pain into their bodies before releasing it to the ether. I'd just never met one in real life. In fact, I'd never met anyone magickal other than wee Oban.

And myself, of course.

But we were a dying breed, after all, and that was the main reason it infuriated my father that I'd chosen to take a position at a rural hospital in Scotland. Not only did he think the job was beneath me, but he liked me close, believing he deserved a say in my life. The "continuation of our line" was only part of *that* equation.

No matter how adamant he was, I would not be pushed. *I should get to control more of my future, should I not?*

It had been over a year since I'd moved to Loren Brae, and in my time here I'd learned two things.

The first?

Loren Brae had deep magickal roots, and for all I had been worried about concealing my identity when I'd moved here, I had quickly learned that Loren Brae had far bigger problems on hand than me.

And the second?

For all my father pushed me to settle down and find a wife, I'd come to realize just how much I enjoyed the freedom of being away from my tight-knit, and heavy-handed, family.

It turns out, I was a lone wolf at heart.

CHAPTER FOUR

Faelan

A few weeks passed in a flash. I hadn't realized when I'd bought the vet practice that it was one of the only practices in the region, nor that there would be a demand for care for everything from livestock to fish. Each night I collapsed into bed, exhausted, promising myself I'd hire an assistant soon, before sleep claimed me.

But it was the dreams each night that woke me, at exactly 3:33, tawny golden-green eyes and a wicked jawline flashing me awake. I'd lie there, heart hammering, and remind myself that everything was fine.

I hadn't heard or seen Dr. Luch Carmichael since he'd left my practice that day, Oban curled in his arms, suspicion draping his face. And I was fine with that. For a few days after the visit, I'd been on edge, jumpy, but the chaos of running a practice on my own had finally demanded my attention and I'd shoved any worries about Dr. Carmichael far into the recesses of my brain.

Except for at night, that is.

The witching hour.

The time I woke each night didn't escape me, nor the gentle nudges my mother was trying to send me from the other side of the veil. It was just that I, quite frankly, didn't have the time or energy for Dr. Carmichael.

Even though I'd googled him over one hurried lunch hour recently. I'd eaten my sandwich standing at the kitchen counter in my flat, and had scrolled my phone, discovering that Luch worked at the hospital about thirty minutes outside of Loren Brae. He was an emergency physician and had a very appealing headshot on their website. Aside from a few nods to his esteemed degrees, there hadn't been much more information that I could find about him.

At the very least, it likely meant that Oban was in good hands and hopefully had healed up nicely from his accident. I'd carried the bruises of his healing on my bum and thigh for a solid week after the incident, moving gingerly through the day and sleeping on one side. I was used to it by now, the cost of a hurried healing, and had a month's supply of arnica creams and Tiger Balm tucked away in my cabinet.

But today, *today* was my first proper day off, and I was using it to get out in nature, before going to dinner at the castle tonight. Lia, the chef at the castle restaurant, Grasshopper, had invited me to her Sunday "family" dinner and I figured it was a good way to finally meet some of the people of Loren Brae in one fell swoop. I'd been meaning to build some connections, as I knew it would be vital to helping me stay here without suspicion, but I'd just been too busy. I'd made a promise to Gloam that he could show me around some of his favorite haunts, and it was important to me to uphold that. I got the sense that Gloam was itching for some playtime in the forest, as he'd been all but stuck to my side as I'd navigated the challenges of running my own clinic. He didn't come down to the practice during the day, instead disappearing into the woods or napping upstairs, but I knew he wanted more time with me. We were still learning about each other, my familiar and me, and what better way to do that than to let him take me for a walk through the forest that blanketed the hills around Loch Mirren?

"I can see why you love it here."

We'd been hiking for several hours, with no particular direction in mind, and I'd just trusted Gloam to lead me where he wanted to go. Now, we'd stopped at a low stone wall which ran through a long line of tall trees and dipped and curved down the hills toward the shores of the loch. Taking off my small pack, I dropped to the mossy ground and leaned my back against the wall, then pulled my water bottle out. My muscles twinged, but in a good way, because even though I was on my feet all day at work, I hadn't done any proper exercise for a while. Digging in my pack, I pulled out a collapsible bowl, popped it open, and dashed a bit of water in it for Gloam.

Gloam sauntered over, lapping at the water, before curling up at my side, his eyes alert as he watched the land around us.

"It's home."

"How did you end up here, Gloam? Do you have family?" Reaching over, I scratched at his favorite spot behind his ears. I'd learned he didn't like me touching his paws or his tail, but that he loved ear and tummy scratches and was a champion cuddler.

"I did. But it was time to follow my call. To find you."

"You were old enough to leave?" I realized I had no idea how old Gloam was.

"I was. We tend to be solitary unless we're mating and raising our young."

"Do you want babies?"

Gloam made a soft chuffing noise, which I'd learned he did when he was amused at my line of questioning.

"We don't think like that. If we find a mate, and the time is right, we'll have kits. But it's not a ... yearning. Not in the way that humans think of it."

"Is your whole family magickal? Or is it just you?" It had never occurred to me that there could be a whole line of magickal foxes just wandering around helping wayward witches and healers in need. But once the idea had sunk its claws into my brain, I couldn't help but think of some magickal academy for training familiars to meet with their witches.

"My father was as well. Not all of us. It's a choice."

"Ah, so there *is* an academy. Do you go to school for this?"

At that, Gloam rolled over on his back, letting out high-pitched yipping noises, his little body shaking with it.

"You're laughing at me."

"That's because you think funny." Gloam rolled back over and slanted me a look, smiling slyly at me. *"It's magick,*

Faelan of the flowers. Like you are. You're either connected or not connected."

His words echoed a sentiment my mother had often discussed. She'd likened our power to source energy, a river of sorts, and one could just cup their hands and drink from it if they chose to do so. I'd never not known magick, and it wasn't a conscious thought anymore when or how I used my power. It just was.

"My mum often said the same."

"*She's crossed over?*"

"Aye."

"*Where were you before this? Why did I have so much trouble finding you?*"

"You were looking for me?" I straightened, surprised at the thought that Gloam had known about me before I'd even arrived. "Did you plan to get hurt? Was that your way into meeting me?"

Another soft chuffing, and Gloam shifted, leaning into my thigh.

"*No, I'd never intentionally hurt myself. An unlucky coincidence. But, aye, lass. I've been seeking you out for a while now. I'd catch your scent, but then you'd be gone.*"

"I moved a lot." I took another swig from my water bottle, my eyes going to where the late afternoon light filtered through the branches of the trees. The breeze picked up, rustling the leaves, bringing with it the soft scent of dirt and moss. Earthy smells. I took a deep inhale, feeling myself connecting to the energy that flowed beneath the ground here, and tension eased from my neck and shoulders. "Turns out, people aren't super friendly when they think you're a witch."

"You are a witch."

"I am. As was my mother. And her mother. And all the women before us. Healers by heart, magickal by nature."

"Not everyone accepts that."

"No." I chuckled, threading my hand through the soft fur at Gloam's neck. "That's the truth of it, isn't it?"

"Was it bad for you?" Gloam angled his head, and I deepened my scratches behind his ear.

"Single mum, child in tow. Questionable activities. Unexplained situations." I closed my eyes, remembering my childhood's instability. Hard stares in the supermarket. Mothers tugging their children away from us. Our magick was both a gift and a curse, and though it had made me a resilient child, it had also made me a lonely one. "I made do. The best I could really. It's all past now, anyway. Water under the bridge."

Gloam jerked under my hand and, startled from my reverie, my eyes sprung open.

Holy hell … was I dreaming?

A unicorn ducked its head out from between the trunks of two massive trees, faintly glowing in the murky light of the forest, its eyes an incredible opalescence.

She was magnificent and my thoughts scrambled. *Was I really seeing a unicorn?*

My lungs tightened, as though I wouldn't be able to draw my next breath, and Gloam stood, his head dipped low almost as if he was bowing to this majestic creature.

Tears pricked my eyes.

She trotted a few steps forward, tossing her mane, and angled her horn at me. Having a mother as magickal as mine had made me privy to certain parts of this world unknown to many others, but *this?* This was awe-inspiring. The unicorn's coat shimmered, as though someone had crushed up thousands of diamonds and pearls together, and then painstakingly hand painted them across her flanks. I brought a hand to my heart, hoping she could feel the power of my admiration for her, and gave her a gentle smile. I'd worked around animals long enough to know to keep still, and to radiate as much goodwill and kindness as I could. The unicorn trotted even closer, coming to a stop, her front hooves almost touching my feet.

"She's hurt."

My eyes rounded at Gloam's words as the unicorn lifted her front hoof to me.

"May I see?" I asked, not daring to move until I had permission.

The unicorn dipped her head, nodding, and I scrambled forward until I was on my knees. Reaching for her leg, I started as my hands touched her coat. Her power was extraordinary. It was as though I was mainlining magick, attached directly to the source, and the power rocketed through me. My hands shook as I curled her leg so I could have a proper look at her hoof, and I tried to stay focused on the task at hand.

No wonder unicorns hid themselves from the world.

They were too powerful, too majestic, for any human to truly harness their abilities. Frankly, this level of power would likely drive the uninitiated mad.

And yet, when blood dripped from her hoof onto my hand, a white shimmering glowing drop, I realized she was not infallible. A rusty nail was buried in her hoof, and I would need to extract it.

"Och, you poor thing. I'm going to do my best to pull this nail out. But I need to grab a tool. It's likely going to hurt." I looked up at her, but she only dipped her head again, seeming to understand my words. Leaning back, I dug in my pack until I found my Leatherman multi-tool that I carried just in case I ever needed it. It wasn't the best tool for the job, but it had a small set of pliers that might do well enough, with the added bonus of my own power. Working quickly, I popped the pliers out and then returned to the hoof. "Here's what's going to happen. This nail has lodged itself in your hoof. I'm going to use my pliers to extract it in one smooth motion, but I'll also use my power to help. Hopefully the combination of both will work. If not, I'll go get the right tools and come back to you. But let's just try this first and see how it goes. Um, please, you know, try not to kick me or anything if it hurts too much. I am just trying to help." The last thing I needed was to take a magickal hoof to the face.

Bracing her leg against my knee, I took a deep breath and called upon my own magick. I often envisioned it as this ball of power inside me, a flower bud still closed, and when I needed it, the magick would unfurl and open the petals. But when I was connected to her? Something astounding happened. Everything bloomed inside me. I was Faelan of the Flowers, protector of animals, healer connected to Earth's natural energies. Power positively flowed through my body, and with just one good tug and my healing abilities immediately stopping the flow of blood, the sweet unicorn was free from pain.

I scrambled backward, detaching myself from her, knowing to linger in her power for too long would be too much even for me. Plus, I suspected it would also be considered rude. She'd given me a great gift by allowing me to heal her, let alone touch her, and overstaying my welcome by her side would be a significant faux pax. I wasn't entirely sure of the protocol, but I knew that I didn't want to break *any* rules when it came to interacting with a unicorn.

Shaking, I held out my hand to the unicorn so she could see the nail I'd pulled from her, the tip coated in that shimmering white blood.

"Should be right as rain now." The unicorn dipped her head, blowing out a happy-sounding breath, and surprised me by lightly touching my hand with her horn. Happiness flooded me, as pure as a puppy's joyful bark, and then she angled her head toward the forest. Bobbing it twice, she stamped a hoof, and I followed her line of sight.

Something shifted in the shadows.

With a soft whish of air, the unicorn disappeared silently into the forest, heading the other way from where she'd drawn my attention.

Gloam stood. His body was tense, his tail straight.

"Is someone there?" I whispered, curling my hand around the nail and tucking it in my pocket. The nail was now highly magicked, and I would keep it with me as a protective charm.

"*Aye.*"

Straining my eyes, I held my breath and waited.

The breeze picked up, shifting the branches, and for a moment I caught a glimpse of golden eyes and shaggy fur.

For one, laughable second, I could have sworn I'd seen a wolf.

But wolves hadn't been in Scotland for ages now.

"A husky," I said out loud, letting my breath out slowly. "Someone must have lost their dog."

The wind picked up, howling across the loch, and whipping through the trees. I blinked, and the dog was gone.

"Hey, come back," I called, making kissing noises, just to see if I could help the lost dog. "Do you need help?"

"We should go."

Gloam didn't have to tell me twice. Everything about this moment had been fantastical, and as the first drop of rain hit my head, I realized I was about to get doused. A storm must have rolled in while I was healing the unicorn, and now I'd need to traipse back home in the wet and cold, if I wanted to make it in time for dinner at the castle.

Dinner at the castle.

Shaking my head at my thoughts, I pulled my rain jacket from my pack and bent my head against the increasing pressure of the wind. Following Gloam, I trailed my hand along the stone wall, when the clouds opened up and let loose a nasty barrage of rain. Stumbling, I raced after Gloam down the hill, but the conditions quickly worsened and I could barely see in front of my face.

"Go on!" Gloam looked behind him at my shout. "Get cover. I can't run as fast as you. It's too slippery."

I'd just have to stumble my way carefully down the hill, holding on to the wall for safety. Oh well, it was just rain. Icy cold and coming down impossibly fast, but still, I wouldn't melt.

Lightning flashed, thunder cracking the air quickly after it.

"Bloody hell."

So much for a peaceful day off. I inched my way along the wall, feeling with each step, not wanting to take a tumble and twist my ankle. My energy was already somewhat sapped from a day of hiking, I was a touch jittery from healing the unicorn, and nerves were making me uncertain in my steps.

"Hey!"

I lifted my head to see a man in a black rain jacket, the hood pulled over his head and shadowing his face, standing at a gate in the wall.

"Come on then, I have a wee dry space to ride out the rain!" The man beckoned to me, and only as I drew closer did I see who it was.

My heart sank.

Dr. Luch Carmichael.

I didn't know if I was safer just toughing out the storm, but when Gloam streaked inside the gate that Luch held open, I figured it was safe. He wouldn't lead me astray. Or at least I hoped he wouldn't. Swallowing my nerves, I stumbled the rest of the way through the pounding rain to where he stood, holding the gate open, staring after Gloam in astonishment.

"Nice day for a walk, isn't it?" Luch asked, amusement dancing in his eyes. *Good God, the man's handsome.* I'd tried to avoid noticing when I'd treated his pup, but close up like this? He left me a little breathless. *Or that could be from the excitement of helping the unicorn.* I grinned.

"Och, aye. Bloody brilliant."

CHAPTER FIVE

FAELAN

A fairy tale cottage, all mossy stones and smoking chimney, was tucked in a clearing surrounded by trees. Gloam disappeared behind the cottage, and I had to assume he'd find shelter somewhere close.

Hurrying against the rain, I ducked inside the door Luch held open for me, feeling like I stepped into another world. Water dripped in long streams from boughs of the trees surrounding the sturdy stone cottage, and moss clambered up the stone walls. Warm light flickered from the windows, a welcome respite in the storm, and I stepped inside the door to scents of garlic mixed with woodfire. Colorful art lined the walls, with brash colors and strong strokes, and a thick burlap-style rug covered the wide-planked wood floor. A fire crackled merrily in the fireplace.

It was all so homey and directly at odds with the harsh

edges of my initial assessment of one Dr. Luch Carmichael. Nerves warred with curiosity in my gut.

Would I have to push him into the fire to make my escape? Shaking my head from thoughts of grim childhood fairy tales, I smiled at where Oban woofed his greeting.

"Och, there's a fine gentleman. Look at you," I cooed, standing on the mat by the door, as water ran in rivulets down my legs. I didn't want to take one step farther, lest I mess up anything in this nice cottage.

"Caught the worst of it, didn't ye?" Luch hung his jacket by the door and slipped his shoes off, before disappearing through a doorway to another room. I was grateful for a moment to gather my nerves, and to study the space around me. To the right was a cozy living room, with a dog bed in front of the fire, and wide-paned windows that overlooked the forest and the loch below. To my left was a streamlined kitchen and eating area, with a pot simmering on the stove. It smelled delicious, something garlicy and Italian maybe, and my stomach growled.

Luch walked back out in just a pair of loose tartan pajama pants, and I almost swallowed my tongue. Thick muscles rippled down his abs, a sprinkle of dark hair leading to his waistband. He toweled his hair with one hand and held out another towel to me with the other, which I immediately buried my face in. Taking a few deep breaths so I could gather some control over my wayward thoughts, I pretended to take my time drying my face and hair. My clothes, however, were soaked.

"Let me get you something to change into."

"Och, it's fine. I'll just be on my way. Surely this will pass soon."

Thunder rumbled at my words, mocking me, and I sighed. A glimmer of a smile tugged at Luch's lips.

"Clothes?"

"Um, sure." Otherwise I was just going to be left standing here dripping on his doormat, looking at the ceiling so I didn't burst into flames from staring at his chest. The man was massively ripped—I'd counted at least a six-pack—maybe eight—before I'd torn my eyes away. How was that even possible? Who had the time to work out that much? Surely his work kept him busy? Did he chop his own wood for the winter or something?

I swallowed and tried to act like I was having any thoughts but lusty ones when he returned, pointing to a door he'd just come out of.

"Loo's through there. I left a stack of clothes on the sink."

"I'm wet though." I pointed at my legs.

A tiniest quirk at the corner of his mouth and just the hint of a raised eyebrow had my face bursting into flames. *Could I have chosen any other words? Any at all?* Mentally slapping my face, I kicked off my trainers and sailed past Luch, almost slamming the bathroom door behind me. Bloody hell, but why did the man have to be so ripped? Just like the other week when I got the impression that he sucked up all the molecules in the room to make space for him, I was once again overly aware of his every movement. It was a palpable thing, this energy radiating from him, and it put me on high alert. Before, I'd been certain I was in danger, but now my thoughts were going an entirely different direction. What I needed to do was trust my first instinct, which was to run in the opposite direction of him, not be in his bathroom changing into a pair of loose joggers and a faded button-down flannel shirt.

I couldn't help myself. I buried my nose in the collar of the shirt and took a deep inhale. It smelled like him. Like fresh soap and a hint of something earthy. Cedar maybe.

Pausing to look at myself in the mirror, I sighed. My hair was a bedraggled mess, and two bright pink spots stood out on my cheeks, highlighting my thoughts. The curse of Scottish skin, I supposed, where any flush stood out against my fair complexion. Luch's shirt draped to my knees, and even that surprised me. I was not a small woman and even so, I had to roll up the arms and the waistband once on the pants to keep them up. Realizing that this was the best I could do, I gathered my damp clothes, tucking my pants and bra into my wet trousers and shirt, rolling it all into one neat ball so he wouldn't see anything. Yes, I was aware we were both adults and had likely seen underwear from the other sex before. I wouldn't call my sports bra the most enticing of undergarments either, yet … I trailed off my mental debate and blew out a breath.

"Get it together, Dr. Fletcher." Good reminder that I was a professional and could handle difficult situations. *A necessary pep talk at times.* Holding the ball of clothes, I cracked the door open to see Luch, thankfully with a T-shirt on this time, at the counter pouring two cups of tea. I swallowed. I just wanted to get home, not have a cozy cup of tea while the storm thundered outside.

Oban trotted over to me and pressed his nose to my leg.

"There's a good lad. Looking well enough, aren't you then?" I scratched his ear and then crossed the room to tuck my wet clothes in the pack I'd left by the door.

"Cuppa tea?" Luch asked as I straightened. The rain still slashed against the windows, and I hoped that Gloam had found himself a cozy spot somewhere to hole up against the sudden storm.

"I should really get—"

"Happy to drive you home shortly. Best to wait until it lets up a bit though," Luch said. He was right. When the rain came down in heavy sheets like this, it made driving particularly tricky.

"Right. Tea would be grand, thanks."

"Milk? Sugar?"

"A touch of both, thanks." I crouched next to Oban, needing something to do with my hands, and stroked his silky coat. Checking my sutures, I was happy to see they'd been removed, likely by Luch, and the scar was healing nicely. "Oban's looking well. Has he had any behavior issues since the accident?"

Oban huffed, slanting me a look, and I grinned. Animals often knew I could understand them even though their owners didn't know I could.

"Och, he's as cheeky as ever." Luch rounded the kitchen table and gestured toward the couch by the fire. "By the fire?"

"Here's fine." I pointed at the kitchen table and waited until Luch sat and then took a seat a few chairs away from him. Space was needed, not cozying up on a couch by the fire. *I was already warm enough just being near this man.* A thought I'd really need to file away for further examination. Later. *Much* later.

"So what brings you to Loren Brae, Faelan? Can I call

you Faelan?" Luch leaned his elbows on the table, propping his chin in his hands.

"Aye, that's fine." I shrugged one shoulder, blowing on my tea. "I'd seen the practice was for sale and the area looked like a nice spot to settle in. So far it's been grand. People are friendly, it's a pretty town. Today was the first day I got out for a proper wander, and it was lovely. Out in the hills, gorgeous forest. No complaints so far."

"Och, Loren Brae's a belter, isn't she? It's got a bit of everything—the loch, a few good hiking hills, the woods. I've been really pleased with it myself."

"Are you new to the area?" I asked, casually, as though I hadn't researched him on the internet.

"Just over a year here." Luch shifted, and something flashed behind his eyes.

"Where were you before this?"

"Here and there." Luch took a sip of his tea and leveled me a look. "And you?"

"Here and there," I echoed, burying my nose in my mug.

"Is that right? Is there much call for traveling vets?"

"Certainly. Just as much as there is for traveling nurses and doctors. You'd be surprised the need, particularly in under-served communities such as this one. I'll be hiring help soon enough."

"Not necessarily a bad problem to have. As a business owner, that is." Luch leaned back in his chair, crossing his arms over his chest, and I couldn't help but notice the way his biceps popped with the movement. I swallowed thickly and took another sip of my tea.

"No, not really. Though I don't particularly like

managing people, I'll admit." I laughed softly, twisting my mug in my hands. "But it's helpful to have someone on hand when we have distraught owners come through the door. In emergency situations, that is. What kind of doctor are you?" I wanted to switch the conversation back to him and away from me. There was something about the way he continued to stare steadily at me that made the hairs at the back of my neck stand up.

"A&E. I can certainly understand your need for help in emergency situations. The nurses are a godsend when it comes to managing panicked families and getting the patient ready for any surgery. I'd be lost without them."

At that, I gave him a warm smile.

"So you're not the egomaniac doctor that everyone hates?"

Luch laughed and ran a hand across his jaw.

"I try not to be. Some of the nurses have worked there for decades. They know half the people coming through the door, and how to deal with them. I welcome their advice."

"I imagine that makes you very popular." *Plus the fact that you're drop-dead gorgeous.* I suspected every woman within thirty meters of him was likely having indecent thoughts. I couldn't blame them. It was a struggle for me not to let my mind go elsewhere, even though there was something about this man that worried me. He was just *so* masculine. If charisma had a name, it was Luch.

Luch smiled, showcasing a line of white teeth, and my insides went warm and liquid.

"So why animals and not people?" Luch asked, changing the subject.

"They don't judge me." It came out before I could stop

it and I flushed, annoyed at myself for letting that thought slip.

"Ah." Luch didn't say anything else, and his silence made me nervous, which in turn made me chatter.

"It's just that animals are pure, you know? They are joy and kindness and love. And not that humans can't be that, because of course they can, but not in the way animals are. Even ones that are wary or scared, they're still good, you ken? I consider it a great honor to help them."

"I can understand that. Wee Oban's my best pal." At his name, Oban trotted over and pawed at Luch who bent and pulled him up. I let out a soft sigh. Once again, a strong man cuddling a wee pup just did something to me. "Any pets for you?"

"No." My thoughts went to Gloam. I wouldn't technically call him my pet, as he could come and go as he pleased, and was magickal. He definitely fell into a different category. "Moving around doesn't really allow for pets. Many landlords won't rent to you if you have animals."

"Such a shame." Luch smiled when Oban tilted his head and licked his face. "But you're here now. For good it sounds like, since you bought the practice. Or are you leasing?"

"I purchased it." Not only did I have my own savings, but my mum had left me a small inheritance as well. Nothing flashy, but enough to invest in my future. If I could stay in one place long enough. I'd had good feelings about Loren Brae, and I sincerely hoped Luch wouldn't turn against me. "It'll be my first time properly running my own practice and I'm hoping to make my home here. I think I can do a lot of good for Loren Brae. I'm sure Oban would agree with me."

I didn't mean the words to come out slightly threatening, but I could tell Luch took them as such when his eyebrows rose.

"Aye, I'm sure he does. Really quite a miraculous healing. Wouldn't you say?" Suspicion threaded his words, but I kept my expression calm, guileless even. I'd long had practice in responding to people questioning me.

"I'd call it luck more than a miracle. Either way, I'm happy he's on the mend." Glancing out the window, relief filled me. "Rain's let up. I've got to be on my way, as I've dinner plans."

"Hot date?" Luch rose, putting Oban on the floor and clearing the cups from the table. I stood, uncertain if I should change back into my wet clothes or just offer to drop his clothes off another time. This put me in the position of having to see him again. From a very base female side of me, I wanted to see him again. From a "protective of my secrets" standpoint, I needed to stay far away from him. Indecision warred.

"No." I didn't offer any other details. It was none of his business what I did with my time. I went and picked up my pack, uncertain of how to proceed.

"Do you want one?"

"What?" I glanced up and realized he was close, closer than I'd expected. I hadn't even heard him cross the room. Now he loomed over me, all muscles and machismo, and excitement mixed with nerves. My eyes caught on his mouth as he angled his head, leaning into my space.

"I asked if you'd like one."

"A one what?" All coherent thought left my brain as he leaned even closer, and I caught that faint scent of soap and cedar.

His lips quirked, amusement flashing in his eyes.

"A date. Even a hot one, at that."

"With *you*?" The way I said it made him laugh and I blanched.

"Some women have been known to enjoy a date with me on occasion."

"I'm sorry, I didn't mean it to sound like that." Automatically, I reached out to squeeze his arm in apology. My hand met hard muscles and that current of electricity zipped between us again. Luch looked down at my hand and then up at me.

He bit his lower lip.

It was quick, but it was enough to make heat flash through my entire body, and ... I needed to leave. Now.

Turning, I slammed my head straight into the closed door.

A door that I'd thought I'd opened.

"Och, shite. Hold on, let me look."

"No, no, I'm fine." I blinked as tears automatically flooded my eyes. I had properly smacked my forehead against the wood and now I wasn't sure if the tears were from the sting of pain or the embarrassment. Luch's hands found my shoulders, and he turned me, cupping my chin so he could look at my forehead. I didn't meet his eyes, but that didn't help me because then I just focused on his mouth.

His ridiculously kissable mouth.

Tearing my gaze away from his lips, I looked up and froze.

His eyes bored into mine, mossy green, with golden flecks.

"You have the most unique eyes," Luch said, echoing my thoughts about his. "It's like they can't decide what color they want to be."

"Is it my eyes or my forehead you're examining, Dr. Carmichael?" My voice rasped, and I eased back, breaking away from his touch.

"I can do both." Luch smiled. "Let's get some ice on your forehead, particularly if you want to look good for your date later."

I didn't contradict him about having a date. It was better this way. Luch crossed to his freezer and wrapped some ice in a paper towel and handed it to me. Picking up my pack, he made a great show of opening the door.

"You'll find it easier to exit this way."

"Noted." I hopped in the front seat of his Jeep, my cheeks burning. Thankfully, Luch remained silent on the drive, the only sounds that of the light rain and the radio turned low. By the time he pulled in front of my flat, I felt composed enough to function like an adult human being again. Luch popped out of the Jeep quickly, and rounded the bonnet, my pack in hand. Opening the door for me, he smiled.

"How's the head?"

"Och, just fine, I'm sure." I moved to exit gracefully and make my getaway.

Instead, I slammed back into the seat, caught by my seatbelt.

"Bloody hell." I closed my eyes and shook my head, Luch's chuckle rolling over me. I stilled as his hand, warm at my side, found the buckle, and he released me. Tucking his arm through mine, he eased me from the car, and once again stood just a smidge too close to me.

"You still didn't answer my question."

"About what?"

"Can I take you on a date?"

"Why?" Suspicion crept up. The last date I went on was ... possibly over a year ago. What city had I been in? Anyway, it didn't matter. I hadn't dated much, especially given most men seemed somehow intimidated by me. *So, why does Luch want to take me out on a date?* I wasn't exactly ... sweet.

"Because I think you're one of the most beautiful women I've ever seen, we have similar interests when it comes to professions, and you intrigue me."

My mouth dropped open. I hadn't expected such a direct answer to my question and now I had no idea what to say.

"I have no idea what to say." *Smooth, Faelan. Smooth.*

"Say 'yes.' Dinner, this week? I'll call you when I know my schedule." Luch eased back, and I shrugged one shoulder, noncommittal. "I'm taking that as a yes."

"We'll see." I needed to figure out what it was about Luch that threw me off so much before I went to dinner.

"That's not a no. I'll take it. Now I'm leaving before you change your mind." With a quick flash of that lightning-bolt smile, Luch hopped in the driver's seat and drove away, leaving me standing in his clothes in the lightly misting rain. A couple in rain jackets, their arms full of bags from the market, rounded the corner and looked me up and down. I immediately realized that I probably looked like I was just coming home from a one-night stand and I bolted for my flat.

Small towns had their reputations for a reason. The last thing I needed was any gossip about me ... even if it was something as innocuous as who I was dating. I'd learned to keep my head down, stay out of gossip, and do my job. It was the only way that I could last for any amount of time anywhere.

Gloam chattered at me from where he sat by my door, his coat still damp. He must have run home when the rain stopped.

"Och, poor lad. Let's get you dried off and some food in you." Animals gave me purpose. *They* were my world. My life's work. It was a helpful reminder and as I focused on getting Gloam cleaned up, I pushed thoughts of Luch Carmichael to the side.

It was the path I'd chosen to walk in life. A friend to animals, a healer to all, and though it was frequently a lonely, solitary path, it was mine.

"I think you're one of the most beautiful women I've ever seen, we have similar interests when it comes to professions, and you intrigue me."

Luch's intrigue wasn't good. Was it?

"You can't make attachments to men, Faelan. You know this. Especially a man who's making roots in this wee town." I took the damp towel and tossed it in the washing machine. There were a lot of self-lectures today, but living on my own, I was used to talking to myself.

Alone. The safest choice for me to make ... which was why I needed to steer clear of Luch.

It was far harder to hide in plain sight if I let someone get close to me.

CHAPTER SIX

LUCH

I was too keyed up to sit still after I dropped Faelan off and returned home to my cottage. The rain had left, and a silvery light filtered through the trees around my cottage, catching the glimmering droplets clinging to the leaves.

"Fancy a run, lad?"

Oban trotted over from where he'd been finishing his dinner in the kitchen and tilted his head up at me.

"That kind of run?"

I shrugged. I knew I needed to work off some energy but wasn't sure yet just how much I needed to burn through.

"Best not. I'm still on the mend and it's probably smarter for me to take it easy."

"That's fair. I shouldn't have asked you." I winced.

Oban typically loved to go for a run with me, but obviously the wee lad was still healing even though he seemed largely back to normal. Some wounds didn't show on the surface, did they?

"Nae bother." Oban trotted over to his bed by the fireplace. *"I'll just cozy in here for a bit."*

"I shouldn't be too long." I rolled my shoulders as I tied my running shoes. "I just need to work off some energy."

"Don't blame you. The cute healer has you all stirred up."

"She doesn't have me ..." I glared at him, his little body shaking with his silent laughter. Oban loved nothing more than to get a rise out of me. "Wheesht. It's not like that. I've just got a lot on my mind."

"Like a beautiful woman who turned you down for a date?"

I stood, annoyed, and went to the door. "I'm leaving."

"Have fun. Try not to creep Faelan out if you stalk her."

"I'm not going to stalk her." I whirled at the door. Right, so maybe I *had* planned to run through town, but it was often where I went for a run. It wasn't my fault that her flat was on the main street, was it? "That would be weird."

"Maybe pick a different direction for your run then." Oban buried his nose in his paws, his eyes drifting closed, and I shot two fingers in the air at him before stepping outside.

"Bloody mutt."

"Heard that. I'm full-breed, you know."

Rolling my eyes, I turned the corner of the cottage and took off up a trail that wound through the woods and away from the street that lined the loch.

The last of the day's light dimmed, but I was steady on

my feet as I pounded up the hill, my breath leaving me in measured bursts. Confident on my feet, I enjoyed the strain in my muscles as I ascended the hill, and stopped as I always did, admiring how Loren Brae spread out below me.

A town to call my own.

Leaving Scalloway had been the right choice, I was sure of it in my very bones, and every time I looked down at Loren Brae, it only strengthened my determination to keep my life here.

Away from my family, away from the old ways, to start a life that wasn't based on rules and obligations, but one that was based on my choices alone.

"You're selfish." Even now, I could hear my father's words as I'd left home. But I tended to believe there was a distinctive line between selfishness and establishing boundaries. Others may not see it that way, but that was the problem with boundaries, wasn't it? The people who chafed against them were likely the ones you needed them for the most.

The castle sat, ever watchful, its windows lit with warm light, a sentinel over Loren Brae. The town needed her, that much I knew, but I still hadn't discovered the root of the magick that threaded its way through the earth here. I could feel it, out on my runs, the soft thrum of energy that told me that something more surrounded me.

The screams of the Kelpies at night could have told me the same as well.

But they were different.

Different energy, that is.

Taking a deep breath, I continued my run down the hill and over the next, drawn closer to the castle, where car doors slammed, and laughter carried on the wind. They must be having an event of sorts, or the restaurant was particularly busy tonight. I took the path that ran the perimeter of the property, following a line of hedges, through a gathering of trees that ran parallel to a small burn, and past the construction site for the new Common Gin distillery. A group of people laughed outside the castle, and for a moment, my heart twisted. They all looked so ... content ... together. Though there were times I craved that togetherness, I wasn't quite sure I was ready for it. The suffocating pressure of my family bore down on my shoulders, and I couldn't help but attribute that same feeling to any potential groups of friends I'd make.

Frankly, I didn't want the responsibility of answering to anyone but myself right now.

As I neared the castle, I followed the dirt path along the gardens that ran behind a tall line of hedges that hugged the drive to the castle car park. Movement through the branches caught my eye and I held my breath as a figure marched up the road, having a conversation with ... *a fox*.

Not just any person, though. It was Faelan, and she was definitely deep in conversation with a fox. I pulled farther back into the bushes. Already I could hear Oban berating me for stalking the poor woman, but how was I to know she was going to be at the castle? Now I just had to stay as still as I could, wait until she passed, and then hightail it out of there. The fox lifted its nose and turned, staring directly through the bushes, and I stayed still, praying it didn't draw any attention to me.

When they continued on past me, I let out my breath in a soft sigh of relief and crept down the path away from the castle and back toward my cottage. My intention certainly hadn't been to spy on Faelan, and now I had even more questions about her than before.

Like why was she talking to a fox? Hadn't she told me she didn't have any pets?

An image of her, flushed and flustered, a bruise welling on her forehead, came to my mind. I'd wanted to kiss her.

Even though the very idea of me dating a healer would send my father over the edge.

Yes, she was a healer. But so was I, wasn't I? Even if I relied strictly on science to do so.

"They don't judge me."

Faelan's words came back to me as I pounded the pavement, pushing myself hard, needing to work through why I was so attracted to this woman. There was a sweetness to Faelan, a vulnerability that I could see in my own eyes when I looked in the mirror.

The reality was outsiders recognized outsiders.

Did two outsiders make a group? Was it possible that Faelan could be my first real friend here? Even though I'd be lying if I said I wasn't attracted to her. It would be hard to be just her friend, not when her very scent made me think of long sweaty nights and my name on her lips. Groaning, I pushed harder, working to ignore the lust that ran through my body.

I was used to ignoring my needs, had done so for a couple years now since I'd discovered the last girl I'd dated had actually been a plant from my father. I should have known. She'd had a perfect pedigree, and he'd be able to boast to everyone that he'd finally made an unequaled match for his wayward son.

Instead, I'd packed up and started my life over, needing to put space between us.

As though on command, my phone rang, and I grimaced, suspecting it was my father calling.

Instead, my mum's name lit up on the screen and I slowed to a walk just down the road from my cottage and swiped the screen.

"Mum, how are you?"

"There's my sweet boy. You sound out of breath?"

The question hung, and a corner of my mouth turned up in a wry smile.

"You caught me at the end of my run. Everything good?" I could never quite calm down in a conversation with my mother until I knew she was well.

I always wanted her to be safe.

"Of course, everything's just fine. Your father's away in surgery, and your brothers are all doing well enough."

"But?" I could hear the hesitation in her voice.

"Och, it's just that I miss you, my wee boy."

"Mum, I—"

"No, don't you start. You need to do this. Ignore your father. He's stuck in the old ways, Luch. You know that."

"I wish he could see that there are ... other options."

"He will. Eventually. He did with me, didn't he?"

I unhooked my gate and then made sure to carefully lock it behind me.

"But ..." I couldn't bring myself to say it.

"Och, not you, too. What happened to me is not because your father broke the rules, Luch. Honestly. How can I be surrounded by highly educated doctors of all things and yet you all still cling to this superstition?" Annoyance laced my mother's tone, and I winced, not wanting to upset her.

"You're right. I know you are. Say, Mum, let me tell you about what Oban did the other day." I launched into a story about how Oban had shredded a brand-new toy I'd bought for him, leaving so much stuffing around the house it looked like it had snowed inside, and by the time I ended the call, she was back to her ever-cheerful self.

Her laughter was enough to ease any lingering tension I had, and her faith in me for making the choice to leave home was the sole candle in the darkness of my family's judgment.

And despite what Oban said earlier, I had *not* been stalking the lovely vet tonight.

But I also hadn't been willing to turn down an opportunity to satisfy my desire to know more about one Dr. Faelan Fletcher. The problem, though, was now I felt like I'd only just scratched the surface. There were deeper forces at play here, and while I usually didn't mind letting people keep their secrets close, I realized that wasn't going to be the case with Faelan.

Her shy smile, flushed cheeks, and whip-smart mind intrigued me, and even if it made more sense to stay away ... I already knew it would be impossible to do so.

CHAPTER SEVEN

Faelan

I'd barely made it to dinner in time last night before I'd been immediately put to work, helping to deliver a hedgehog's babies. It had been a chaotic, albeit fun, evening, and I'd walked back from the castle with a smile on my lips and another date.

A date, that is, to meet with the American woman, Sophie, who had inherited MacAlpine Castle.

The castle itself was perched on a hill, a stately dame lording over Loren Brae, and where I'd expected fancy airs and polite conversations, I'd instead been treated to a genuinely cheerful evening. I hadn't had much actual dinner, instead taking my food on the side while overseeing the birthing process, but various people had rotated through to chat with me while I had monitored my patient.

It turns out the dinner had been a baby shower for the

hedgehogs. Their owners, Shona and Owen, were over the moon that Edith had gone into labor at the party and had been just as nervous as if it was their very own children. I can't say I'd ever attended a hedgehog baby shower before, but everyone in attendance seemed deeply invested in the wee hedgies, and I, for one, always supported anyone that celebrated animals. If they wanted to throw a party for the new babies, why the heck not? The whole evening had been odd, unexpectedly relaxing, and I'd made some new connections.

I was also fairly certain there was magick at the castle.

I had been too distracted to delve deep into the sensations I was getting, but there was a certain buzz in the air, a vibration of sorts, which made me suspect that there was magick about. It had been that same energy that had pulled me to Loren Brae, making me hope this idyllic small town situated on Loch Mirren's frothy shores would be a place I could finally call home.

I guess I'd find out more when I went back to the castle after work today.

"Are you staying up here today or having a wander about outside?" I asked Gloam as I ate my porridge and filled my travel cup with coffee. Gloam stretched on the couch and then padded over to me, bumping against my legs. Reaching down, I scratched his ears. His fur was extra soft today, as I'd given him a good bath yesterday to rid him of the mud from the storm. I'd even taken some adorable pictures of him wrapped in a towel in the bath, his nose sticking out of the towel, mouth hanging open in a smile. And even though they were the cutest photos ever, it was times like these that I missed Eriska the most. I didn't have *my people* to send them to, and that stung a little, as it always did.

So I'd slept in Luch's flannel shirt.

Not that I'd ever tell him that. But his faint scent had soothed me to sleep, and I'd felt cocooned and comforted all night. It was the first really peaceful sleep I'd had since I'd arrived, and I'd even missed the 3:33 wake-up call that had been bothering me of late.

If his shirt was what it took to get a good night's sleep, I might just hold on to it a while longer.

"I want to stay here. I like to sleep during the day."

"Yeah, that makes sense. There's water in the bowl, food, and all that. I've cracked the bedroom window as well." I hated thinking about keeping Gloam locked in the flat all day, and I'd learned if I left the back bedroom window open, he'd be able to get out onto the small balcony and down the stairs from there. That would at least give him some freedom to come and go as he pleased.

"Will you meet with Luch?"

"Ah. Not sure." I paused as I pulled the straps of my tote bag over my shoulder. I hadn't yet decided if I'd go on a date with Luch. I mean, a part of me was encouraged by the idea—to ride that ride as long and as hard as I could, and then never call him again. But the more subdued, awkward side of me, couldn't quite follow through on those thoughts. I'd always wished I could be a femme fatale, but the only person I was a real danger to was myself.

As exhibited by the bruise on my forehead that I'd hastily covered with makeup this morning. It was a stark reminder that I was awkward at dating, having only rarely hooked up with men when I desperately craved intimacy—

and even then, it was always on my way out of town. But given both Luch and I were keen to make Loren Brae home, it wasn't as if I could do that and sneak away in the night.

"His cottage is warded."

At that, I paused at the door and turned to Gloam. He'd hidden in a shed behind Luch's house the day before and had nosed around the space.

"It is?"

"Aye."

"From him? Like his own wards?"

"Hard to say. Just that there's protection there."

"Huh. That's strange." Mulling it over, I opened the door and stopped.

On my doorstep was a bundle of wildflowers, still damp with dew, wrapped in a simple twine bow. Picking them up, I turned them over, but there was no note to be found.

Were these from Luch?

Or maybe it was a "thank you" for helping with the hedgies the night before?

Pursing my lips, I took the flowers with me to my practice, placing them in a cup of water on the front desk where I could see them.

Faelan of the flowers.

Eriska endlessly knotted flower chains together and draped them over my head as a child. I hadn't thought about that in years.

"You're most at home in nature, wandering barefoot through the woods, flowers in your hair, chattering nonsense to the animals, Faelan of the flowers. It's a gift."

And though I'd grown out of the barefoot wanders and

flower chains in my hair, I was thankful my affinity with animals had only grown stronger.

And my love of flowers had never left me.

After she'd died, I'd had a delicate tattoo of a peony, her flower, and a water lily, mine, inked on the inside of my left wrist. Sometimes I rubbed the tattoo when I needed strength, or just to feel close to her once again.

"Good morning!" Shona, the owner of Edith, my hedgehog patient from the evening before, poked her head in the door carrying a wicker-style picnic basket. She was my first client of the day, even though I suspected there wasn't much for me to do other than tell her that Edith would likely take care of her babies just fine. "How are you today? Pretty flowers."

"They are, aren't they? Are they from you?" Shona was a gardener, so it wouldn't have surprised me if she'd left a bunch for me as thanks.

"Um, no. Though now I feel a right shite for not bringing you some." Shona's face dropped and I rushed to reassure her.

"No, no. It's fine. They were just ... on my doorstep with no note today. I couldn't help but wonder if they were from you for helping with Edith. How is she today?" I waved them back to the exam room, hoping to move the conversation smoothly past the mystery of the flowers.

"A secret admirer, then. How nice." Shona beamed at me, her blue eyes twinkling. She was a pretty woman with straight blond hair, happy eyes, and work-roughened hands. I peered into the basket, ignoring her comment. Inside, Edith slept, curled around her babies.

"Och, aren't they sweet? I'm reluctant to awaken them. Have you been monitoring them? Is she feeding?"

"Yes, though I've really tried not to disturb her."

"That's really for the best. Mums can get easily stressed. The best thing you can do really is give her a safe and quiet space to rest and nurse. The less disruption she has, the better."

"Oh no. Do you think the party last night was bad for her?" Worry crossed Shona's face.

"She seems all right. If it had been too much she would have abandoned them out of fear. Give her a quiet few weeks, and I suspect she'll bring them along well." I eased the top of the basket closed, not wanting to bother the new mum too much.

"You're meeting with Sophie later?"

"I am." I tilted my head in question at her. That was odd. Why did she know that?

"Maybe you could stop by this week. After your chat. You could see the garden and I'll make you a pretty bouquet for your table."

"Sure, if time permits. It's been a bit hectic lately."

"No problem. Soon then." Shona gently lifted the basket. "What do I owe you?"

"It's nothing." I waved it away. I hadn't really done anything, the night before or now, that Edith hadn't been able to handle on her own.

"Definitely come by then. I have a greenhouse too. We'll get you some fresh veggies for a nice salad." I smiled. I could see myself becoming fast friends with Shona. I felt genuine warmth from her, and that was extremely welcome. And a salad with fresh produce sounded divine.

"I'll do that." My next client was already coming in the door, and my focus turned to my patients.

One of my favorite things about running a vet practice was that there was little time for outside thoughts or distractions. Instead, I was forced to respond immediately to the problems at hand, and I loved how immersed I could get in my work.

By the end of the day, I was ready for a quiet meal and a glass of wine curled up on my couch with Gloam, but it would be rude to cancel on Sophie at the last minute. Plus, I needed to make sure I ingratiated myself with the people who lived here, and judging from the tight-knit group on hand at the hedgehog baby shower the night before, building a friendship with Sophie would certainly benefit me. With one last lingering look at my couch, I left my flat.

I'd chosen to walk, as the castle was just up the hill from my flat, and Gloam prowled the bushes near me as I strolled up the road. Silver light trailed across the calm waters of Loch Mirren and once again my eyes were drawn to the perfectly circular island out in the middle. Though I was one for the flowers and forest, there was something about the water that fascinated me. Perhaps it was that same undercurrent of otherness that clung to Loren Brae's underbelly, but I was certain that Loch Mirren held her secrets close.

Humming, I followed the perfectly manicured hedges that lined the drive up to the castle, and I let myself go loose. That's how my mum had always described it, when she dropped her shields and tuned into her magick. It was almost like taking a pair of sunglasses off so you could see the light. I did this now, just to confirm if what I'd been feeling was true.

While I couldn't see magick, as I didn't have that particular gift, I could feel it, pulsing gently across the hills and rolling down rocks that pebbled the shores of the loch. In my mind's eye, I envisioned it to be like a delicate spiderweb that clung to the buildings and trees, dewy and fresh after a misting rain. Gloam made a soft yipping sound, a warning, and I pulled myself back, shuttering my magick, and looked for him.

He stood, his back rigid, his tail pointed straight, eyes focused into the hedges. Stepping close, I aligned myself with him, trying to see what had put him on alert.

"There's something following us. Again."

I didn't respond to Gloam's thought in my head, but held my breath, not daring to move or make a sound. *What did he mean by again?* The wind tickled the back of my neck, and fine goosebumps broke out across my skin as my adrenaline kicked up. I'd taken self-defense classes, which had then turned into a stint of Muay Thai training that I had fallen in love with. Rocking backward so my weight was on my heels, I shifted slightly, bringing my hands up.

Golden eyes glimmered in the fading light and then they were gone.

Had whatever it was not blinked, I would have missed it entirely, as the breeze strengthened, sending the hedges rustling, blocking my vision. Straining, I leaned up, searching for what I'd seen, but I couldn't get a read on anything.

"It's gone."

"What was it?" I glanced down to where Gloam bumped against my leg, his posture now relaxed.

"I'm ... not sure, to be honest. I can't get a read on its scent."

"Human? Animal? Magick?"

"I don't know."

That was odd. Wasn't it? Shouldn't a fox be able to get a read on what was following us?

"You're certain it was following us? Or was it just passing through?"

"Hard to say. But it's gone now. Listen. You can hear the birds again."

I paused, and realized he was right. The sounds of wildlife putting themselves to bed for the night had returned to the early evening air. A raven swooped over us, and landed nearby on a branch, cocking its head and studying me with its shiny brown eyes.

"Good evening, sir," I said, automatically, as I pretty much talked to every animal that I met.

"Good evening."

My mouth dropped open. This wasn't Gloam's voice in my head, but another. Deeper, with a rasp around the edges, like someone slowly ripping wrapping paper.

"Is that you speaking to me? Raven? What's your name?" I glanced over my shoulder to make sure nobody was about. The last thing I needed was for people to hear me talking to animals.

"Murdoch."

"Wait, Murdoch. Didn't I treat you a few weeks ago? Are you with Kaia then?"

"I am."

Confusion had me furrowing my brow. Could Kaia speak to animals too? Was Murdoch a familiar? If so, did that mean there *were* witches in Loren Brae? Before I could ask any of my questions, Murdoch took flight, swooping high above my head and disappearing over the top of the castle.

"Well, now, isn't that interesting?" And exciting. This new development gave me hope that for once I might be able to settle in one spot and stay a while. Bolstered, I continued my walk up the drive, daydreaming about what color I'd paint the walls in my flat. I'd never really decorated my home before, yet oddly enough I found myself endlessly watching videos on decorating and housing renovations. It was the forbidden fruit, I supposed, that dream of settling down and making a cozy space for myself.

My last home I hadn't even lasted three months before I'd been met with a knock late at night, angry men at my doorstep. It was an age-old story, and one I'd grown tired of, but self-preservation had me able to leave any place I lived within an hour.

Being misunderstood was tiring.

And my cross to bear.

Leaves rustled, Gloam yipped a warning, but it was too late.

A massive glowing Highland coo thundered from the bushes, bellowing, and despite my training with magick and self-defense, I shrieked and ran.

Pounding up the hill, I skidded to a stop in front of the castle as two dogs raced to meet me, a chihuahua and a corgi mix, barking with excitement. An older gentleman, with bushy white brows, a newsboy cap pulled low over his shock of white hair, and faded denim trousers, stood with a shovel in hand and a smile on his face.

"Clyde get ya?"

"I ... I have no idea what a Clyde is." I brought my hand to my chest, and steadied my breath, trying not to look like a mad woman screaming up the hill to the castle doorstep. Gulping, I reached up to pat my hair and take a moment to settle myself.

I was one hundred percent certain that the coo that had just terrified me was a ghost. But I wasn't about to admit that in front of this gentleman, a man I faintly remembered seeing pacing the halls last night during Edith's delivery.

"Our resident ghost coo. He gets a real kick out of frightening guests. It's like he learned how to ghost from watching television and now takes it as his sole responsibility to perform his duties correctly."

I raised an eyebrow at the man, but he didn't seem to be having me on.

"A ghost coo?"

"Aye, lass. Ye heard me." The man's bushy brows dropped and I realized it was best not to argue with him. "He's right there."

I glanced over my shoulder to where he gestured and found Clyde poking his head from the bushes, like a toddler peeking to see if his practical joke had worked.

"Bloody hell, you're right. It is a ghost coo." I shook my head, and now that I was no longer in a panic, I could find the amusement in what he'd done. One of the dogs, the chihuahua, caught sight of Clyde and took after him, his jaws contorted in a snarl.

"And they're off. That's Sir Buster and his sidekick is

Lady Lola." The man chuckled as the coo leapt from the bushes and the two dogs chased it across the expansive lawn, their excited barks reverberating across the hills. "They do this pretty much every night. It's a great game for them."

I couldn't blame them, it looked to be grand fun to race around the gardens.

"I don't think we've properly met. I'm Dr. Faelan Fletcher." Turning, I held out my hand and was given a firm handshake in return.

"Archie. My wife, Hilda, and I are the castle caretakers. We're pleased as could be about your help with wee Edith. She had us worried."

Bemused, I tilted my head at Archie. I wouldn't have suspected a man like him would be that invested in a hedgehog's delivery.

"She did everything right. She's going to be a great mum."

"Aye, lass. I believe that to be true. Well, now, come on through. We're just having a simple tea tonight in the lounge. Leftovers from last night. Lia spoils us all with her cooking. Don't say anything, but once in a while it puts Hilda out a bit as she doesn't have to cook as much as she once did."

"I won't say a word." Largely because I'd only met Lia, the owner of the castle restaurant, in passing last night.

"Welcome, again, to MacAlpine Castle." Archie left his shovel by the door, wiped his boots on the mat, and ushered me inside. "The castle was built in the 1600s and has always been occupied. Forty years ago, part of the castle was converted into a tourist attraction, in order to encourage more visitors to Loren Brae. This side of the castle has family and staff apartments, and the other has been turned into a historically accurate museum that reflects how life was once lived here, as well as displaying items and art from years past. It's been quite popular, well, it used to be, that is."

At that, I glanced at him and caught a flash of frustration on his face. Not feeling comfortable enough to ask him what he meant, I defaulted to silence as he led me down a stone corridor with electrical sconces that mimicked real flame torches. Portraits of what I presumed were family members from days past lined the walls, and voices carried to us from an open doorway at the end of the hall. Though Scotland boasted its fair share of castles and historical keeps, and I'd been to loads of them, I couldn't help but admire the care for preserving the history here.

"Faelan's here," Archie announced unceremoniously at the door, and I followed him into a lounge. Along one wall were tall windows that looked into the well-lit garden, a fireplace with two armchairs bookending it, and faded rugs covered the stone floors. On another side of the room, a kitchen table and chairs were tucked against cabinets, and in the middle of the room were two impressive couches where Sophie sat, speaking to her boyfriend, Lachlan, and the woman I believed to be Hilda. Archie confirmed that when he walked past, dropped a kiss on the top of her head, and took a seat in one of the faded tartan armchairs by the fireplace. Immediately, he lifted a box from the floor onto his lap, opened it, and pulled out what looked to be a feather. Before I could ask what he was doing, Sophie popped up to give me a hug.

"Yay! You're here. I've been dying to get a chance to really talk to you, but we've been a bit slammed of late. Have you met my partner, Lachlan?" Sophie gestured to Lachlan, who stood and reached out a hand.

"Aye, we met briefly last night. Nice to see you again."

"Thanks for all your help with Edith. We're all over the moon about the new additions to the family." Lachlan beamed at me and then put his arm around Sophie's shoulders and she snuggled into him. They were quite the couple —her shorter and curvy, casual in a jumper and UGG boots, and him tall and stately in neatly pressed trousers and a fitted button-down. But their easy affection made me instantly like them together.

"I can't say I've ever attended a hedgehog baby shower before, but it was quite the party." I smiled as the older woman stood and came forward, her hand outstretched.

"I'm Hilda. Can I get you a cup of tea? Or a glass of wine?"

"Wine would be great, actually. It's been a long day."

"Och, I told you we should have done this on a day she doesn't work." Sophie shot Lachlan an accusing look, and he just shrugged.

"You said the sooner the better."

"But she's clearly tired."

"You're in charge here, darling, not me."

At that, Sophie's cheeks flushed, and she turned to me with a pleading look on her face.

"Say you'll stay for a bit? You're not too tired?"

"I can stay for a bit." *Just what did they mean about "the sooner the better"?*

"You're certain? We don't want to put you out." Hilda waited, concern on her face.

"No, please. Go ahead. I would have just been at home on my couch with a glass of wine as well. Plus, there are really no days off in my practice. Not when you're a solo business owner. It's kind of hard to say 'no' if there's an emergency, you ken?" I sat down on the couch across from where Sophie and Lachlan had been sitting, and they sat as well while Hilda went to get me that glass of wine.

"That's got to be exhausting, isn't it? To always be on call and never have a break for yourself?"

"It is. But it's rewarding. And there are slow days and mad days. It really just depends. Since I'm new here, it takes a bit more time because I need to inventory the office, put orders in for areas that are lacking, all while still seeing patients."

"Did the last vet not leave it in good shape?"

"It wasn't horrible, but he left quite quickly. Almost like he was running from something."

The room went quiet and I realized that I'd messed up.

Somehow, I must have stumbled on the thing that Loren Brae was hiding. The very thing that I'd heard whispered about through the region. Apparently, the problem that was driving tourists and locals alike out of town was well known to the people gathered here.

"Och, he was. Running, that is." Archie cleared his throat, his eyes on the feather he was working on. I realized he was tying flies for fishing. "Coward."

"You can't be blaming the man, can ye? Certainly one can only take so much." Hilda came forward with a full glass of red for me in one hand, and a bottle in the other.

Handing me the glass, she topped up Sophie and Lachlan's glasses before taking the armchair across from Archie.

Silence fell across the room, and I twisted the wine glass in my fingers, my eyes dropping to the rich red liquid. Was this even safe to drink? What was happening here? My stomach twisted, nerves putting me on high alert. Were they going to kick me out of town already? I'd barely made a go of it here.

"We should just tell her." Sophie twisted to look at Lachlan.

"Tell me what?" Sadness fell on my shoulders. I'd been on such a high from a fun night at the castle the night before, and now they'd found out what I was.

"Lass, we think you're magick," Hilda said, her tone serious.

There it was. I'd hoped it wouldn't come, not here, but once again, I'd misread the situation. Loren Brae was just like every other small town, chasing away what they didn't understand, needless worry overshadowing reason.

But one thing I would no longer do, that I'd sworn to myself that I would never do again, was lie about what and who I was again. Lifting my chin, I set my glass down on the table and stood.

"Aye, I am. A healer by heart, a veterinarian by profession. Magick is my gift, but hard work and ethics is my guide. It's a shame you can't be understanding of that." Turning on my heel, I marched to the door.

"Och, lass. Settle down. It's nothing to be stomping off over. We're all magick here."

I stopped, my back to the others, my heart thundering

in my chest. Glancing over my shoulder, I saw the whole room watching me, smiles on their faces.

"You are?"

"Well, some of us are." Lachlan crossed his arms, an annoyed look on his face.

"He's just grumpy that I got the power." Sophie squeezed his arm, laughing, and I turned fully around, my eyes widening.

"Come, sit down, lass. Have your wine." Archie waved a feather at where I'd just been sitting. "Welcome to the Order of Caledonia."

CHAPTER EIGHT

FAELAN

It turns out, the Order of Caledonia was made up of women with power, all different from mine, but each unique and powerful in their own right. Sophie was the first Knight of the Order, tasked with finding the others and completing the final ritual that would protect the Clach na Fìrinn, the Stone of Truth that lay buried deep in the ground on the wee island in the middle of Loch Mirren. I'd been right to be fascinated by the loch, as it was highly magicked, and until the Order of Caledonia was complete and the protective wards had been restored, the Clach na Fìrinn had unleashed its Kelpies as a defense against any suspected predators that would seek to steal it from its resting place.

I was on my second glass of wine, nodding along with everything that they were explaining, trying to soak it all in.

A magickal order of women. *Had Mum known about this? Especially given it was passed down through generations.*

Dangerous Kelpies that were intensifying in their behavior the longer it took to lay the wards for protecting the Stone of Truth.

A sentient truth stone that knew the secrets of the universe and could destroy anyone who sought to keep it.

And me, Faelan of the Flowers, a direct descendant of those who had served on the Order before me.

It was a lot to wrap my head around, but at the same time, it wasn't difficult at all. I'd cut my teeth on magick, and though Eriska had told me many a fantastical story through the years, she'd never once mentioned the Order of Caledonia. What could have kept her from telling me about this? Or was this what she'd been running from all along? Would it bring harm to me to join this order of women?

"You don't seem all that surprised by this," Hilda observed, as I'd sat quietly, soaking in parts of my family history I'd had no clue about. *But why?* That was the question I was wrestling with.

"I'm not," I admitted, but then shrugged. "And yet, I am. Magick doesn't surprise me. My ancestors' involvement in this Order does."

"So you already know you have power then?" Sophie bounced on the couch, lightly clapping her hands. "Oh goodie, that makes life so much easier. It's kind of wild to try and accept something when you've never had magick in your life before."

I smiled at her, amused. She was from California and hadn't been raised with all the myths and legends of Scotland seeped into her bones. Raising my hands, I held them palm forward in the air.

"I'm a healer."

"Ohhhhh." Sophie slapped her forehead. "That's what you meant when you said a healer by heart. I thought you just meant you were compassionate."

"I am." My lips quirked. "But I can also lay hands on an injured patient and repair ripped tendons and knit skin back together or expunge illness."

"Badass." Sophie gave me an approving nod. "Hilda, can we do a cheese platter? I'm a bit peckish."

"What about a few leftover pizzas from last night?" Hilda stood and I gaped at them as they casually discussed food after I had bared my secret to them all.

A secret that had kept me running for years now.

I cleared my throat.

"Um, doesn't that bother you?" I asked, bewildered.

"Do you not want pizza?" Sophie's eyebrows shot up.

"No." I laughed softly. "The healing with my hands. My magick. That doesn't bother you?"

"Why would it bother us, lass? You're an asset to Loren Brae," Archie barked, and I pursed my lips, honestly confused on how to respond to this.

My gift had rarely been welcomed by others in my life.

In fact, I could count on one hand the number of times I'd shared it and had been celebrated for it. Three of those times had been after I'd been unable to shield my gift from owners while healing their animals. However, I'd lucked out in those cases, as they'd been so grateful for my help they hadn't cared how I had managed to do it.

And then there was the fourth time.

My ex-boyfriend.

My first love.

In the beginning, he'd been excited about my gift. A fellow student in my vet classes, Stuart had loved knowing that I had this added tool to help animals. Until I'd started getting more accolades than him. I'd tested higher on the exams, was picked more often in demonstrations, and even scored an internship that he'd also coveted. It had all proven too much for Stuart. One night, after second year exams were done, he'd tried to expose me to the other students. Luckily, Eriska had taught me the art of deflection and there was enough alcohol flowing that I'd been able to flip it into a joke. Everyone had laughed at Stuart, and the next day he'd broken it off with me. The following year, I found out he'd switched to a different program, and that had been my first lesson in sharing secrets with someone I loved.

Protect thyself first. Eriska had warned me of that, herself having been burned by my own father. In most parts of the world, magick was not met with fanfare and well wishes.

And yet here I stood in a room of people blithely telling me that magick existed, they each had it, and that I was part of some sort of ancient magickal Order. Suspicion formed, and I put my glass down, ignoring Sophie's chatter about pizza.

"What's wrong, lass?" Archie's sharp voice cut through the conversation, and everyone turned to look at me.

"How do I know this is real?" I asked, holding my hand out to the room. "This Order of Caledonia. Ancient truth stones. Magick."

"I mean, it's a valid question. One that will probably disappear the minute a Kelpie shows up on your doorstep."

Or a talking fox.

"If you want the full history, Agnes of Bonnie Books has the historical records. But largely, I can tell you as keepers of the castle, it's our job to restore the Order as soon as we can. The last Order had fallen defunct, with Sophie's uncle being the last of the standing Order. When he passed, it triggered the Kelpies to appear more often."

"If you're the keepers, why did you allow the Order to get down to just one person?" I asked, and Hilda winced, while Archie's brows drew low over his eyes.

"Och, it's not something I'm real proud of, to be sure of it," Hilda murmured. "We'd grown a touch complacent, hadn't we? The Order had hummed along nicely enough and we were optimistic that even though the Order was no longer complete, that there were enough surviving members to maintain the necessary protections."

"Until Lachlan's mum."

I glanced to Lachlan and he rubbed a hand over his face. Sophie leaned in, murmuring something in his ear.

"It's all right, Soph. It's not a secret." Lachlan folded his arms and looked up at me. "My mum died in the loch. Drowned by Kelpies. It took me a long time to accept the truth of it. I wanted something real to blame, you understand? For a long time, it was her. I was so mad at her for swimming in that icy cold water. I'd convinced myself it was just something that happened. Water too cold. Leg cramp. Drowning. But it wasn't. It was the Kelpies, and now the only way for me to avenge her death is to banish them forever and protect Loren Brae from further harm."

It was the quiet righteousness in his voice that convinced me.

And the flash of very real pain I saw in the shadow of his eyes.

I recognized a wounded animal when I saw one.

"I'm sorry. It's terribly hard to lose someone you love, particularly your mum. I've lost mine as well."

Sophie's eyes went soft in that way of people who want to express condolences and I held my hand up, stopping her. My grief was a scab that I tried my hardest not to pick. Rubbing my thumb across my tattoo on my wrist, I thought of Eriska.

She would have loved this.

Despite the number of times she was run out of town, spat on, and shunned for her magick, she'd been an endless optimist. She'd also been willing to give people the benefit of the doubt far more often than I had. If she were here right now, she'd be urging me to join this unique little magickal club and to fight the good fight and all that.

Maybe I should.

This could provide the answers to the many things that plagued me. Sophie owned the freaking castle here, which meant people looked up to and respected her decisions. If I was a part of her group, so to speak, it would be less likely that I'd be run from town on suspicions of witchcraft. In fact, if Loren Brae was as open to magick as I was beginning to think it was, I might finally have found my haven.

The practical side of me that had just invested my life savings in my new vet practice stood up and cheered.

"I'll join." I looked over at Archie, who gave me a sharp nod of approval. "What do I have to do?"

"There's a ritual ..." Sophie began and I raised an eyebrow at her. She winced. "I know, I know. It sounds awful. But it's just a ritual where you go to the four corners of the property with your weapon of choice, pledge to protect the Stone of Truth, and then once you pass your three challenges, you're a part of the Order."

"Challenges?" I picked my wine back up and drained it. I didn't like the sound of this. Challenges were for video games and side quests. Not for a very busy vet who didn't want to attract undue attention around town.

"More like challenges of the heart," Sophie said.

"Or character," Archie added.

"Explain." I shook my head when Hilda offered me more wine. A commotion at the door sounded and Hilda left the room, as barking could be heard from outside.

"The Stone of Truth needs to know you're pure of heart in order to protect it. It doesn't present challenges like in a Highland Games or something, you'll just know if you passed because a symbol will show up in your weapon."

"Aye, this weapon you keep mentioning?" I gave Sophie an exasperated look. "Weapons and challenges and all that sound pretty intense."

"A symbolic choice, really. It's *your* weapon of choice. It should matter to you."

"My scalpel," I said, automatically. Not only was it a lethal weapon if wielded as such, but it was a symbol of my skill as a surgeon for helping animals.

"Perfect. So you take your scalpel in the ritual and once you pass a challenge, something will show up. For some it has been jewels, others gold bands in the handle ..." Sophie trailed off and gave Lachlan an exasperated look. "I'm bungling this, aren't I? You'd think after having to explain this several times over, I'd be better at it."

"Several times over? How many are there?" I asked, not having considered the others in this ritual.

"There's myself. Lia. She's a kitchen witch and owns Grasshopper. Shona. She's a garden witch."

"Shona?" I asked, surprised. Now it made sense why she wanted to speak with me after I came to see Sophie. I *was* going to be a part of her club now. *Shona*. So easy to like with her mild-mannered personality, garden witch knowledge, and definitely someone I'd like to be closer friends with.

Friends. Even the idea of growing close with people was a touch off-putting, but I could almost hear Eriska screaming in my ear to be brave.

"Yup, Shona. Whom you've met, of course. Then there's Orla, Kaia, and Willow."

"Seven. Including me, that is."

"Correct. We need nine." Sophie gave me a pleading look. "You're certain you'll join? We lucked out by you coming here and didn't have to search down the next in line. But the Kelpies are escalating. It's why the last vet ran, I believe. We had quite a showdown right on your doorstep. In broad daylight."

"With the Kelpies?" My mouth dropped open. So that was why Dr. MacAllister had turned tail and ran. It wasn't because he was covering up some scandal of sorts, it was because a mythological water beast had come knocking on his door.

It all made much more sense now.

All his nervous looks out to the loch.

His insistence on me staying inside at night.

His absolute refusal to show me around town.

Feeling calm for the first time since I'd moved here, now that someone had finally let me in on the secret, I let out a small sigh of relief.

Magick I could handle.

Even in the form of massive water horses.

They were just another type of animal, weren't they?

"Yup, with the Kelpies. They've been quiet since. Kaia got the bridle off one, and we think it freaked them out, though I suspect they'll only lie dormant for so long. The sooner we close our Order, the better."

THE SOONER THE BETTER. Well, that part made sense now. But getting a bridle off a mythical creature? The fact they wear bridles was surprising in itself. A horse can weigh anything from 300 to 1000 pounds, so a mythical version could be even more. *How did Kaia manage to get the bridle off the beast?* It was all so fascinating, and I wanted to be a part of this, especially if it placed charming Loren Brae back on the map.

"I'm in. Let's do this. What's the ritual involve? Do you need my blood?" Blood didn't make me squeamish and I smiled when Sophie made a gagging sound.

"Gross, no. We can do it when you're ready. You'll need your weapon."

"I'll just pop home and get it."

Hilda walked back in, Sir Buster and Lady Lola at her heels, and smiled when she heard my words.

"You're joining us?"

TRICIA O'MALLEY

"Aye."

"Welcome, Faelan. We're lucky to have you." The way Hilda beamed at me warmed my soul, almost as if she could be a stand-in for the motherly energy I missed in my life. Nobody could replace my mum, but it was nice to feel the approval from a woman that the people in this room looked up to.

"Thank you. I'll just be right back."

I needed a moment. Whether it was the emotions of being welcomed instead of chased away, or the realization that maybe I had finally found my home, but either way a quick walk in the brisk night air would help me to breathe more easily. *As long as Clyde doesn't scare me again playing boo.*

Gloam joined me the instant I was passing the gardens, slipping out from the bushes to prowl along at my side.

"Why didn't you tell me that there were Kelpies here?"

"Didn't want to scare you off."

I mulled that over. Though the lack of communication annoyed me, it also warmed my heart to know that Gloam had wanted me to stay.

"I'm stronger than I look. And the women? There's magick here."

"You knew that. It's what called you here in the first place." Gloam paused, his tail going straight, his nose lifted to the wind. *"Something follows us."*

"Is it Clyde again?" I asked, unbothered this time now that I knew the castle grounds were haunted by a ghost coo.

"I can't say."

"You can't say or won't say? Or you don't know?"

86

Gloam didn't answer me, and I scanned the dark hills, hoping to catch a glimpse of movement. When nothing happened, I continued to my flat. There wasn't much I could do about something following me. So long as it didn't pose a threat to me or Gloam, I had to assume it was just something curious about the newcomers in town. At least I hope that is what it was.

I liked to think that if I was in danger I would feel it.

But maybe that could be survivor bias speaking.

Either way, I made it to my flat without a surprise ghost coo attack or a Kelpie screaming across the water toward me, so I considered that a win.

By the time I made it back to the castle, scalpel sheathed in my pocket, inky night had drawn close, and warm light flickered from the torches that Archie and Lachlan held. The group was standing outside the castle doors, waiting for me, and had I not known better, I could have been convinced we were villagers off to kill the beast.

"We'll start with the east," Archie directed, pointing toward Loch Mirren, and I fell in line as he led us to a narrow footpath that wound around the stables and over gently sloping hills. Sophie chattered about Scotland as we picked our way along the dark path, choosing our steps carefully in the light of the torches.

"Here we are." Archie crouched and brushed wild grasses away over an old stone plaque with a Celtic insignia on it.

"A Kelpie?" I asked, leaning closer.

"Here you go, lass." Hilda held out a bundle of dried thistle wrapped in twine, and I took it.

"What's this for?"

"It's just an added layer of protection. Keeps the bad stuff out." Hilda winked at me. It made sense. My mum always "saged" every new place we moved into.

I lit the bundle, thinking briefly about the handful of flowers on my doorstep earlier that day. More flowers. Maybe there were signs everywhere and I'd just been ignoring them. A thin curl of smoke emanated from the bundle of dried flowers, and I held it over the stone, watching as the smoke curled into the night sky.

"I, Faelan Fletcher," Archie said, "a Charm Witch in the Order of Caledonia, announce my arrival."

I paused and looked up at Archie, the reflection of the flames dancing in his eyes.

"Charm Witch?"

"For the animals. You have a charmed spirit as a healer of animals," Archie explained.

The title warmed me, and my shoulders straightened unintentionally, as though I was gaining a new confidence with this rite. My mum had always told me I was charmed, even though I'd brushed off her words.

I repeated his words, waving the bundle of smoking flowers over the stone.

"I accept the responsibility of protecting the Clach na Fìrinn and promise to restore the Order to its fullness. In doing so, I show myself worthy of the magick of Clach na Fìrinn."

I mirrored Archie's words, feeling my magick ripple through me, excited at a new challenge.

"It is with these words I establish the Order of Caledonia as the first line of protection for the Clach na Fìrinn and alert the Kelpies to my arrival. I accept the power bestowed upon me."

When nothing happened, I glanced at Archie.

"Well done. On to the south." Archie nodded once, and we all turned as a group and plodded toward the next marker stone. The breeze kicked up, and the smoke from the bundle of flowers I carried mixed with that of the torches, adding an even more mystical touch to the evening.

What would Luch think of this?

Him, a doctor, rooted so staunchly in science. *And why did Luch Carmichael just pop into my head now?* Was it because of the thought of flowers? His clear suspicion of how I'd healed Oban? Yet he'd lived in Loren Brae for over a year now. If what Sophie said was true about the Kelpies screaming in the night, surely he would have had to suspend some disbelief over the presence of magick in the world?

I pulled my thoughts away from Luch as we finished the ritual, Sophie beaming at me like I was her new best friend. And maybe I was. Well, *a* friend, at least. The idea of having friends again excited me, instead of inciting the usual anxiety and worry, and my thoughts were confirmed when she gave me a huge hug.

"Welcome, Faelan. I'm so glad you're a part of the Order."

"Thanks, I think I am too." I laughed when Sophie scrunched up her nose. "I mean, it's still very new to me. But I'm sure I'll be glad to be a part of it. Though I'm not really certain how I'm supposed to wield this." I held my scalpel up in the air.

A band of diamonds glittered in the handle, and I almost dropped it on my foot.

"How have you already passed a challenge?" Sophie gasped, grabbing my wrist and dragging my hand forward. The others gathered, the light from the torches glinting off the diamonds in the handle of the scalpel.

"Have you healed anything unusual, lass?" Archie asked, scratching his chin.

"Just a ..." I paused. Could I really say I healed a unicorn out loud? I knew we were all about magick here, but even that might be too farfetched for everyone.

"Just a what?" Hilda leaned closer, lowering her voice.

"A unicorn." I pressed my lips together, straightening my shoulders, ready to be laughed at.

"Ohhhhh, you saw her?" Sophie squeezed my arm, excitement on her face. "Were you with anyone?"

"No, I was alone."

"That's *interesting*." Sophie exchanged an unreadable look with Lachlan.

"And she was hurt? Such a shame." Hilda shook her head.

"I fixed her up though, as she'd had a nail in her hoof. She was pretty incredible. It was like trying to hold a star in your hands."

"It's a rare treat it is, to be seeing the likes of her. That's a blessing for you, lass." Archie nodded his head briskly in my direction.

"See? You really are charmed." Sophie beamed at me, and I smiled back, feeling the warmth of acceptance flow through me.

For the first time in ages, I finally felt like I'd found a place I could call home—and even more than that? A place that would finally welcome me.

I hoped, wherever she was, Eriska would be at peace knowing I'd finally found my place in the world.

CHAPTER NINE

LUCH

"**E**asy one today, Dr. Carmichael." Lynn, a nurse practitioner who often shared the same twelve-hour shift as I did, pulled on her coat, and stretched her arms over her head. She'd been around long enough to know everyone in the hospital's names, including their immediate and extended family members' names as well.

"Aye, lucky enough." I quickly glanced at the clock to make sure we were indeed done with our shift lest she jinx us, and car crash victims came rolling in. "Gave me some time to follow up on a few patients, make some extra notes on a few charts."

"You're so great at that." Lynn's approving smile made her sixty-year-old eyes crinkle, and it was welcome. "Most people don't expect a call from the A&E doctor himself."

"It makes less work for the nurses." Sometimes admin

could pile up on a doctor if we had back-to-back emergency situations, but I really did try my best, often staying after hours, just to make sure all my observations were noted for each patient, as well as examining any that I'd had additional concerns about. The charting protocol was such that notes should be entered in real time, in order to help with any follow-up care or next steps for the patient, but there were times where we just couldn't get to it.

"And that's why we all love you."

I smiled, patting her shoulder lightly as I passed, holding the door open for her as we stepped into the chilly night air.

"When are you going to start wearing a coat, Dr. C?" Jacob, the security guard, who was old enough to be my grandfather, shook his head at me.

"I told you I run hot."

"That's the truth of it, isn't it, handsome?" Nan, the night cleaner, blew me a kiss from where she chatted with Jacob. Nan was almost as old as Lynn, but colored her hair to hide any grays, and wore cakey black mascara to make her brown eyes pop. She fluttered her eyelashes at me, and I just grinned. Her flirting was harmless, as she was happily married, and she complimented everyone who came across her path.

"New haircut, Lynn?" Nan asked.

"Just a trim." Lynn patted her hair that I was certain looked the exact same as it had the day before.

"It's nice."

Lynn paused to chat, and I raised a hand in goodbye to them, trotting out to my car. I wasn't very good at small talk, at least at work, but did my best to mask it by always being polite and working hard. In the end, that had won most people over and once my colleagues had gotten used to the fact that I was a quiet sort, they'd more or less let me be. I never opened up about my personal life at work, nor with anyone really, as I found it just made my life run more smoothly. I kept my work life in one box, and my home life in another. It was easier that way, less complicated, and it allowed me to fully check out once I got home.

I let myself unwind on the drive home, my headlights slashing through the velvety night, not meeting another car on the thirty-minute drive back toward Loren Brae. Oftentimes, I'd listen to a podcast or put on soothing music on the drive, but today I craved the silence.

It gave me some uninterrupted time to obsess over my newest fascination.

One Dr. Faelan Fletcher.

I just couldn't get her out of my mind.

Never had I been so instantly intrigued with someone.

Sure, I was attracted to her. I was a red-blooded male, wasn't I? And Faelan was gorgeous in the way of people that didn't seem to know that fact about themselves. Not that I didn't think she was confident or aware of herself as a woman, but I sensed that she might not care that her unconventional, striking beauty lingered in someone's mind. *It's like being able to see the light from the sun even when you've closed your eyes.*

Her skin flushed when she was nervous—a soft petal pink that warmed her face—and if you were close enough you could see the smallest smattering of freckles across her cheeks.

She didn't like when I drew too close.

I made her nervous.

Which meant, she wasn't unaffected by me. That or she was nervous about the secret she kept from me.

Or maybe not just from me—I shouldn't give myself that much credit—but from the world at large.

Oban had told me what she was.

A healer.

Scoffing, I ran a hand over my chin as I pulled into the gravel lane that led up the hill to my cottage in the forest. Healers were the stuff of childhood fairy tales, and even if she was real, she certainly couldn't do what I could do—with science as my backing. Call me stubborn, or call me egotistical, but I was convinced that with the right tools and the right medical education, a person could work miracles.

I just couldn't bring myself to believe that healing with magick could do the same.

It bugged me that Oban liked her so much.

It wasn't that I didn't believe in magick, not with Oban in my life, it's just that I didn't trust it. Science I could rely on. Medical training I could believe in. But magick? To heal? It was unpredictable, volatile, and there were too many hacks that royally screwed it up. No, I'd stick to relying on what thousands had before me, with procedures and methods that stood up to medical scrutiny.

The dog in question trotted around the side of the cottage when I pulled the car up, the gate to the drive sliding closed behind me. I'd installed a doggy door so he could come and go as he pleased while I was at work, and he knew where his bin of food was when he was hungry. The only thing I couldn't provide for him on my long days away at work was companionship, but he'd repeatedly promised me that, like me, he enjoyed his alone time as well.

Seeing him, I forced my thoughts away from Faelan, as she was an enigma I wasn't going to solve in this moment. Or over a date, either, since she hadn't yet taken me up on my offer.

"There's my wee pal. How'd you get on today?"

"Well enough." Oban bumped his nose against my hand, and I reached down and scooped him up into my arms, having no qualms about giving my buddy a cuddle. *"Kept the rabbits out of the garden."*

"Och, they're tenacious, aren't they?"

"They'll stay back. I consider it my duty to protect your plantings."

I smiled as I carried him inside, flipping on a few lamps, and putting him on his favorite cushion by the fire.

"It's late. Are ye wanting your tea or did you see to it yourself?"

"I wouldn't say no to a wee bite."

I smiled. Oban never said "no" to a snack. But he was an active dog, and in good health, so I never minded giving it to him. After a quick shower, I changed into comfortable clothes, and I turned my Sonos on and ordered up a chill playlist to listen to while I cooked. I'd picked up some salmon fillets the day before that would be perfect with a little lemon and olive oil in a pan. Digging them out of the fridge, I also grabbed some fresh asparagus and a few potatoes. A simple meal, easy enough to prepare, and nothing that took too much energy after a long day. Filling a pot with a little water, I tossed the potatoes in to boil, and then pulled out two pans, one for the fish and the other for the asparagus.

I enjoyed cooking, when I had the time to do so, and preferred simple, rustic meals. I didn't eat meat, fish only, so that limited some of my choices, but made life easy for me.

Would Faelan let me cook for her?

I'd enjoyed having her in the cottage that one night, looking delectable in my shirt, cozied at the table. She'd kept her distance from me, wary, and rightfully so. She wasn't heedless, which was another reason she was avoiding my invite to dinner.

"Have you heard from Faelan?"

Oban joined me in the kitchen, his pointy ears jutting to the side as he tilted his head at me in question. I chuckled.

"Nope. It's only been a few days, but I'm going to follow up. If it's a firm 'no' then I'll have to back off."

"Och, that must sting. Women don't usually turn you down." Oban made a soft huffing sound, his grunty wee laugh, and I slid him an annoyed look.

"We have chemistry. I can feel it."

"Maybe it's one-sided."

I shook my head. It was my job to pay attention to people, to see if they were in pain, or hiding something. I'd felt, hell, I'd *seen* the spark of energy between Faelan and me.

"I don't think so." I added more water into the pan before dropping the asparagus in to cook. "But you may be right. I'm not going to creep on her if she doesn't want to go on a date. I can accept rejection, you ken?"

"Not well." Oban did his grunty wee laugh again and

then took off across the room when I lunged at him, pretending to chase. He skidded to a stop, butt in the air, paws down, ready for a chase.

"One time, mate. *One* time."

"You cried."

"Och, I'll get you for bringing that up." With that I chased him around the house, and he took off running, looking over his shoulder with a cheeky doggo grin. I skidded to a stop by the stove where the asparagus sizzled.

"You're lucky I have to cook, you clarty bastard."

"Like you could catch me anyway." Oban lolled on his cushion, watching me with his tongue out.

Laughing, I shook my head and turned to the stove. Oban wasn't wrong, but he was a wee shite for bringing up the one time I'd been head over heels for a lass I worked with. She had left me all pie-eyed and tongue-tied around her. I'd felt like a schoolboy all over again, with a crush on the prettiest lass in class. We'd gone on two dates before the head of surgery had taken her on a helicopter ride over Edinburgh, and then she had been finished with me. And I hadn't *cried*. There'd just been a speck of dust in my eyes is all.

It didn't much matter.

It wasn't like I could have brought her home to my family.

I couldn't bring *anyone* of my choosing home to my family.

It was one of the reasons I'd left.

I just wanted the peace to live life on my terms, doing a job that I deeply cared for, with a few hobbies in what little downtime I had. It might be a simple life, but it was free of family demands, and though the cost to live this way was high, in the end, it had been worth it.

My phone pinged with a text.

My stomach dropped. I didn't need to hear from my father today. Or from one of my brothers. It was the same request, just phrased differently depending on who it was coming from.

LUCH, I know you have a job there, but it's time to put your foolishness to bed. You have a responsibility here and having spoken to Dad today, he's worried about your protection. You're unprotected and at risk without us, putting us in jeopardy. It's time to come home.

"SUBTLE AS A BRICK THROUGH A WINDOW, BRO."

Sighing, I flicked the screen only to see a photo with a bundle of flowers that I'd left for Faelan.

ARE THESE FROM YOU?

I SMILED, my mood perking, and slid the salmon into the pan before answering.

MY, my, popular lady. First a date with someone else, and now a secret admirer?

. . .

My date was with Sophie.

I think Sophie's taken, but I'm not really up on the gossip in Loren Brae.

I laughed when Faelan sent a rude gesture emoji back at me.

"Who are you talking to?" Oban sidled closer, likely not used to me smiling at my phone. Typically I was swearing and tossing it across the table. If I wasn't on call, I'd turn the damn thing off half the time.

"None of your business."

"*I can pee on your pillowcases when you're gone, you know.*"

"Bloody hell, you're a wee shite at times, aren't you, Oban?" I glared at him and he chuckled. "It's Faelan, all right?"

"*I like her.*"

"I know you do." I'd transferred the asparagus to cold water and now tossed them back in the pan with some butter and garlic. "Because she healed you. Or so you claim."

"*You know it as well as I do. I'm telling you, Luch. I was close. Too close.*"

At that, I inhaled through my nostrils, steadying myself. I hated knowing I'd almost lost him. He was my best friend, confidant, and a damn good dog.

"I know it. It's terrifying to think about."

"She pulled me back. She's more powerful than you think."

"Maybe. Or maybe it was just luck. Not everyone can play with magick, Oban."

"I don't get the sense she's playing."

My phone pinged again.

You didn't answer my question.

And you didn't answer my question.

What question was that?

Can I take you to dinner this week?

I'm not sure.

Is that a yes or a no?

It's an I don't know.

Are you open to persuasion?

. . .

LIKE WHAT KIND?

I TURNED TO OBAN. "What kind of pose would you do to make Faelan feel bad for me and go out with me?"

Oban tilted his head and thought about it before rolling on his back and holding his paws in the air.

"That's perfect, mate. You're an excellent wingman." I snapped the photo and sent it.

OBAN MISSES YOU.

I'M happy to go on a date with Oban then.

UNFORTUNATELY, we're a package deal.

HMMM.

I GOTTA RUN, my dinner's almost ready. Night, night, Faelan.

I CLICKED off and deliberately ignored the next text, knowing she was probably annoyed that I hadn't answered her about the flowers. A little mystery was good in life, though, and I hoped it would keep her intrigued enough to consider a date with me. But I pondered Oban's words for a moment.

"She pulled me back. She's more powerful than you think."

If Oban was right, I'd need to keep a careful eye on her.

"All right, lad. One perfectly seared salmon coming your way."

CHAPTER TEN

FAELAN

T he rock hit me right beneath the eye, splitting my skin, and causing a trickle of blood to roll down my cheek.

"Witch! Dirty witch!"

"At least I'm not a bloody eejit!" I bent to pick up a good-sized rock when my arm was seized and I whirled around, gaping at my mum.

"He's not worth it, Faelan." Eriska dragged me past the cottages where families stood on their doorsteps, their faces drawn. Eriska waved her fist at them. "Shame on you. Shame on you all."

People drew back inside, ducking their heads as we passed, their whispers following us. Once we were outside town, and back at our car, Eriska pulled me into the back seat and wiped my face. Immediately, I felt the pain beneath my eye lessen as she used her magick to heal the cut.

"I'm not a dirty witch, am I, Eriska?"

"No, Faelan. My sweet, powerful child. You're charmed is what you are."

"Cursed," I mumbled, wiping my nose with the back of my hand.

"No, you listen to me, Faelan of the flowers. Don't listen to what anyone says. Ever. You're charmed. Kissed by the fairies, you are. It's a gift what we have, and that's the truth of it. My wee lucky charm."

She'd kissed me on the nose, we'd packed, and then left town within the hour.

I woke up from the memory, missing my mother sorely, and smiled when two eyes gleamed at me from across the room.

"You're up?"

"Foxes are nocturnal."

I glanced at the clock. It was just shy of seven in the morning, but at least I'd slept through my witching hour wake-up call. Tugging Luch's shirt more tightly around me, I rose and walked to the bathroom to splash water on my face. No sense in trying to go back to sleep when I'd be up soon enough anyway. Even on the weekends, I was hard-pressed to sleep past seven. Pausing, I studied my face in the mirror.

Just a hint of bruising was left on my forehead from when I'd slammed my head into Luch's door the other day. Even thinking about it again brought a rosy flush of embarrassment to my cheeks. I'd panicked, like a mouse caught in a cupboard, and had tried to flee. I hadn't healed the bruise on my forehead, as much as I was tempted to do so, because it reminded me every time I looked in the mirror that I needed to keep my guard up around him. Particularly now that I know he wanted to take me on a date.

Typically I prided myself on being able to handle situations that made me uncomfortable. I'd developed a thick skin through the years—more as a matter of necessity than a desire to do so—and I aimed to be an oasis of calm in all manner of situations from hysterical clients to suspicious neighbors. Yet with Luch, none of my prior training seemed to matter.

He bothered me.

Slipped into my dreams at night.

Soothed me with the scent of his shirt when I went to sleep.

Put my back up with his questions and all-seeing eyes.

Desire pulled me closer even as my self-preservation demanded I stay away. I sighed as I plaited my hair back from my face, securing it in a bun at the nape of my neck. Luch hadn't responded to my question last night, and though I was now fairly certain he was the one leaving me flowers, I also didn't want to make any assumptions. Three bouquets now decorated my practice, and I'd kept a fourth bunch to put in a small glass next to the picture of my mum on the windowsill.

It was a silly thing, yet I found myself charmed by the simple bundles left on my doorstep. There was something softly sweet about the handpicked wildflowers, carefully curated and wrapped with twine. I couldn't help but get the impression that each flower was picked meticulously, as they all melded together in a symphony of colors and textures.

Gloam brushed against my leg as I walked to the

kitchen and I took that as his invitation for a cuddle. Since I was up earlier than usual today, I made myself a quick cup of tea and then took it to the couch, patting the cushion next to me as I curled up with a blanket. Gloam jumped up and settled on the blanket, curling up at my side. When I began to scratch his ears, his eyes slitted, and his mouth hung open in a sleepy half smile.

The first silvery light of morning was trailing across the surface of Loch Mirren, the water a slate gray edging to soft blue, the green hills across the way smudged in its reflection. The little island, which had captured my attention before, now held more serious meaning to me, and I let myself consider the Stone of Truth a little more deeply than I had since a few days ago when I'd first learned of it.

"A sentient truth stone," I murmured, taking a sip of my tea.

"*Objects can have power.*" Gloam slanted me a look.

"I know that, wee one." I threaded my fingers through the thick fur at the back of his neck. "It's just the sentient part that kind of throws me. To think, this inanimate object can make decisions to protect itself—like calling the Kelpies as a line of defense."

"*It has to. It's too powerful. With that comes great knowledge of what will happen if the wrong person wields it. It didn't used to be so powerful. But through the centuries, it learned, ever growing, and with it came the understanding that it needed a safe resting place. It could no longer be used, at least not by humans, as no one person could be able to withstand all its power.*"

"So it put itself to bed?" I asked, almost amused at the thought.

Out on the island, a light flashed, just the smallest of flickers and I straightened.

Could the stone hear me?

"In order to protect humanity, and others on Earth, the stone has removed itself from the hands of those in power. It's a gift it has chosen to give us."

"Huh. An altruistic sentient stone of great power." I pursed my lips, studying the wee island. "Fascinating."

"Not entirely altruistic. If the wrong person obtains it, the likelihood is they'll destroy the earth. The stone along with it."

"Fair play to the stone then. You can still do good by others even if it also serves you."

Another flicker of light, this time warmer in color, and I wondered if the stone really could hear this conversation. Maybe it could, considering it seemed to know all the things and held all the power of the universe and whatnot.

No one person should ever hold that much power. If it was my duty to protect it, albeit in whatever magickal ways the Order of Caledonia needed me to, then I would certainly do so. If only because as a healer, I'd taken my own vow to help others where I could.

After a quiet cup of tea with Gloam on the couch, the rest of the morning flew by in a series of patient appointments. I only opened for a half-day on Saturday, and due to how busy I was, I'd have to extend hours once I hired more help. Many people couldn't afford to take time off work during the week to take their pets into the vet, so the weekends were prime time for them to bring them in. Even with my half-day posted hours, it was almost mid-afternoon by the time I could close up for the day.

Maybe I should close on Monday and Tuesday and

open on the weekends? Mulling the thought over, I went to lock up after my last patient and saw Oban sitting in the middle of the waiting room.

"Oban! What are you doing here? And don't you look very handsome?" The wee Scottie had a red and black tartan bowtie around his neck. Oban trotted over and I crouched to scratch his ears and laughed when his rough tongue swiped up the side of my face. "Och, what's this?"

There was a note with my name on it fastened to his collar. Unpinning it, I stood and opened the note.

"'You've given me no choice but to send in my greatest weapon,'" I read out loud and peered over the note to see Oban had rolled onto his back and put his paws in the air. "'Plus, you have to eat. Join me for a picnic?'"

I looked out the front window to see Luch leaning against his car with his arms crossed, a smile on his face. He looked like he could be in an outdoorsman advertisement, with a flannel shirt rolled to his elbows, and thick-soled hiking boots on his feet.

"You're pretty damn cute, Oban. And so is your owner. Well, cute is an understatement for your owner. 'Hottest man I've ever seen' fits the bill, quite honestly. Not that I'd let him know that." I rubbed Oban's belly. Indecision warred. I was sorely tempted to turn my back on Oban and Luch, because a part of me understood that there was something about these two that would have a significant impact on my life. It was like standing at a fork in the path—one way, predictable, a road I've always taken before, and the other, dangerous, lit with pitfalls and danger but at the end might just be a hidden waterfall. Was discovering a secret waterfall worth the potential dangers in the path along the way?

"Get a hold of yourself, Dr. Fletcher." My thoughts were like I was about to jump out of a plane, not going on a simple picnic date with a cute client. It was *just* a date. What could be the worst thing that happened?

"All right, Oban. You've got yourself a date. But I'm going because of you, not him."

"I always tell him that I'm better with the ladies than he is."

My eyebrows shot up. Had I just heard Oban's voice in my head? It wasn't entirely unusual for me to catch an animal's stray thoughts or to be able to communicate with them in times of high stress, but this was much more direct and conversational. Like Gloam. Which meant ... what exactly? Was Luch a witch and just hiding it from me? Was that the reason he was so suspicious of my healing powers? Intrigued, I raised an eyebrow at Oban.

"Is that right? You're quite the ladies' man?"

"What can I say? Some of us are born charismatic." Oban proceeded to shake his head and lift his snout, as though he was preening for me.

"Why can I hear you talk?"

"Because you're magick, aren't you, Faelan?" With that, Oban trotted to the door and waited, glancing back over his shoulder to see if I would join him.

"I have so many questions."

Oban didn't respond and I took that to mean that he wouldn't be the one answering them. Which was fine, really, as it wasn't his job to explain the workings of the magickal world to me, and Eriska had always impressed on me to be grateful for any communication that an animal chose to give me. Hounding them for answers rarely worked in my favor, and if anything, closed them off more.

Opening the door, I stepped outside and crossed my arms over my chest, raising an eyebrow at Luch.

He just gave me a cheeky grin.

Damn it, but why was this man so good-looking? A part of me wanted to slurp him up like an icy-cold lemonade on a warm summer's day. But I was going to ignore that part of me and wait for him to speak.

"Good afternoon, Dr. Fletcher. Fancy a picnic?"

"I suppose so. As you mentioned, I do have to eat." I surprised myself by answering. I'd been certain I'd tell him that I was busy, yet that smile of his was weakening my defenses.

"Fantastic. Need a moment to change?"

"I do." I glanced from where he leaned against his car to the stairs to my flat. It would be rude to leave him sitting outside if I planned to go out to lunch with him. A normal person would invite their friend inside to wait. I was taking a stab at normalcy here, settling in, making friends and all that, so it would be the expected thing to do to ask him to come upstairs.

"Would you like to come up while I change?" I asked, reluctance obvious in my voice, and his grin widened.

"Love to. Thanks." Luch snapped his fingers at Oban. "Come on, lad. The dragon is inviting us to her inner sanctum."

"Bloody hell. I am not a dragon," I growled and Luch chuckled, the sound warming my core, and I stomped upstairs. I was *not* my normal self around this man. I ran into doors, growled, and always felt like I was off-kilter. Or one step behind. Either way, he unsettled me.

A bundle of flowers sat at my doorstep.

Grabbing them, I whirled, and came face to face with Luch. I was one step above him, the height difference aligning our eyes, and my breath caught.

"Are these from you?"

Luch's lips quirked.

"Charming flowers for a charming woman."

My eyes squinted. Did he know? Why did he phrase things that way?

Fumbling with my key, I unlocked the door, trying to ignore his large presence at my back even though every nerve in my body seemed to tingle when he was around. There was this palpable energy about Luch, like he was a fire to warm my hands with, and I blew out a breath as I stepped inside my flat and flipped the kitchen light on. Crossing inside, I put my tote bag and keys on the kitchen counter and turned to Luch.

"I'll just be a minute."

"Take all the time you need." Luch wandered toward the windows that overlooked the loch, Oban sniffing the blanket on the couch. The dog's ears perked, and he turned his head to meet my eyes.

I suspected he smelled Gloam.

Bloody hell, I'd forgotten to warn the fox we were coming. He was nowhere to be seen in the living room, but that didn't mean he might not be curled up in the bedroom. Darting over to the bedroom door, I eased it closed behind me and looked desperately around for Gloam.

"Why are there dogs in here?" The way Gloam said it told me everything I needed to know about his thoughts on dogs. Mortal enemies the two were.

"I'm sorry," I whispered as I crossed the room to stroke his head. He was curled between my pillows, just his wee snout sticking out. "For what it's worth, I think he's one of us."

"I'm not interested in finding out." Gloam glowered at me, and I couldn't blame him in the slightest.

"Just stay here then. I'll get them out quickly."

Gloam buried his head again, effectively hiding himself, and I dug out a pair of jeans and a loose blue jumper to change into. Pausing to look in the bathroom mirror, I debated unplaiting my hair and running a brush through it, but then I didn't want Luch to think I was trying too hard for this date. Even so, I couldn't help but dash a bit of mascara on and put a touch of gloss at my lips.

Stopping at the bed, I reached into the pillows and gave Gloam's ears a scratch, before I grabbed my handbag and left the room, pulling the door almost all the way closed.

Luch stood by the windows, arms linked behind his back, staring out at the loch.

"I'm ready."

He reached down and picked up the picture. "Is this your mum?"

"It is."

"She's beautiful."

"She was, yes."

"Och, I've stuck my foot in it, haven't I? I'm sorry, Faelan."

I shrugged one shoulder, never certain what to say

when people I didn't know all that well offered condolences for someone they'd never met. Luch put the frame down and turned to gesture at the bare walls of my flat.

"How long have you been here now?"

"Um, I don't know. Two months?"

"Place is a bit spartan."

That was the understatement of the year. Aside from the flowers I had in a vase by the picture frame of my mum on the table, I had no other decorations in the room. Remembering the new bundle of flowers he'd given me, I went to a cupboard and opened the door, considering my options. There were more coffee mugs than glasses, and even at that I had five to choose from. Picking a chipped green mug, I filled it with water and added his new bundle of flowers, crossing to put it on the windowsill.

"I haven't had much time to decorate."

"Is that so?" His tone suggested he had a lot of questions. "You didn't move any of your household stuff with you? Rugs? Art?"

I shrugged again, noncommittal. "My practice consumes my life."

"I get that. But even I have had time to decorate."

"You don't run your own business, though, do you?" My voice had a sharp edge, warning him to back off, and he seemed to understand he was treading on difficult territory.

"What would you do here?"

"Huh?" I turned from admiring the flowers to see him staring at the blank wall next to the small bistro table set.

"Like in here? If you had the time to decorate?" Luch waved a hand at the living space and even though I really wanted to bundle him out the door, particularly because

Oban was sniffing around my bedroom door, I paused to answer his question.

"Paint," I said, tilting my head at the plain white wall. I'd lived in enough boring places now to crave color and character. "I'm sick of white walls. I'd do something dramatic, like maybe a deep navy. And then pop colors with pretty rugs and cushions, maybe some colorful art prints."

"Do you lease? Did this come with the practice?"

I moved to stand by the door, picking up my keys and jingling them, the international signal for I'm ready to leave.

"It's mine."

Luch whistled for Oban, and I opened the door, ushering them out, and then closed and locked it behind me, letting out a small sigh of relief. I couldn't say what would have happened had Oban found Gloam, but the last thing I needed was for a chaotic dog and fox chase around my flat all while trying to explain to Luch why I had a pet fox.

"Surely you can paint then? Since it's yours?"

"Huh? Oh, the decorating?" I pulled my thoughts back to the conversation as I followed Luch down the stairs, trying not to fixate on his broad shoulders. "I suppose I could, yes, if I find the time."

"What are your hours?"

"Every weekday. Half-day Saturday. Closed Sunday, though I've been putting in half-days because I often end up dealing with emergencies anyway."

"Busy lady." Luch held the back door open for Oban, and the dog jumped dutifully in the back seat. He hadn't spoken to me again, keeping his thoughts to himself, but I still had so many questions for Luch. If I could work up the courage to ask him. Did he know his dog could talk? Maybe not. That was also a strong possibility. Maybe I was assigning potential ideas to Luch that weren't even a possibility. Now that I thought about it, surely there were plenty of pet owners that had no idea that their animals could communicate. Luch was likely one of those, not some hidden witch like I was, which was also why he was so suspicious of my powers. If he was a witch, or had any type of power, he'd just identify himself and ask me about it.

Like Sophie had.

Getting into the front seat, I waited as Luch rounded the bonnet and slid inside the car, turning to smile at me.

"Ready for an adventure? We can't go far, as I'm on call, but just a wee hike to show you a favorite spot of mine."

"Sounds good. If the weather holds." Glancing at the sky, I noticed the clouds that clustered over the hills in the distance. The only thing predictable about Scottish weather was that it was unpredictable, having a mood all its own.

"Don't worry. It's not far, and I've got umbrellas."

"Prepared for everything, are you, Dr. Carmichael?"

Luch slid me a grin, his eyes full of heat, and winked.

"Always."

CHAPTER ELEVEN

Faelan

Luch had driven about fifteen minutes or so out of Loren Brae, following the road that wound along the rocky shores of Loch Mirren toward the hospital, before pulling off onto a nearly hidden dirt and gravel lane that rolled up the sharp crevice of a hill. Once we'd reached the top, he'd parked and hooked a backpack over his shoulders that he'd pulled from the boot of the car.

"This is beautiful, Luch."

"Aye, it's a favorite for sure." I followed him down a thinly trodden trail, the wind rustling the long grasses and flowers that brushed at our sides as we walked. Oban all but disappeared in it, and I laughed when I saw him bound, his little head popping over the top of the flowers before disappearing once again. I recognized many of the flowers as those of the bouquets I'd been receiving, and my heart warmed as I thought about Luch walking out here, gathering wee blooms for me.

Damn it, but I didn't *want* to like this man. My instincts were signaling that something was up with him. But from the outside, he was handsome, had a super dog, took care of people for a living, and gathered flowers for a newcomer in town. There were a lot of green flags here, and what would it hurt for me to give him a chance? If I was meant to be settling down and starting a life here, wouldn't a romance be the next thing in order? Particularly now that I was also making friends. At the very least, I could maybe talk to Sophie about it. She'd know who Luch was and would tell me if there were red flags to be wary of. That was the benefit of small towns. You could get the backstory on your dating companion pretty quickly.

"Did you know there are standing stones out here?" Luch asked.

"I didn't know that. But I'm not surprised." There were standing stones all over Scotland, many rich with history, even more with magick. I tended to steer clear of them, never sure if I wanted to dance with any power that played there, and hoped he wasn't taking me to a circle now.

"I'm told the locals believe you can make a wish at Christmas and it will come true."

"Is that right? I hadn't heard of it." Even more reasons to believe that Loren Brae was the place for me if the locals believed in a Christmas wish at the standing stones. They'd probably not blink an eye at one more witchy woman being added to their mix. The thought cheered me and I smiled.

"Do you believe in that stuff? Magick and all that?" Luch asked. There was a note to his voice that suggested he most definitely did not, and I tried not to bristle at his line of questioning. Despite my initial hesitancy toward him, I truly doubted he thought I was magick, and especially given his medical and science background, it made sense that he doubted magick's existence. So there was no reason to take offense to something not stated. Being questioned about magick was my own private trigger, borne of years of speculation and distrust from others.

"It's more fun to believe, isn't it?"

"It depends on your definition of magick," Luch said. I waited for him to elaborate, but he didn't.

"And what would your definition of magick be then?" Luch scrambled down a few boulders and then turned and held his hand out to me for assistance as I followed. I almost hesitated touching him, since the last two times had resulted in a visceral shock, but it would have seemed even more odd of me to refuse.

My hand clasped his.

Our palms warmed together, that crazy heat trailing up my arm and through my belly, and my heart fluttered in my chest.

He didn't move back as he helped me down, and I almost bumped against his chest as I found solid ground again. Raising my eyes, I held his gaze. There was a question there. And a challenge.

Flecks of gold shone in those mossy-green eyes of his, and my thoughts scrambled as he loomed over me—all muscles and man and rugged confidence.

"This."

"This what?" I'd completely forgotten about my question but then his lips were on mine and any thoughts I had scattered for the hills and all I could do was feel.

Bloody hell, but this man could kiss.

I'm talking instant heat, everywhere in my body, curling up from my toes, all the way to the roots of my hair. His kiss was a possession, and ownership, as though he had the key to unlock every secret of my body and had no problem whatsoever using it. I went limp against him, and he dropped my hand, wrapping his arms around my waist, and pulled me more tightly against his muscular chest.

A chest I'd dreamt about every night since I'd seen him without his shirt.

Mewling into his mouth, I licked deep, my arms going around his neck to pull his head closer. He slowly tasted me, as though I was an exquisite dessert, his kiss both slow and plundering, and somehow, sweetly exploratory.

He'd push, opening my mouth wider, licking deeper, and then retreat to nibble softly at my lips while we both caught our breath. Then another kiss, this one soft, before sinking his teeth into my lower lip and causing me to gasp with excitement. It was a dance, a thorough seduction, and one he led masterfully. By the time we separated, little dots floated in front of my eyes, and I slapped a hand on his chest to steady myself.

"Holy hell. I need a moment." I wasn't lying. I was thrown completely off course by his kiss, unsteady but in the best way possible, and all I could think about was getting this man into my bed. Or to the ground. Or to whatever available surface would allow us to explore, in great detail, whatever the hell chemistry this was. A fine tremor rippled through my body.

"Would it be rude of me to say that I'm pleased to hear that?" Luch took my hand and turned it over, placing a kiss in the center of my palm, sending a tingle across my skin. Then he folded my fingers over my palm, as though he was giving me a kiss to keep for later, and tugged my wrist to continue to follow him.

Bloody hell, this man was going to do my head in. I'd known it from the moment I'd set eyes on him, hadn't I?

"I'd say it's a touch egotistical, but since you've proven your kisses are worthy of a big head, I'll allow it."

"She loves my kisses? A compliment?" Luch shot me a delighted grin over his shoulder as he continued down the path. "I'll take it." *How is he able to simply walk on? My heart's beating frantically and I want more ... and yet he's sightseeing?*

"As I've only got *one* kiss to go on, I can only offer feedback on one instance. Correlation does not imply causation."

Luch whirled, grabbed my shoulders, and pulled me sharply against him before claiming my mouth once more. This time, he feasted, taking me straight into the heat, and I gasped for air as his kiss stole every thought from my mind. I became one big nerve ending, craving his touch everywhere, my body warm and liquid with need. When he broke away, a knowing grin danced across his lips as he took in my likely shell-shocked expression.

"There. More data for your study."

"Who said I was conducting a study?" I asked. Though as studies went, it was a touch more interesting than the one I'd been reading on pain receptors and arthritis in aging dogs.

"You're the one who brought up causation," Luch pointed out.

"Well if I'm conducting a study, then I'll need a larger sample size, won't I?" I held up a hand when Luch turned back, his eyes almost feral as he reached for me again. "Nope, I didn't mean a sample size of kisses. I meant perhaps I need more participants."

"But that would change the scope of your study, wouldn't it?"

"Not necessarily," I argued, following him down a small gully and around a turn in the path.

"Surely it would. If you're positing that all my kisses leave you breathless and needing to 'take a moment', then the only way to expand the sample size is to add more kisses. If you're positing that *all* kisses from *all* men leave you breathless and craving more, then, yes, you'd need a large sample from a variety of different participants."

This is what I got for arguing with a fellow doctor.

Luckily, I was saved from answering when Luch stopped around the corner of the bend we'd just taken and held out his arm.

Holy shite. What was this place?

"Oh, wow. Okay, just wow. I see now why this is your favorite spot." I brought a hand to my heart as I took in the view before me. We were at the bottom of a gully of sorts, cocooned on both sides by hills covered in wildflowers, with a rocky outcropping that formed a ledge covered in soft green moss. About five meters below the ledge, the waters of Loch Mirren lapped against sharply-edged rocks jutting out of the surface.

It was like being cradled in a blanket of wildflowers while floating on the water.

It was dizzying, almost as dizzying as Luch's kisses, to be surrounded by so much beauty, the earth, loch and sky, all meeting together in one perfect spot.

"It's a cracking wee spot, isn't it?" Luch sounded pleased that I was so taken by his choice.

"It's glorious. Is this where you've been collecting my flowers from?"

"It is. I imagined you here. Wait ..." Luch bent and, plucking a white wildflower from the ground, he reached up and tucked it in my hair. My breath caught. It was a casual gesture, but so like the one my mum used to do. I hadn't let anyone else close enough to do something like that again. "Much better. Faelan of the flowers. A beauty among the beauties."

"Why do you call me that?" I asked, my cheeks heating, as Luch slid the backpack from his shoulders and dropped it to the ground. He unclipped a rolled blanket attached to the top and shook it out before laying it on the ground. Oban promptly walked over and sat on it, and I grinned.

"I don't know. It just rolls off the tongue, I suppose?"

"My mum used to call me that." I said it before I realized I had, caught up in the moment, where the emotions were swamping me. I didn't usually mention my mother to people, as I was never comfortable receiving awkward condolences, so I kept her memory to myself. As though it was my own precious pearl to pull out and admire when I was alone.

"Did she? It suits you. Do you want to tell me about

her?" Luch asked, and I glanced at him, surprised. There were no condolences now, just genuine interest.

And despite my usual reticence to talk about myself— *the necessity to hide my past, my life from people*—sometimes I'd wished for opportunities for people to know about Eriska. *She was such an amazing woman.* And for the first time in such a long time, I did want to tell someone about her. I wanted to ... share a part of myself with the man in front of me. *To show him where I come from, if only briefly.*

"We're rooted, you and I, Faelan. Like the flowers that bloom in the spring and the ancient trees that sing in the wind. Beneath the sky, face to the sun, is where you'll always find me." My mum's words whispered to me across the pages of my memories.

"She'd love this moment, for one." I laughed as I thought about her. Luch took my hand and guided me to a seat on the blanket before uncapping a thermos and pouring me a cup of tea. "She was endlessly romantic, sometimes to the point of foolishness if I'm to be honest. But she always wanted to believe the best in people. It made her an easy mark at times, for the wrong boyfriends, but her one saving grace was she also had a backbone of steel. The minute someone mistreated her, she booted them."

"Good for her." Luch busied himself taking a few containers and packages of tinfoil from his bag, spreading everything on the blanket before us. "What about your dad?"

Robert Thomas. Reckless fool. Sperm donor. No one to me.

"He was one of the bad ones." I cupped the mug of tea in both hands and took a sip, my gaze going across the loch to the island. "Lived fast. Died young. He'd been drinking and had eight-month-old me in the car with him. She took me and moved on the next day. He was dead within the year. To my mother's credit, I never missed having a father. She was ... everything. All-consuming. Beautiful, funny, whip-smart. And constantly, endlessly, joyous."

"That's an incredible talent, to hold joy in the face of adversity," Luch observed, popping open the lids on the containers.

"I think that's part of being a mother, isn't it? Creating these pockets of joy and happiness, even if sadness burned in her heart? She never let me see it, even though, intuitively, I often knew she felt it. She worried over me. That I was too serious. She didn't want me to take the sadness of the world on my shoulders."

"Why did she think you were too serious?"

"It was a defense mechanism, I suppose. I didn't, well, don't, trust easily. It takes me time to let people in. And she was always an open book, from day one of meeting her. She'd invite friends and foe alike to dinner, never batting an eye, always happy to have people surrounding her. I think, maybe, because our family was so small. So she constantly opened the doors to the world, even when that same world didn't open the doors back."

"Why not?"

I blinked at Luch, surprised I'd said so much. I fell back on a lie, unwilling to tell him that most people didn't accept witches into their lives. I wasn't ready to share that information with him. Yet. Or ever, maybe.

"The world isn't often very kind to single mothers."

"That's such shite." Luch's eyebrows drew together in a

glower. "Why do the men get off on being shite fathers, but the women bear the brunt of it? Ridiculous."

"Aye, it is at that." Oban shifted, licking my palm, and I raised my hand to scratch his ears. *I need to change the subject.* Luch's phone pinged, and I paused, waiting while he pulled it from his pocket and glanced at it.

"Sorry, I have it on for work."

"No problem. Feel free to take it." I could understand better than most about the needs of work.

"No, it's fine. Just my father."

"Oh, go ahead." I waved a hand as his phone pinged again, but he just silenced it and put it back in his pocket. I studied his face as he pressed his lips together, frustration flashing behind his eyes. "Everything okay?"

"Yeah, it's fine." Luch reached for a tinfoil package. "I wasn't sure what kind of sandwich you'd like, so I made several."

"Luch. What's going on? Is everything okay?" It annoyed me, just a bit, that I'd opened up about my mother and he was going all clench-jawed and quiet about his father. "Tell me about your family. Please."

"Fine. But tell me what sandwich you like first. I have a tomato and cheese, egg, and tuna salad."

"Are you vegetarian? I am."

"I am too!" A grin chased the clouds away from his expression. "But I do eat fish."

"I'll take the egg salad. Thanks." Pleased that I didn't have to discuss my reasoning for being a vegetarian—it was hard to eat animals when I devoted my life to treating them —and I didn't like to press my views on anyone else, I happily unwrapped the sandwich.

"My family is ... complicated to say the least. I have four brothers, and I'm the youngest. My father is a surgeon, all my brothers are as well, and when I went the comprehensive emergency services route, they were stunned. They're a tight-knit family, demanding, and the egos are intense. They always think they know what's best for everyone else, I suppose that's a casualty of their occupations, but it also makes them difficult partners, friends, and frankly, family members."

"Ouch," I said, taking a bite of my sandwich. "That does sound tough. Your mother?"

"A goddamned saint." Luch sighed, but some of the tension left his face when he spoke of her. "She's in a wheelchair. From my birth."

"Oh, Luch, I'm sorry. Was it nerve damage?"

A look I couldn't decipher crossed Luch's face, and then he shook his head, his expression clearing.

"Aye, it was. I was a large baby and it was a long labor, twenty-one hours to be exact."

I'd heard of it, though I wasn't largely familiar with it. The ins and the outs didn't matter, just that I could understand why it would be hard for him, particularly in a family that sounded as difficult as his. Was there blame placed on his shoulders for his mum's injuries?

"I'm sorry to hear that."

"She'd chosen a healer for her labor. One that used magick."

A healer that used magick. Oh.

My eyes tightened at the corners as I forced my emotions down.

"Like a midwife?" I asked, casually, and made myself

take a bite of the sandwich. "Or like someone using crystals and whatnot?"

"Something like that."

The air felt heavy between us, and I wasn't sure how to navigate going forward.

"Your father? He wasn't able to assist?"

"He wasn't at my birth."

"Ah." Again, I wasn't sure how to swim through the undercurrents of what he was telling me, so I just took another bite and sat in silence. I often found that saying nothing prompted the other person to continue speaking and save me from saying anything that could cause distress, or in this case, be potentially harmful to me.

The reality was, if his mum used any type of healer that professed to use magick to help during labor—and it had gone wrong—Luch's opinion of non-traditional healers would be horrible forever. Particularly coming from a family who dedicated themselves to modern medicine.

It didn't matter if the man kissed like a god, there was no path forward for us.

I could never be honest with him about who I was.

And he blames healers forever for harming his mum.

This relationship was dead in the water before it started.

And even though there's a pinch of disappointment, I was glad to know that now before I became too invested in Luch.

"I love my mum." His voice cracked as he looked out over the loch. "Fiercely. But I also had to leave them behind to start fresh. It was ... they are ... too much. Too many rules. Too controlling. I can't, no, I won't, follow in what they believe to be right."

"And what do they believe to be right?" I reached over and stroked Oban's ears, needing to soothe the tension that roiled in my stomach.

"Everything has to be a certain way. Done by the rules. Approved by my father. Down to even the person I marry. They follow a very specific set of guidelines on what is allowed and what is not."

"Sounds stringent. Militaristic, almost?"

Luch's eyes met mine, and he smiled, though it didn't reach his eyes.

"Yeah, something like that."

He's hiding something. Part of his truth. I couldn't fault him for not opening everything about his world to me, as I was guilty of the same.

"So you left and came to Loren Brae. Starting fresh. And they're furious about it, I gather?"

"Pretty much." He shrugged and polished off his sandwich in two bites.

"That's got to be fun for you."

Luch barked out a laugh and leaned back, stretching his legs out in front of him.

"It's been over a year. I'm hoping they'll accept it, while they're hoping I accept my destiny."

I tilted my head at that word. Destiny was an odd choice, wasn't it? I wondered if his family just had a flair for the dramatics or if they really felt he was destined to follow whatever role they'd laid out for him. Either way, it sounded stifling and cold, and certainly no way to raise a child.

"And your mum? She feels the same?"

"My mum is an angel of a woman who somehow

manages to put up with my father. She is the light, the sun, and everyone revolves around her."

"What did she say about you leaving?"

"She misses me, but she's proud of me. She thinks I need to do this, but she won't say that in front of my father."

"Ah." I reached out and squeezed his arm. "Sounds like a good woman."

"The best." Luch covered my hand with his own. Then his hand circled my wrist and I gasped as he pulled me quickly to sprawl on top of his body. The strength of this man was mind-blowing.

"Luch!" I gasped, laughing down at him, as Oban gave an indignant huff and stalked off through the flowers. "What are you doing?"

"I want to kiss you again, Faelan of the flowers. Will you let me?"

How was I supposed to let this man kiss me when I'd just learned his entire family hated healers? It wasn't fair, to either of us, to take this a step further, but when he reached up and cupped the back of my neck, and pulled my head closer, I succumbed.

I didn't usually give in to my weaknesses, but Luch's kisses were terribly addictive, his body was rock hard under mine, which—*naturally*—made me think all sorts of dirty thoughts, and bloody hell, but I just wanted this moment to never stop. It had been ages since I'd let myself have any sort of fun, let alone go on a date, and my body was already responding to every unmet need I'd denied myself. When his other hand wrapped around me, cupping my bum and pulling me hard against where he very obviously wanted me, I rocked into him as he caught my mouth in a searing kiss.

Everything faded behind us, and all I could do was feel. A long pull of liquid lust went through as I shifted, straddling my legs around him, and tilted my hips forward.

"Och, lass, that's just it, right there." Luch's voice rasped against my lips, his tongue hot against mine. Shamelessly, I rubbed myself against him, rocking back and forth, loving the heat that spiraled inside of me. I'd been craving a man's touch for so long now, and between his mouth, hot at my neck and trailing his tongue along the edge of my jumper, and his hand rubbing fast circles over my bum, dots of desire danced across my vision.

I couldn't believe how close I was to tipping over into an orgasm.

It shouldn't be this easy.

I shouldn't be responding this fast to a man.

But something about the open air, the flowers spread around us, his tongue slick against mine, was causing desire to spear through me. When he slid a hand to the edge of my jumper, and toyed at the waistband, I nodded against his mouth.

"Yes, och, please, yes." I wanted his hands on me.

He slipped a hand beneath my jumper, cupping a breast, and thumbed a nipple into a perfect peak as I rode against him, the spiral going higher, higher, higher. When he tilted his head, angling his kiss deeper, and pinched me at the same time, I came apart.

I simply came apart.

Crying into his mouth, I rocked around him, my

orgasm tipping over the edge and flooding waves of liquid pleasure through my body until I shook with it.

And Luch?

He laughed.

He laughed into my mouth, kissing me softly as he wrapped both arms around me, pulling me tight to him in a hug. I felt cradled and safe, protected from the world outside, as he continued to chuckle.

"Bloody hell, Faelan. But you're fucking glorious. I'm going to have dirty dreams about that for a week."

"Och, wheesht, Luch." I buried my face in his shirt, embarrassed about how responsive I was to his kiss. I'd gone off like a rocket, basically.

"I'm serious. That was sexy as hell. You're amazing. Simply amazing."

Looking up, I realized he was serious, and I had to look away. *What about when he finds out who I really am?*

Then he'd hate me forever.

The thought alone was like dumping a bucket of cold water over my head and I eased back, needing to put some space between us. How would I gracefully make my way out of this without hurting his feelings?

For once in my life, I was pleased when the first fat drops of rain hit the back of my head. In seconds, the skies opened up. Luch packed up the remains of the picnic, scooped Oban up, cradling him close, and we hustled back to the car.

Saving the awkward conversation for another day, I begged off any more time with Luch by explaining I was freezing, and exhausted from work. When he dropped me off, saying goodbye with another searing kiss, I ran inside and slammed the door behind me, my heart pounding in my chest.

How? How had he made me come so effortlessly? How had Luch's touch, his kisses, his reverence made me hotter than I'd ever felt before? *And why had I finally found someone I felt so connected to when he couldn't be mine?*

Because no matter what I felt, the reality was, I couldn't take this situation—I refused to call it a relationship—with Luch a step further.

He is so utterly dangerous for my soul ... and possibly my heart. And I simply hated the fact that I knew, deep in my bones, by my own feelings or his potential actions, this man was going to hurt me.

CHAPTER TWELVE

LUCH

As expected, I'd woken up with my cock in my hand and the taste of Faelan's kisses on my lips.

Bloody hell, but she was incredible.

I couldn't shake the feeling that Faelan was meant for me. I wanted to uncover all her secrets, have her bare her soul to me, to learn everything that she was holding back. And if yesterday was just a small taste of how responsive she was to my touch, I could only imagine what it would be like when I convinced her to make love to me.

Although ... she hadn't told me she was a healer.

And after revealing my mum's painful reality yesterday, I doubted she'd tell me anytime soon. Why would she? I hadn't exactly painted Mum's life in a good light, and I'd made it tremendously clear that my entire family hated healers.

Well, just one in particular, the chancer who hadn't helped my mum in her greatest time of need.

It was a sore spot, for all of us, and yet here I was, lusting after the very type of woman that we'd sworn to forever hate.

What was wrong with me?

Was this just some sort of big "fuck you" to my father? Was I thumbing my nose at their beliefs? Forcing them even further back from me? I felt a little like the straight-A schoolboy who'd never broken a rule in his life falling for the tough girl who smoked cigarettes and broke curfew.

Except, from what I could see, Faelan didn't really seem to be all that bad.

She'd healed Oban, hadn't she?

I was beyond confused, because meeting Faelan was challenging long-held beliefs, and I still couldn't talk to her about it, because she hadn't given me *her* secret yet.

But she would.

I was determined to get her to tell me, so we could discuss it out in the open, and then, maybe from there, I might be able to learn something new.

As a doctor, it was important to practice what you knew, until new information—hopefully well studied and scientifically presented—became available and changed your way of practice. It happened quite often, which was why we were always taking continuing education courses and learning about new methods, so it would be hypocritical of me to not also give Faelan a chance to change my mind about healers.

Though, I suppose it would be good if I made her feel

more welcome to do so other than blurting out that a healer had paralyzed my mother.

Wincing, I pulled my car to a stop in front of the B&Q hardware store. I was here on a mission. Not only did I need to give Faelan an excuse to open up to me more, but I also needed to convince her to stay in Loren Brae longer.

I paused, my hands gripping the steering wheel.

"What am I doing?"

"About Faelan or your life in general?" Oban asked from the back seat.

"Faelan."

"I think you like her."

"But I can't. For too many reasons."

"Admittedly, you do have several roadblocks to get around."

"Gee, thanks for the vote of confidence."

"It's not confidence you'll be needing."

"Approval?" I shifted to look at Oban. "You know my father would never. She's not one of us."

"And maybe that's okay."

I huffed out a laugh and shook my head, turning back to stare at the store.

"Is it? Didn't work out so well for my mum."

"I thought your father blamed the healer. Not the fact that she's different."

Intrigued, I pursed my lips. More research would be needed.

"After what I've told Faelan about our experience of healers, I think she might hate me."

"And she might not. I mean, she did mention how hot she

136

thought you were." Oban made a gagging sound and I laughed.

"Did she really?"

"Aye. But you're not off to a good start. What were you thinking? Telling her about your mum?"

"Och, I know. I know. Bloody hell, it just came out. Stupid." I punched the steering wheel. I'd been berating myself for it the whole night.

"It's not exactly the best way to get her to open up to you. Particularly since she already senses you don't trust healers or magick. Then you lay the mum story on top of it? There's no way in hell she's talking to you now. You dug your own grave on that one, boyo." Oban made that soft huffing sound that always indicated he was laughing at me.

"You find this funny?"

"Kind of. I like seeing you flustered. You're too used to pissing excellence all the time."

"I'll take that backhanded compliment, thank you very much."

"You've got a lot of work to do if you think you'll win her over."

"She likes me. I told you we had chemistry."

"Yes, the entire hills heard your chemistry yesterday. Give a dog a warning, would you?"

"Don't tag along on my dates then." I laughed when Oban pretended to vomit. "All right, let's go in. I'm starting my plan to win her over."

I got out of the car and opened the back door for Oban, and he trotted next to me into the store. I had an idea in mind that I sincerely hoped Faelan would welcome. Or she'd think I was too much, kick me out on my sorry arse, and that would be the way of things. Either way, I had to try.

I'd never been like this with a woman before, not where I'd wanted to or had been willing to try. There were very few women that I'd been able to date of my own volition. Every other woman had been paraded in front of me, my father choosing them and rolling them out like we were on a dating show, and it had soured the idea of love for me.

But Faelan was different. I could feel it in my bones, even if I didn't fully understand why.

Hauling my supplies up her steps, I knocked on her door, and hoped she was home. It was early still, only nine in the morning, and she'd told me that Sunday was her day off, if she wasn't working an emergency. When the door cracked open an inch, and one suspicious eye peered out, I grinned.

"It's the Loren Brae welcome committee."

"Didn't you welcome me enough yesterday?" Her cheeks pinkened at her words and my grin grew wider. She opened the door a bit more, and I almost did a happy dance when I saw she was wearing my shirt.

"I'm not done welcoming you." I winked at her and gave her body a lazy perusal. "Nice shirt."

"Ugh, I find you both infuriating and arousing. How is that possible?" Faelan mumbled, pushing her tangle of hair back from her face.

"I'm not sure, but I'd dearly love to explore the latter part of that statement if possible."

"No. We're not doing that again. Yesterday was an anomaly."

"Was it? I think we should talk about it. Preferably

inside." I squinted at the moody clouds that were just starting to release rain. "You wouldn't want poor Oban to get wet again, like yesterday, would you?"

Faelan slanted a glance down to Oban who obediently sat and lifted one paw, the picture of a needy pup.

"Och, fine, come in." Faelan shut the door briefly and I looked at it in confusion as I heard her mutter something behind the door. But then a moment later, she opened it wide and ushered us inside. Oban immediately trotted across the floor and stood at her couch, looking from her to the cushions.

"Yes, you can jump up." Faelan sighed and piled her hair in a messy knot on top of her head. She wore my shirt, loose joggers, and fuzzy socks.

I wanted to unwrap her like a gift on Christmas morning.

"What is all this?" Faelan gestured at the bags in my arms.

"Well, first, and most importantly, breakfast." I brandished the small bag in my right hand. "I've got croissants and egg and cheese sandwiches."

"I'll accept." Faelan grabbed the bag and went to her kitchen counter, pulled out two mugs, and two plates. "Tea?"

"Please." I bit back a smile. The first battle was won. I was inside her flat, I was feeding her, and soon I'd be on to the second stage of my attack. One which required we spend the entire day together. During that time, I hoped to break down her walls, get to know her better, and maybe that would help me understand why I was so drawn to her despite the many reasons I shouldn't be.

"I'd be mad at you for showing up uninvited on my day off, but I'm starving and didn't get a chance to go to the shops."

"Ah, for once a grueling schedule works in my favor." I smiled at her, hoping to chase that mulish expression from her face. What I wanted to do was to kiss it away, but since she seemed tetchy this morning, I figured it was best to keep my distance.

For now.

I also wanted to talk to her some more. I needed to see, for myself, if the thoughts and feelings I was having were real, or if it was just excitement over someone new and pretty in my life. If I told my family about her, they'd show up on my doorstep and try to run her out of town. In theory, I should take an immediate dislike to her.

And yet.

She'd healed my wee pal.

She'd taken the pain inside herself, healed Oban without a second thought, and had ushered me out the door without an explanation.

A person didn't do that if they were evil. Or taking advantage. If she'd used her magick for nefarious reasons, as I'd been taught from my father that all healers did, she'd have charged me an arm and a leg for healing wee Oban. But fifty quid and I was out the door? Something wasn't adding up here.

And it could very well be everything that I'd been taught from a young age. I'd always been the most open-minded of my family, aside from my mum, that is. My brothers all fell in line with my father's opinions, whereas I always had asked the most questions. It was just the way my brain worked. I wanted to know the "why" behind every-thing. It was another reason I'd not followed my father into cardiology, instead enjoying the diversity and nuance that came with dealing with emergency situations. By not specializing, I was able to constantly ask "why" in every situation that came through the hospital doors.

But now it was time for me to apply this same critical thinking to my own circumstances. Faelan had captured my interest for a reason, and while my initial instinct had been suspicion, a few talks with Oban had made me pause on that path. What I needed was more information and a better understanding of who Faelan was before I would get out my pitchfork.

Just the thought alone brought an acrid taste to my mouth. It was one of my biggest issues with my father—how he could be so willing to persecute others, when we, too, had been persecuted. He had a blind spot, that he did, and one could even say he was a hypocrite at times.

My phone pinged in my pocket. Pulling it out, I noted my father's name and switched it to silent. I wasn't on call today and could happily avoid any conversation with my family.

"Work? Or family?" Faelan asked as she poured hot water from the kettle into the mugs.

"Family."

"Hmmm."

It was a perfect opportunity to address the story I'd told her yesterday about healers, but I wasn't quite sure how to bring it up without sounding obvious.

"Have you always wanted to be a vet?" I asked, instead, taking the mug and plate of food from her and going across the room to the wee bistro table. I barely fit in the chair and I felt like we were eating at a doll's table, but this seemed to be the only option.

"Pretty much." Faelan shrugged one shoulder as she brought her plate to the table and sat, tearing off a piece of the croissant. "I've had a natural affinity for animals from a young age."

"They don't judge ... you said."

"It's true. They don't. Mostly." A smile drifted across her pretty face. She was clearly remembering a secret joke I wasn't privy to. "But also, it's hard to ignore their companionship. You're never really lonely, are you, if you have a pet?"

I looked around the flat.

"But you don't have one?"

"I didn't say I was lonely, did I?" Faelan scowled, neatly putting me back in my place. "What about you? If your whole family are medical professionals, was that just the only way forward for you?"

"Honestly, I never really tried something else." I took a bite of my egg sandwich and chewed while I thought it over. "It wasn't a burden for me. I genuinely like learning. I was an inquisitive child, more so than my brothers, and constantly asked questions. It also made me a touch annoying."

"You? Annoying? Never." Faelan gestured with a hand to the bags I'd dropped just inside her door.

"Hey, you'll think I'm less annoying once I tell you what your surprise is."

"And will you be telling me that now?"

"Nope, not yet. So, back to childhood. Basically, I like

figuring out how things work. I like logic. Science was a great way for me to fulfill that part of my inquisitiveness. I've always been uncomfortable with things that I can't explain."

"And has there been a lot in your life that you can't?" Faelan picked up her mug with both hands and leveled me a look over the top.

"Aye." Not that I was ready to share what those things were with her. "But I suppose that's what humanity is about, isn't it? The pursuit of answers."

"Or meaning." Faelan's eyes took on a haunted look.

"Och, now that's an area I struggle with." I leaned back and crossed my arms over my chest. "I take meaning in being able to treat injuries. To help others. But then I also struggle to understand when a child dies on my table."

"I understand." To my surprise, Faelan reached out and squeezed my arm, sympathy on her face. "Not to the extent of losing a child, but to many, their pets are much the same. It's horrific to not be able to help in those instances. Us healers, we're a special breed, aren't we? There are only certain types suited for this line of work."

"Healer. That's an interesting way to put it. Don't you mean doctor?" I asked, raising an eyebrow at her.

"Doctors are healers. They were healers long before the term doctor ever came about. Isn't that what you've been taught? How to heal?" Faelan neatly sidestepped my question, and I gave up. I was beginning to understand there was no normal way to directly ask someone if they used magick in their healing. Which meant I either had to get up and leave, or I had to listen to my gut instinct that Faelan was a good person ... *with a secret.*

Because, at the end of the day, I was hiding one from her as well.

"I guess so. Which is why I'm here to 'heal' a wound of yours." I grinned when Faelan's eyes narrowed.

"I don't recall asking for help. With anything." Faelan gestured with the cup, her lips pursing into a scowl.

"Remember when I said I could be annoying at times?" I laughed and stood up, crossed the room to the bags, and brought them back to the table. Putting them on the floor, I nudged them to her. "Go on. Open your prezzie."

"I don't wanna." Faelan pushed out her lower lip and I laughed again. She was cute when she pouted.

"Aren't you the least bit curious?"

"Oh, for sure. Dying of curiosity." Faelan's laugh was rich and warmed my gut, sending little tendrils of desire curling through me. "But then if I open it, I have to accept it, and something tells me a B&Q bag means a project, and a project means you'll stick around longer than I had planned to have company today."

I held a hand to my chest, and made puppy dog eyes, the picture of a wounded male.

"Are you telling me that you're sick of my company? Already?"

"I should. Just because I suspect not many people tell you that." Faelan smirked when I gave her a shite-eating grin. "I knew it. You're the type of man people rarely say 'no' to, aren't you?"

"That's not true. Patients tell me 'no' all the time." I laughed when she squinched her nose up and made a sound of disgust.

"You know what I mean. In your personal life."

"I couldn't say. I don't have much of one."

"Is that so?" Faelan toed the bag, and I knew I was getting closer to her opening them. "No lonely ladies waiting outside your door?"

"Nope. Oban would just chase them off. He's very protective of me."

Oban huffed from the couch and Faelan chuckled.

"What about you? I'm surprised you don't have a line of men at your door."

"Why?" Faelan asked, tilting her head to study me.

"Why? Because, for one, you're drop-dead gorgeous. But past that, you're clearly intelligent, caring, and capable of running your own business. It doesn't appear that you're after a partner for money, or frankly, to even complete any aspect of your life. You seem largely fulfilled, content with your work, and willing to take risks. All really great traits of a partner."

Faelan's mouth formed a tiny O of surprise.

"That's quite the assessment, Dr. Carmichael."

"First one's free. Next time, I'll have to charge you."

Faelan's laugh warmed me once more, and this time she did bend over and tug the handles of the shopping bag open. She jolted and looked up at me in surprise, before pulling out a can of paint.

"You bought me paint?" Faelan asked, incredulous.

"Aye, lass. We're going to paint your living room. Today."

"But ... I can't." Faelan looked around her flat. "I haven't planned anything. I don't have paint brushes. What if I hate the color you picked?"

"I brought all the supplies. If you hate the color, I'll go

145

back and get another color. But you did mention a dark navy and I picked the blue that the paint guy recommended. He said it's dark and dramatic but has some cool undertones that are really nice."

"But I don't even know why I said navy. It might look stupid. Or make the place look too small." Faelan glanced around the room, stricken.

"It's just paint. How about this? We'll try one wall and see how you feel about it."

"Just one wall?" Faelan gave me a look like I was offering to give her a haircut.

"Just one wall," I confirmed. "It's easy enough to cover up if you hate it."

"Hmm. You know what? I'll do it. This is a good step for me." Faelan nodded her head sharply, like I was teaching her how to swim or something much more serious than painting a wall in her flat. Only then did I really understand how important this might be to her. I'd certainly heard the yearning in her voice when she'd mentioned never really settling down before, but the way she eyed the paint cans suspiciously and then gave herself a determined nod, as though it was okay to finally make a living space her own, made me want to understand her even more.

"It sounds like it. Shall we crack on?" I was ready to be standing up and out of that tiny chair I was certain would break under me at any sudden movement.

"I don't even know where to start." Faelan turned, hands on hips, and studied the wall. "I've never done this before."

"Luckily, there's not a steep learning curve." Digging in the bag, I pulled out a roll of tape. "We start here."

"Tape?" Faelan shot me a confused look.

"We tape the edges. So those pretty baseboards of yours don't get dirty. And around outlets. And windowsills. Got it?"

"Ahh, I see. What else do I need to know?"

"Cover these wood floors. There's a plastic sheet in the bag. We'll start there. You'll be a pro in no time."

"We'll see about that." Faelan dug in the bag and then paused to look up at me. "Thanks. This is really sweet of you."

I'm not sure why, but a compliment coming from her made me feel like a million bucks. I got the impression she wasn't used to giving them out very often, let alone sharing her space or home improvement projects with anyone else.

"And most importantly?"

"Aye?" Faelan paused as she was pulling out a strip of paint.

"Don't wear anything you don't want to get paint on."

"Oh." Faelan glanced down at the shirt she was wearing. *My shirt.* "I'll just go change."

I smiled the entire time she was in the bedroom.

CHAPTER THIRTEEN

FAELAN

I loved the paint.
Loved it.

I loved the process of it, the taping of all the wood, the careful application, the roller brushes. We even ended up painting the ceiling, and what I had worried might end up looking dark and gloomy ended up looking charming. The navy managed to pop the gorgeous undertones in my floors and kitchen cupboards, and I could already see how a cool rug and some funky art on the walls would make this space much more livable and interesting.

A home, really.

"I can't believe how different it looks," I exclaimed, hands on my hips, surveying our work.

"As you've said now. For the third time." Luch laughed

at me from where he hammered a paint lid back onto the can.

We'd talked. The entire time. In fact, I couldn't remember the last time I'd talked so much with one person before. As if in mutual agreement, we stuck to easy topics— favorite concerts, best meals, recent books we'd read. But I was finding Dr. Carmichael to be a surprisingly interesting companion. His interests were varied, he read widely, and he asked questions when he didn't know the answer to something.

Which made it all that much harder to try and stop thinking about our kisses the day before. Or how his touch had rocketed me over the edge into one of the easiest orgasms I'd ever had. It would be embarrassing, except Luch had given me no reason to feel embarrassed, and since he hadn't tried to touch or kiss me since I'd told him we wouldn't be doing any of *that* anymore, he'd respected my boundaries.

Which, if I had to admit, I was now finding a bit annoying. I was just *so* happy. I had a place to call my own, and even though it seemed silly, the coat of paint drastically changed my view on what I could do with my own space. I was proud of what we'd achieved here today. Proud enough that I wanted to reward Luch for all his help.

Except I'd already drawn the line in the sand about no more kissing. So would I have to be the one to cross it? Uncertain of how to proceed, or what, exactly, I wanted ... I took my time packing up the supplies.

Dinner.

I could ask him to dinner. Feeding the man seemed an appropriate way to thank him for helping me today.

"Hey—"

"Can I take you to dinner? It's been a long day. Fancy a bite at the pub?"

Damn it. He'd beaten me to it.

"Um."

Luch's lips quirked. "Why have I annoyed you?"

I crossed to the kitchen and put the empty tape roll in the bin under the sink. Straightening, I turned and almost bumped into Luch's chest.

"Oh, jeez. Hey."

"Why have I annoyed you?" Luch repeated and lifted my chin with his finger, and I pursed my lips, now annoyed both with him *and* myself for *being* annoyed.

"Because I was debating how to thank you and taking you to dinner was one of the ways."

"Ah." A grin spread across Luch's handsome face, and my skin flushed. "And what was one of the other ways?"

I shrugged and looked away.

His laughter made desire curl through my body.

"Can I take a guess?" Luch prodded.

"Nope." I was not about to say that I was dying for a kiss. I'd boxed myself in and had to live with the consequences of my choices.

"Was this one of them?"

I looked back at him in time to see him lean in, and then his lips were on mine. He ranged himself over me, his hands on either side of me on the counter, and I felt like I was being shown the way home. Cocooned. Sheltered. He was just so big and broad-shouldered and even though it should feel like he was looming over me, instead it just made me feel protected.

Like I was his, and his alone.

His kisses tasted of the mints I'd seen him pop periodically through the day, fresh and sweet, and heat raced through me as he licked into my mouth. I met him, taste for taste, as he feasted on my lips.

"Have I told you how much I enjoy kissing you?" Luch said, surprising me when he picked me up and placed me on the counter, moving to stand between my legs. Bloody hell, but the man was sexy. It shouldn't have been such a hot move, the way he effortlessly lifted me—*no one has ever done that to me before*—and yet I couldn't help but respond to something so basic.

And yes, the muscles in his arms flexed when he picked me up.

How did I know?

Because I was hanging on to him like a barnacle clinging to a ship, my legs wrapped around his waist, my arms now twined over his shoulders. I threaded my hands in his hair, needing more.

"You haven't mentioned it, no. But feel free to conduct your own study."

Luch laughed, his teeth flashing white in his face.

"Are you still collecting your data points? For your study?"

"Absolutely. I'm certain I'll need a much larger data set before I can make a ruling on your kisses."

"It's certainly best to be thorough in your research." Luch laughed into my mouth when I moaned and rocked against him. I swear I didn't even know who I was with this man. I'd gone so long without dating and now I was ready to come undone over the first sexy man I'd touched in ages.

Granted, he was pretty damn hot.

"Maybe we should expand your data." Luch toyed with the top of my waistband, tugging a little downward to indicate what he meant. "Just to make sure you can report on all of my kisses."

"Oh. *Ohh*." I blinked up at him as he tugged at my leggings again. Bugger it. Even if I was a fool, I didn't care. Inching forward I lifted my hips and let him slide my clothes down my legs and rip them off.

I didn't even have time to think before his mouth was on me.

It was such a shock that I almost crushed the poor man's head when I brought my legs together, leaning back on the counter as I thrust forward, and when he laughed against me, the vibration of it almost sent me over the edge.

"Easy there," Luch said. Reaching up, he pressed my thighs wider and looked up at me with a relaxed smile on his face.

Bloody hell, I would never forget the image of handsome Dr. Carmichael kneeling between my legs with a devilish smile on his face. I almost came right then. Turning, he pressed a gentle kiss to the soft skin of my inner thigh and then trailed a hand up until he slipped one finger inside me. I jerked at the intrusion and then moaned as he added another finger, curling to find the perfect spot inside me.

"Oh, right there. Yes, that's it." I was beginning to shake with need, fine trembles rocketing up my body, and when his mouth found my most sensitive spot again, his fingers circling gently inside me, I dropped my head back and moaned. I didn't even care that I hit the back of my head against the upper cabinet. All I cared about was this man's touch. His mouth was that of a god, his fingers that of a warrior. And no matter what, he owned me.

Luch suckled, and then licked leisurely, as though he had all the time in the world, gently twirling his fingers inside me. Over and over he played with me, lingering when I began to shake harder, going even slower when I jerked against his mouth, finally, when I couldn't take it anymore, I cried out.

"Please, Luch. Please."

"Please, what, darling?" Luch pulled back, and I was so furious I almost jumped off the counter and kicked him out of my flat.

"I need you. I need you to make me …" I couldn't say it. I knew I was a doctor and all that, but I was already far past my comfort zone. Seeming to understand that was the extent of what he was getting from me, Luch flashed me a cheeky smile before bending his head.

He devoured me.

I arched against him as I came, crying out to my freshly painted ceiling as he worked his magic, unable to believe how good his touch felt. He was everything, all wet heat and perfect strokes, and my pleasure rolled through me until my body went limp with it. *Holy hell. Have I ever come that hard?* Have I ever been with someone so intent on *my* pleasure? I've never felt this … blissful. I sighed.

When I was finished, Luch stood and wrapped his arms around my waist, giving me a lingering kiss.

"Ready for dinner?"

"Dinner?" I blinked up at him, my thoughts hazy and confused.

"You know ... food. At a table. Usually out in public?"

"But ... but ..." I waved a hand weakly. "What about you? This?"

"I'm just fine, darling. Better than fine. I'll be thinking about this all week."

"But don't you need, um, release?" I blushed, even though the man had just licked me like he was devouring an ice cream cone on a hot summer's day.

"This may come as a surprise, but there is no biological rule that says a man must have release after pleasuring a woman. I promise you, I'll be just fine."

"So you just want to ... give me pleasure and then go to dinner?" I raised an eyebrow at him.

"For tonight, yes, that's what I want. Is it what you want?"

"I think you're well aware of what I want." As if on cue, my stomach growled and we both laughed. "And I guess I can't lie about being hungry."

"Dinner it is then."

"But I'm paying," I insisted as I slid from the counter. "I want to thank you for your gift today." *Well, gifts plural, as that last gift was divine.*

"Och, darling. You already have." Luch dropped another quick kiss on my lips, and I blushed, totally out of my element and uncertain how to proceed.

"I'll just go change." Needing a moment, I hurried into my bedroom only to find Oban with his head buried under the pillows on my bed. I couldn't blame the wee lad for escaping to another room. I would have done the same.

"Sorry, buddy, forgot you were there."

"Next time I'll start barking so you can let me out."

I grinned and grabbed some clothes to change into in the bathroom. By the time I came out, Oban was at the door, and Luch had his coat on.

"God, it really does look good out here." I marveled at the change in the living area as I walked back out. Luch had cracked the windows to air the paint, and a cool breeze wafted through the room. "I'm really chuffed with this."

"You'll be making a home here soon enough. Add a few more cozy elements and you'll be happy to coorie in over the long winter."

"I wonder if I could get one of those fake fireplaces? The one that kicks out heat? It might add a cozy bit for the winter."

"Or you could get a gas one installed. Might not be too much trouble." Luch nudged me with his elbow. "See? Look at you thinking like a homeowner already."

"I truly can't believe that it hadn't occurred to me to start decorating in there. Granted, I've been busy with managing the practice, and I'm used to existing with just the basics, so it wasn't really at the top of my mind. But you know what? Decorating is fun. I had *fun* today. Thanks again, Luch," I gushed as we walked down my stairs and around the corner onto Main Street.

"Was that the only thing you had fun with today?" Luch stopped before we turned the corner, and I drew up short as I looked up at him. The loch, silvery with soft evening light spread behind him, and a few pink traces of the setting sun slashed across the sky. His face was shadowed, but those eyes, that unique greenish gold color, reflected the streetlamps that had popped on overhead. It was as though they glowed, all-seeing, and the intensity in his look sent a shiver across my body.

"I think you know the answer to that." Heat flushed my face as I looked up at him.

"Bloody hell, Faelan, but you're gorgeous." He brushed his thumb across my lip, before cupping my chin and giving me a bruising kiss. I felt it all the way down to my toes, like he'd staked his claim, and I surprisingly did not seem to mind.

Perhaps it was the lingering effects of the pleasure he'd already given me today.

Or was it just that I was genuinely enjoying his company?

Either way, I was more than happy to ignore that initial instinct I'd had to turn tail and run when I'd first met him. Perhaps it had been my anxiety about him discovering my magick, or maybe it had just been simply being in the presence of such an overly charismatic male. But now, his edges seemed to have softened around me, and something had shifted quickly with us. I'd gone from avoiding him to craving his mouth on mine.

A remarkably quick turnaround for someone like me. Marveling over it, I pulled back and shook my head, a smile on my face.

"What's that look for?" Luch asked, taking my hand and tugging me down the street. I almost pulled back, not ready to be seen like that in public with him. Small towns, and all that.

"I don't know. I'm not really sure what to think of you, Dr. Carmichael."

"You think that I'm strong. That I'm sexy. That I'm wickedly funny."

"And full of yourself?" I suggested, laughing as he stopped in front of The Tipsy Thistle, the main pub in town.

"Confidence and ego are often mistaken for each other."

"Fair enough." I laughed as he held the door open for me and pub sounds spilled out. The Tipsy Thistle was a pub housed in an old gray stone building with a narrow entrance and doorways low enough to duck through, worn wood floors polished to a sheen, and a circular bar on one side of the room. Tables of varying sizes were clustered around the room, most notably full, and a man stood by the fireplace with a microphone in hand. He wore overalls, had a shaggy beard and ruddy skin, and a younger man—clearly related—stood next to him dressed similarly.

"Och, hold on." The man at the fireplace looked to us. "Are you two joining in then?"

"Um?" I looked around and a woman sitting at the bar with a short crop of swingy curls waved to me.

"They can be on our team, Fergus. We were short anyway."

"Oh sure, steal the two doctors for your team, Agnes," a woman grumbled from across the pub.

"I'm simply being welcoming, aren't I? How was I to know they were doctors?" Agnes fluffed her hair and smiled like she'd already won.

"Do we back out quietly? Pretend we didn't hear them?" Luch hissed at my ear and I glanced up at him over my shoulder, surprised to find a hint of panic in his eyes.

"Why, Dr. Carmichael, don't you like games?"

"Games are fine. It's more the people factor."

"You work with people all day."

"Aye, but that's work. I know what I'm talking about there. Social niceties? I fall apart."

"Come on then, Doc. I've got your back. Plus, I'm starving." Hooking his arm, I dragged him across the room to two open stools next to Agnes. "Hi, Agnes. I'm Faelan, the new vet in town. I think our paths crossed briefly at the hedgehog baby shower."

Luch slanted me a surprised glance.

"Och, that was a belter, wasn't it then? Welcome, welcome. We're just about to start trivia night. It's an off night for us, but Fergus is about to go on a month-long holiday—his first ever!—and he's training his son to make sure he can handle the game while he's gone."

"It's that serious?" Luch asked, nodding to a man who came out of the kitchen carrying a bowl of soup and a basket of bread.

"Deadly," Agnes said, her voice hushed. "I wish I was kidding, but you screw up trivia night and these villagers will cut you."

"You'd be at the head of the line wouldn't you, darling?" The bartender leaned over the bar, tapping a finger to Agnes's nose, and my curiosity piqued. The man was easily one of the most handsome men I'd seen in real life, excluding Luch, of course, and I blinked at him as he turned the full wattage of his smile on me. "Careful of this one. She's adorable, but her claws are sharp."

"Noted." I laughed as Agnes pretended to hiss at the man.

"I'm Graham, welcome to my pub." Graham shot a guilty look to where Fergus cleared his throat into the microphone. "And I'll just very quietly give you a menu to look over if you're in the mood for a wee bite. And I'll get a bowl of water out for your wee pup as well."

"Thanks," I mouthed, and took the menu from him. Luch leaned close, resting his chin on my shoulder as he read the menu with me, and my heart did a funny little flutter in my chest at the intimacy of this moment.

I mean, we'd been wildly intimate an hour ago, but this was different. I couldn't explain it, but that small gesture from him made me both excited and a touch panicky. Suddenly, this felt real. All of this. My new job, my new town, a potential new boyfriend. And with all that came very real responsibilities to these people—including telling some of them my truth. Namely, Luch.

Maybe I was getting ahead of myself.

We could keep things fun. Light. No labels. We were both busy individuals, hardly room for real relationships in our lives.

"See anything you like?" Luch said at my ear, and I turned, his lips centimeters from mine. His eyes caught me again, that beautiful golden greenish, like sunlight hitting a mossy rock garden.

Yes, yes I do.

"Um, vegetable soup and a cheese toastie is fine for me."

"Great." Luch turned and ordered with Graham, glancing back at me. "Red wine, okay?"

"Yup, that'll suit me." I turned back to where Fergus was instructing his son on how to call the questions.

"This first round, we'll all write the answers down. No

phones allowed," Agnes whispered to me, "then we'll discuss. Someone will get mad. There will be arguments. Fergus will put people in line. And then we'll move on to the next round."

"What are the topics?"

"This round is popular media and Scotland, so likely a bunch of questions about crime dramas." Agnes sniffed, crossing her arms over her chest and fiddling with a book charm on her necklace.

"Not a fan?"

"Nothing wrong with a good thriller, I just think Scotland has more to offer when it comes to shows and films. I mean, come on. We live in a land rich with myths and history. Magick. Romance. We can't just keep producing the same television over and over. Surely there's more to cover."

"Agnes. Wheesht," Fergus's command was sharp and Agnes winced.

"Sorry, Fergus."

"Round One begins now. On you go, lad." Fergus nudged his son.

The round went quick, and the pub was dead silent as people whispered answers in each other's ears. By the time my soup and sandwich had arrived, Agnes was on her feet, going head to head with Archie, who I hadn't seen when we'd first come in. He and Hilda had been tucked away in a corner table, but they'd waved when I'd spotted them halfway through the round.

"*Twilight* is not the basis for werewolf stories in Scotland." Hands on her hips, hair flying around her head,

Agnes leaned into the argument. "Haven't you heard of the Wulver?"

"Now, lass. He's talking about modern media. You can't say the Wulver comes from modern day media." Archie's bushy brows drew low over his forehead as he thundered.

"The question was ... what story informed Scotland's modern-day retellings of werewolves," Agnes shot back.

"I love when she gets worked up." Graham pitched his voice low behind me, and I turned to grin at him. Clearly the handsome bartender had a thing for pretty Agnes.

Luch looked ashen.

Surprised, I tilted my head at him, as he pressed his lips together, his eyes tightening at the sides.

"The Wulver is Scotland's most famous werewolf," Agnes continued. "Granted, they aren't entirely werewolves in the traditional sense, but they were *Scotland's* were-wolves, weren't they now? Truly misunderstood, too. Kindred protectors they were. None of that rip-your-throat-out-at-the-full-moon nonsense. They looked after people. Left them gifts at their door. Fish and other presents. Had a responsibility to protect others. That kind of thing."

"Scotland has other werewolf myths," Fergus said.

"*Twilight* is not one of them. It's not even *in* Scotland. How is this even relevant?" Agnes argued.

"Because people may have watched *Twilight* and then written modern-day werewolf stories," Archie said, hands on his hips.

"What people? Name 'em," Agnes demanded.

"Well, lad, how are you going to handle this?" Fergus asked his son, who cleared his throat before raising the microphone to his lips.

"Though Agnes raises a good point, the answer I have is, indeed, *Twilight*, so I'll have to adhere to the card."

"Rubbish!" Agnes threw up her hands, turning to glower at Graham when he laughed.

"Och, darling, you've always been a sore loser. Come on now, a wee kiss will sort you out." Graham leaned over the bar but his face met Agnes's hand.

She pushed him back and then squealed when he licked her palm.

"Gross, Graham."

"Think these two have a thing?" Luch said at my ear, and this time when I looked at him, his face looked relaxed again.

"We do not have a thing." Agnes whirled on Luch and he winced, raising his hands in the air.

"Och, now, come on, love. You have agreed to marry me, if you'll recall?"

"That's ages from now and basically if not a single other man in Scotland would have me!" Agnes fumed.

"Och, is it just Scotland, now, hen? That's fine then. I'll just be putting the word out to all me mates about staying away from you, and I'll be biding my time." Graham's grin widened when Agnes pushed her lower lip out in a sulk.

"It doesn't have to be just Scotland you know. Maybe I'll take a holiday to Greece like Fergus and Meredith are and meet the man of my dreams."

"Why travel all that way to find him when he's standing

right in front of you?" Graham's expression was teasing, but something flashed behind his eyes, and I felt a tug on my heart as I watched them.

"Round Two starts now. The category is Great Sports Moments in History," Fergus announced.

"Och, come on." Agnes whirled, hands on hips. "You had three sports categories last week."

"The heart wants what the heart wants, Agnes," Fergus intoned, ignoring her complaint. "Go on, lad, ignore the riff-raff. You're doing just fine."

We lost by two points, but I considered it a win in my book. Not only had I met new friends, but I'd participated in a pub challenge, navigated a date with Luch without too many awkward moments, and I'd enjoyed a delicious meal. All things considered, the day was turning out to be one of the best I'd had in a long time.

Yawning, on the walk home, I hooked my arm through Luch's and pointed to the almost full moon.

"Did you ever wish on the moon as a child?" I asked, admiring how the soft light filtered through the moody clouds.

"The moon? Not the stars for you, lass?"

"No," I said, wistful as I thought about my mum and me making wishes under the full moon. "It was always the moon. *Mother Moon, how beautiful thou be, we have but a gentle request of ye.*"

"And what would you ask for?" Luch's voice rumbled in his chest against my arm.

"To stay." My heart twisted as I realized I might finally have what I wished for all those years ago. "For a home."

"Looks like your wish might be coming true."

"I think so." I squeezed his arm and looked up at him. "And you? If you could make a wish, what would it be?"

"The moon doesn't grant wishes to the likes of me, lass."

CHAPTER FOURTEEN

FAELAN

Did I check my phone more often than I should hoping I'd see a text from him? Absolutely. But Luch had told me he'd be on nights this week, which meant he'd likely be sleeping all day. That was the life of a doctor, and it wasn't like I was sitting around twiddling my thumbs, waiting to hear from him.

The moon doesn't grant wishes to the likes of me.

He hadn't elaborated on what he'd meant, instead, he'd pulled me into a steamy kiss that had me forgetting everything but his mouth on me. But I'd thought about it more than once since then.

This afternoon I was doing another first for me. A first that Luch had kicked off by helping me paint my living space.

I was going to Shona's garden to pick out a few plants for my house.

The idea alone, of *actually* owning plants to keep alive and nurture, made me slightly giddy. Naturally, I'd always loved flowers and would pick up bunches at the market here and there, but I'd never owned my own plants before. Shona promised me she had some options for me that were dead easy for a plant newbie to manage, and I trusted her word on that. *As long as they weren't dead easy to kill as well ...*

Gloam had elected to stay home, needing to rest before he had a good run in the moonlight that night, and I cheerfully made my way to Shona's, choosing to walk the distance along the loch instead of drive. Not only was it a surprisingly nice evening—clear skies and a gentle breeze—but I sometimes found it difficult to sit after a long day. Even though I was on my feet most of the day, walking helped me clear restless energy and allowed me to sort out my thoughts.

Plus, without my car, I wouldn't be overly burdened with too many plants. I would feel too guilty if I bought several from Shona and then murdered them all with benign neglect. No, *one* plant to start would be best, and that would be easy enough for me to carry home.

Ahead of me, a woman walking a fluffy golden retriever wearing a yellow and white guide dog vest stopped on the pavement in front of Shona's nursery. She'd stopped where the pavement ended and the gravel driveway started, and her dog obediently sat at her side.

"Mitch, wait."

The dog sat and swiveled its head, looking for cars.

"Mitch. Forward."

The dog stepped confidently off the pavement, and the woman followed, adjusting her gait to the difference in terrain. I followed at a distance, not wanting to potentially distract her dog from working, or startle her. It was clear she was either visually impaired or blind, and I watched in admiration as she and her dog worked perfectly together to navigate the rocky path before they reached the grass next to Shona's garden.

Shona's cottage, and her surrounding gardens and nursery, were charming as could be. She'd invited me to visit a few times now, but I'd finally taken her up on it now that I knew she was a part of the same Order I'd just joined. Her cottage, a lovely cream stone building with vines trailing up one side, was positioned just off the road, and her expansive gardens spread out behind it. Rows of plants were staked out in various stages of growth, and at the back of the gardens were several greenhouses and another equally charming cottage. It was a lovely space, and I could imagine spending many an hour digging around in the gardens here, well, if I had any idea what I was doing with plants, that is. Though I was someone who dearly loved being in nature and around flowers, I certainly had no frame of reference for their care.

But that would change.

I was a proper adult. I owned my own business, I owned my own flat, and I even, technically, had my own pet. Though Gloam was about as self-sufficient a pet as one could have, really, so I couldn't quite claim that as a win for adulthood. Nevertheless, I was here, I was building friendships, and I was getting myself a damn plant.

"Mitch, find Shona."

I tuned back in from my thoughts to find the guide dog, presumably Mitch, had gone on alert. He'd found a person, all right, but probably not the kind of person that the woman holding his harness was thinking.

A gnome dashed from the bushes and froze into a statue form when he saw the dog. Covered in tattoos and wearing a leather biker vest, the gnome went from moving to frozen so fast, even I second-guessed if what I was seeing was correct.

Mitch clearly did not know what to do with this development.

Frankly, I didn't blame the dog. What does one do when being ordered to find a person and a gnome appears? His fluffy golden tail wagged, and he dragged his human forward, sniffing the now still gnome statue inquisitively.

Then he gave it a sloppy lick.

Just to see, naturally, if it was real or not.

I bit back a grin as I imagined the fury of this gnome at that lick. Granted, I'd never seen a real-life gnome before, but I had to imagine this was somehow connected to Shona's magick, even as I marveled at the power that must be involved in freezing oneself into a statue form.

Mitch sniffed heavily.

"Oh, do you have to go potty, Mitch? I can hear you sniffing. Mitch, busy. Go bizzies, Mitch."

I gulped as Mitch eagerly lifted his leg, readying himself to pee on the gnome's face.

"Excuse me!" I called, surprising both the dog and the woman, who put a hand to her chest, before turning around, bringing Mitch with her.

With their backs turned, the gnome came to life and lifted a fist in the air, brandishing two fingers at the dog, before dashing back into the bushes.

"So sorry to startle you," I said, smoothly, trying desperately not to laugh at the gnome. "Are you here to see Shona? I'm looking for her as well."

"I am." The woman looked to be late twenties, with lush brown hair, gorgeous amber eyes behind thick rimmed glasses, and a smile that lit up her face. Mitch matched her smile, but he didn't come forward to greet me as most dogs normally would. He was working, after all. I'd treated enough guide dogs to know it was best to not distract him in any way while working, so I kept my focus on the woman.

"We can find her together. I'm Faelan Fletcher, the new vet in town. I say that because I'll probably meet you at some point if you're from the area."

"I am! I just moved back here a few months ago. Mitch will be due for his checkup soon enough, so it's nice to meet you. I'm Zara."

"Hi, Zara and Mitch, nice to meet you both." Mitch wagged his tail, his face still stuck in a doggy grin, and leaned into Zara's side. "I'm here to buy my very first plant."

"Your first plant? Really?" Zara gasped and held a hand to her chest again. "That's almost blasphemous."

"You're a plant person, I take it?"

"I love them. I swear I can hear them speak to me." Zara laughed. "They're slowly taking over my house, yet here I am, ready for another."

"In that case, what would you recommend for a newbie?"

"Hmm, you'll need something hearty." Zara's expression sharpened. "You're certain you'll be able to care for it? Otherwise, if you don't have the time, we'll need to get you something like an aloe or a cactus that needs very little care."

"Ouch." I laughed. "I'm hoping I can tend to it fairly regularly, but until it becomes a part of my routine I may forget at times."

"Right, so you don't want something too sensitive then," Zara mused and turned. "Mitch, sweetie, find the door. We want to find Shona."

Mitch took off across the lawn, heading toward the greenhouse, and I stepped in stride.

"I'm busy with my practice all day, so I could keep the plant down there, but I really do want one in my flat. I'm trying my hand at decorating, and having a plant feels like the cozy thing to do. I can keep it by the window, so it gets light."

"East facing? West?"

"Um, the window? I don't know?"

"Morning sun or afternoon?"

"Morning," I said, relieved that I wouldn't have to reveal my absolute lack of directional skills.

"Hmm."

Movement caught my attention, and my eyebrows rose as two gnomes darted around the corner of the nursery.

Mitch barked and Zara froze in her tracks.

"What's wrong? What's going on? He never barks."

"Um, I think it was just a squirrel that ran through really fast."

"*Really*? That's so weird. He never does that." Zara looked worried.

"I can't see anything that would bother him, but maybe he saw something else?" I didn't like to lie, but in this case, I wasn't sure how to explain the presence of gnomes. I didn't even know *why* there were gnomes running about, but the last thing I was about to do was surprise a stranger with an explanation about magick.

Shona poked her head out from the door of the greenhouse, having heard Mitch bark, and a smile wreathed her face.

"Zara and Faelan! And, Mitch, of course. What a treat." Shona came outside and lightly touched Zara's arm, before giving the woman a quick hug.

"Sorry about the barking. Mitch must have seen something." Zara shrugged and Shona shot me a quick look. I widened my eyes and shook my head slightly, letting her know that Mitch had seen something unusual.

"Not a problem. The hedgies are tucked away in their wee nest, sleeping, so it wouldn't have bothered them at all."

"And how's the wee mum getting on then?" Zara asked.

"Och, she's grand. Really just doing so well. The babies are growing so fast, and as much as I want to be diving in and playing with them all day, I'm giving them their space as Dr. Fletcher suggested. Best to let Mum and Dad handle the babies, and I'll keep my wee nose out of it."

"Just for a few weeks longer. I'm sure once they've grown a bit, Mum will be happy to show you her brood," I promised Shona. "They're just a touch shy and protective about it when the bairns are so wee." It was completely unnecessary to add that I was dying to see the hoglets too. With their white, fluffy faces, soft spikes and pink feet, they're just so adorable.

"What can I help you with today, Zara?" Shona asked, holding the door open and stepping backward.

"Mitch, find door." Zara directed Mitch forward and followed him into the greenhouse. "I want to start a pepper plant, as I think it would be quite fun to grow."

"Och, they're grand, they are. I've got a few options that might suit." Shona glanced at me. "Are you okay to wait a minute? I'll just get Zara sorted and then we can have a look at what you're needing."

"She may just need an aloe," Zara stage whispered, and I laughed.

"I promise not to kill whatever plant you assign me."

Both women regarded me with suspicion and I laughed again. "I swear it. I'll sign whatever I have to. I'll put reminders in my phone to water it."

"There is a really great app you can download. Tells you when to water, rotate, and feed each plant," Zara suggested.

"Yup, no problem at all. I'll add it. I promise."

"Mitch, forward."

When the dog didn't move at first, Zara glanced down, tilting her head. "Mitch?"

Mitch's back was arched and a heaving motion rocketed through him. I didn't have to be a vet to know he was about to vomit.

"Oh no, I think the lad's about to be sick." I came forward and then paused, not wanting to touch the dog without Zara's permission. "We should maybe get him outside, I think he's about to throw up."

"It's fine, he can be sick on the floor here. I'll clean it up," Shona rushed out, worry on her face.

I stiffened as I saw the foam at his mouth. This wasn't just being sick from eating a bit of grass. This was far worse.

"Zara, can we get Mitch out of this harness? I'm worried he's ingested something serious."

"Oh no." Zara gave me a stricken look before bending to unharness Mitch as he heaved. "I swear he hoovers when I'm not looking, but almost never when he's working. What do you think he got into?"

I crouched by the dog, helping to finish removing the harness, and slid a hand under his gums to check. I glanced up in time to see the gnome with the tattoos peek out from behind a table leg, his hands full of mushrooms, a guilty look on his face.

Bloody hell, depending on the mushroom, this could be serious. Sending the gnome a furious look, I glanced up at Shona, indecision roiling.

I didn't have what I needed here to induce vomiting, and even so, the poison could already be working its way through Mitch's system. Reaching out, I grabbed a mushroom from the gnome's hands, startling it into running away, and shoved it at Shona.

"What is that?"

"Bloody hell, I'd been growing these as an option for natural pest control." Shona gave me a worried look.

"Bad?" I mouthed to her.

"Use your magick," Shona whispered at my ear and then turned to a now whimpering Zara.

173

"Mitch! What do we do? Dr. Fletcher, can you help?"

"Of course, Zara. If you don't mind, I'm going to carry Mitch outside where I have room to work on him. Shona, will you help Zara while I get my first aid kit out?" I was entirely lying now, as I didn't have a kit with me in my handbag, but Zara didn't need to know that. I wasn't sure how impaired her vision was, but judging from the commands she gave her dog, I was certain she wouldn't be able to see my use of magick. My pulse hammered as Mitch continued to heave. Mushrooms could be quite toxic to dogs, but if it was the one I was thinking of, not only would I have to work fast, but I'd also have to protect myself.

Otherwise I could accidentally poison myself too.

Bending over, I gathered Mitch in my arms and lifted him, barely strained by his weight. I was used to lifting animals of all sizes, so my muscles were well developed. Rushing outside, I laid the dog out on the grass as he continued to heave and knelt by his side.

His warm brown eyes met mine, a plea in them.

"I've got you, buddy. I know this is really scary, but just hang on for me, okay? Zara needs you."

Threading my fingers through his soft fur at his stomach, I closed my eyes, reaching for the magick I held deep in my core. It always answered my call, like a flower blooming in the sunshine, and I breathed a sigh of relief as gentle healing light flowed through me. My hands warmed, and I sent the power inside Mitch, seeing in my mind's eye how the silvery light surrounded the sticky sludge of poison that threatened him. Slowly, the light surrounded the toxin, crisscrossing over and over, like a spider wrapping up its prey, and when I was certain I'd found all traces of it in his body, I took a deep breath.

"By Mother Moon and Sister Sea, I call on my shield to surround me. Protect my body and my soul, let no pain take its toll."

Normally, when healing, I'd take the pain into me and then redirect it elsewhere, if possible, or deal with the after-effects later—like the bruising I'd had after I'd helped heal Oban. But toxins were different, particularly once magick was involved. They could mutate, enhance, and evolve, and taking them into your system was never a smart thing to do.

Mentally keeping a strong hold on the sludgy ball of poison wrapped in my web of magick, I tugged, *hard*, and ripped it from Mitch's body and whipped it into the air. It tried, briefly, to jump to me, but it bounced off my shield and flew up, before shattering into a swarm of tiny black gnats. They buzzed around my head briefly before a strong gust of wind tore them away, and then Mitch rolled, gagging into the grass, heaving up the mushroom he'd eaten.

"There you go, boy. That's a good lad. You'll be just fine now." Sweat ran damply beneath my jumper, and I stroked Mitch's back lightly as he finished heaving, scanning his body with my mind. I couldn't find any other traces of the toxin in him, and feeling comfortable enough to pull back, I retracted the threads of my power and furled it back inside me, tucking it in its safe space deep in my core.

Mitch turned and licked my hand.

"You're welcome, bud. Scary stuff, eh?" I'd have to have a serious talk with Shona about her gnomes. This was unconscionable, what they'd done, and if she kept them about, they'd properly hurt someone one day.

"Is he okay?" Zara called, her voice panicked. I glanced over my shoulder to see Shona doing her best to comfort Zara.

"I was able to induce vomiting and he seems to be doing well now that he's cleared it."

"But what about toxins? His liver? Aftereffects?" Zara gripped Shona's arm as she stepped forward. "Should I be worried?"

"It really looks like he's cleared it all. If you'd like, I can take him home with me to monitor him for a day, but I don't think it is necessary." To prove my point, Mitch had sprung up and was racing across the lawn to Zara.

"Oh, buddy. You scared me." Zara dropped to her knees and hugged Mitch but turned her head when he tried to kiss her. "Ew, vomit breath."

Shona's eyes met mine over Zara's head. She raised her eyebrows in question, and I gave her a quick nod.

"The mushroom must have been a different variety from what I thought. Thank goodness."

"He's usually pretty good when he's working, but sometimes he can't help himself. I'm just glad it wasn't more serious. Can you grab his harness for me?"

"I'll go get it." I went inside the greenhouse, closing the door behind me, and darting a quick look over my shoulder, I crouched.

The gnome looked up at me, still frozen, and I grimaced.

"Listen, you little shite, if you ever do something like

this again, I'm going to punt you into the loch. Understood?"

The gnome shifted into life and threw his hands in the air.

"Och, I swear I didn't know. I swear it. I was just giving the dog a treat so he wouldn't bark at us. I was worried it was going to give us chase and cause his owner to fall."

"You swear it? Because I saw him almost pee on you," I hissed, holding my hand in a fist over the gnome's head.

"I swear to the goddess! Och, I'm not a fan of the wee beasties. They're always trying to piss on me, but I would *never* harm one. It's against our code. We're garden gnomes. We protect all creatures." The gnome seemed to be serious, and I narrowed my eyes at it.

"I'm watching you." I used two fingers to point at my eyes, and then at him.

"I'm sorry. I really am." He seemed contrite enough and there wasn't much else I could do. Grabbing the harness, I went back outside to where Zara cuddled Mitch on the ground.

"He seems fine," Zara said, rubbing her hands down his side.

"He should be. But I'll give you my number and you can call with any concerns." I handed Shona the harness and she gave it to Zara.

"Listen, Zara, why don't I drop you at home real quick and that way you can cuddle up with Mitch and make sure he's doing okay?"

"You'll want to monitor if he's drinking water and eating normally," I instructed.

"Yes, that's probably best. I'll wander back down

another day this week." Zara dug in her pocket and handed me her phone. "Can you add your number?"

"No problem. I'll save it as 'Vet. Dr. Faelan Fletcher.'" I punched in my number, saved it, and handed the phone back before crouching to give Mitch one more rub. "Oh, I'm sorry. I just pet him with his harness on."

"That's fine. I haven't called him back to work yet." Gripping the harness, Zara stood. "Mitch, forward."

"I'll be just a few minutes, Faelan," Shona said. "Have a look at the greenhouse if you'd like? The hedgies are in their nest in the back room if you want to check on them."

Instead, I plopped down on the grass and gave myself a moment to breathe. Healing was a double-edged sword. It was a great gift, but depending on the extent of power needed, it often left me drained. Leaning back on my hands, I closed my eyes and lifted my face to the sky, allowing the cool breeze to brush my cheeks.

"Is the dog all right then?"

Slitting my eyes open, I saw the gnome sticking his head out of the door and looking both ways.

"Aye. No thanks to you." I wasn't willing to let this wee man off the hook quite yet.

"Do you hear that, Gnorman? You almost killed a dog. What's wrong with you?"

I gaped as the second gnome, a woman dressed in a pencil skirt and a low-cut top, smacked Gnorman on the back of his head and sashayed toward me.

"I'm Gnora. You must be one of us, or Gnorman wouldn't have left his resting gnome stance to talk to you."

"Hi, Gnora. I'm Faelan. It's nice to meet you." That

was questionable as I wasn't yet sure if it was nice to meet these little menaces.

"Och, don't lump me in with the likes of him. I would never do such a thing to a dog. Even if those filthy creatures do try to pee on us." Gnora put her hands on her hips as Gnorman came toward her, red cap in hand, his face crestfallen.

"I didn't know, Gnora. I thought I was giving the beastie a wee treat."

"Mushrooms? What dog likes mushrooms?"

"It was all we had on hand that was easy for me to grab. Truthfully, I just wasn't thinking." Gnorman sidled closer to Gnora, his eyes huge and sad in his face.

"And to think, I was considering carrying your bairn. Not with the likes of that behavior, I won't be." Gnora sniffed and lifted her chin.

"You were?" Hope lit Gnorman's face. "Och, just think what a bonnie lass you'll be with your round belly."

"You think?" This seemed to catch Gnora's attention, and before I knew it, she'd giggled and run off, blowing kisses over her shoulder while Gnorman took chase. Shaking my head, I let out a sigh. Was this my life now? Talking foxes and gnome statues that come to life?

A car door slammed, and I stood, brushing my pants off as Shona crossed the lawn to me.

"I'm sorry about that. I just felt better seeing her home and making sure Mitch was well looked after." Shona glanced around and then up at me. "She knows about the gnomes."

"What?" My eyebrows shot up. "Really?"

"Aye. She's not a part of the Order. But seems she must

have her own rare gift, because she heard you speaking to him in the greenhouse."

"Is she ... will she ... do anything?" I wasn't really sure who you'd report talking gnomes to, but I was so used to getting persecuted for being a witch that my first instinct was to worry for Shona's safety.

"Nope. Doesn't seem fussed in the slightest other than asking me to give Gnorman a stern talking to. Now if Mitch had been seriously hurt, that might be a different story." Shona sighed and tugged on her blond braid, pursing her lips. "Those little shites."

"I couldn't believe what I was seeing when I walked up. I'm surprised Zara isn't fazed by it either," I admitted, as I fell into step beside her as we went into the greenhouse. Shona led me to a table full of trays of waxy-leafed plants.

"I swear they cause nothing but trouble. But I do love them." Shona swept out a hand to the plants. "Now, we can do a spider plant for you which is absolutely fine with its soil going dry and being watered sparingly or if you want flowers like you asked for, I'd give you a geranium or a peace lily, but you'll need to keep the soil moist."

Instantly I felt tension band my gut.

"How do I keep the soil wet all the time? What if I forget?"

"You can use one of these." Shona indicated a cute little frog statue with a long stem at its butt. "Fill with water and it will slowly drip into the soil."

"Oh, well, that seems very helpful." I looked between the three plants, but I kept going back to the bright pink flowers. "I'm sure the spider plant would be more realistic, but I think I want the geranium."

"It's a hardy plant. You'll do well with it, I'm sure of it. Plus, if it starts to look a little worse for wear, just call me and we can triage it."

"Oh no, we're already talking about triage and I've just met the plant." I sighed and ran a finger across a leaf. "I'll do my best by you, pretty lady."

"Give her a name. Talk to her. Soon you'll remember to feed her like she's part of the family."

"Hmm, I don't really have much family. I guess I'll have to build one on my own."

"You do, you know." Shona stopped from where she was transferring the geranium into a small pot. "Here in Loren Brae. With us. It'll take time. Feels a bit weird at first —particularly with the gnomes and the magick and the Kelpies and all that—but we're here. We don't turn our backs on one of ours."

Unexpectedly, my eyes filled, and I blinked down at the now blurry table of plants. *We don't turn our backs on one of ours.* I doubted that Shona appreciated how incredible those words sounded. I'd been on my own for years now, and therefore, hadn't felt part of a family since Eriska passed. *It had been such a solitary existence,* and the more I got to realize that and see the stark difference in Loren Brae, the more I felt both overjoyed and filled with sorrow for the many years on my own. *Hence the tears.*

"Och, you poor wee thing. I'm sorry. I didn't mean to make you cry. I just wanted you to know that we're here." Shona's arms came around me and I leaned into her hug, feeling the kindness radiating from her like a warm blanket. "Come on now. How about a wee cuppa tea or hell, it's time for a glass of wine, no? Let's pour a glass and have ourselves a chat. I want to know more about you."

"And I you. Thanks, Shona." I held up my plant. "And for this, she's really lovely."

"What's her name?"

"Betty," I said, automatically, and grinned when the plant seemed to perk up in my hands. Granted, that was likely just my imagination, but still, it was fun to think she responded to my naming her.

"That's a grand name. Sure, and she's going to love her new home with her new family."

Cheered, I tucked her in the nook of my arm and went to have a glass of wine with my new friend.

A friend that I don't have to hide anything from. It was a refreshing concept, and I realized now just how much my soul had been craving such a connection. I couldn't believe how much time had passed before I realized I had to get home. *Such was the easy company.*

Every day, Loren Brae was helping me to grow roots.

CHAPTER FIFTEEN

Luch

"Got a hot date tonight, Dr. Carmichael?" Lynn stopped by my desk as I was finishing off charts. She asked me this question, or some iteration of it, at least once a month.

"Just with my wee pal, Oban," I replied as I always did, focused on typing out the last few notes of the chart I was working on. When she lingered, waiting quietly by my side, I saved the file and shut down the computer, turning to look up at her. "What's up?"

"Tough one today."

"Aye." I shrugged. That was the nature of working in emergency. There were days where I almost felt like a god, granting miracles to those desperately in need, and other days where I'd question my very existence and the choice of my profession. Today was the latter.

It had been a freak accident. A shed collapse, punctured lungs, and a rip of an artery. The man had been past help upon arrival, but still we'd followed protocol, hoping to change the inevitable. I'd thrown my walls up, pushing my emotions down the best that I could, when I'd spoken with the family.

And still.

It always lingered.

Their grief was mine, even though I wasn't responsible for the accident. I still took a piece of everyone I'd lost on my table with me. I think most medical professionals did. None of us got into our job because we *didn't* want to help people, so when we lost someone, it was personal.

"I worry about you, you know." Lynn fussed with a silk scarf she'd pulled out of her purse to wrap around her hair. "New to town. Going home alone every night. It must be lonely, and a man like you? Surely any girl would be lucky to have you."

I gave Lynn a look, hoping she would let off, and she raised an eyebrow at me.

"Or have I misread the situation? Is it a man I should be looking for to date ye?"

At that, I smiled. Lynn was an eternal matchmaker, determined to find everyone happiness.

"Nae, hen. Your read is correct. I do prefer the ladies. However, I just don't feel like dating right now."

"Why's that? Maybe we can get it sorted out."

"What if I told you that people can be happy on their own? That not everyone needs a partner to be fulfilled in life?"

At that Lynn's brow furrowed. I'd stumped her.

"I'd say to you that if that's the honest truth of it for you, then I'll not say another word about dating. I think you've the right of it—some people really are happy on their own. There's certainly nothing wrong with it. Take my mum. She lost my dad when I was just out of uni, and she's never bothered to date again. Not once. Said she'd enjoyed love once in her life and now had a million other experiences to have. She's in Italy right now. On a woman's retreat where they teach you how to make the perfect loaf of bread. Isn't that something?"

"Och, it is." My stomach grumbled, loudly enough that Lynn laughed. I shrugged, sheepish. "I do love a good loaf of bread."

"Who doesn't? When she's back, I'll get her to make some loaves for us. We'll have a wee party in the break room and pretend we're sipping wine in sunny Italy."

"You know what, Lynn? It's a date." I winked at her and Lynn crowed, slapping me on the shoulder.

"I'm telling you, Dr. Carmichael, if I was thirty years younger and single, I'd make a play for you meself, and that's the truth of it."

"Your husband's a lucky man, Lynn."

"Safe home, Dr. Carmichael. I'll see you tomorrow." Lynn tightened her scarf and waved goodbye as she left. Grabbing my coat, I put my phone and laptop in my bag and then hooked it over my shoulder. Strolling out into the night, I nodded at a few people in the car park.

Lynn would likely go wild with joy if I told her about Faelan. I could already see her telling me all the different ways I needed to charm Faelan, and I just wasn't sure I had the stomach for my relationship to be under the microscope at work.

Not that we were in a relationship.

But what I felt for Faelan was pretty damn real.

Just thinking about her taste on my lips had me fumbling and dropping my keys at my car. Sighing, I shook my head and bent, remembering just how good it felt to be with her.

How excited she'd been once we'd launched into painting her living room.

Her breathy moans as I'd brought her pleasure.

Her soft kisses that seemed constantly surprised by her attraction for me.

I couldn't stop thinking about her and hated that I'd been so busy that I'd had to stay away from her the last few days.

"It's normal to have space when you first start dating someone," I muttered to myself as I unlocked my car. My body was almost overheated, thinking about her mouth on mine, and I rolled the windows down as I left the car park, waving to Jacob on the way out.

I just liked her.

She was easy to be around. There were some people that took up too much of my bandwidth, but Faelan? I felt recharged after spending time with her. She was resilient, and I loved watching her talk about things she was passionate about, and then quietly pull into herself when she hit a subject that was too close to her vulnerabilities.

Every moment I spent with her, I was more and more convinced that a healer's magick was not something to be shunned. There was just no way that Faelan was a grifter.

Or if she was, then she was the best of the best, because nothing she'd said yet had pinged my radar as a lie. Except for the one she'd told me about Oban being in shock when she'd healed him. But I'd read that lie so easily, I just couldn't imagine she was playing people for fools. I truly believed she just wanted to help animals.

And if that was the case? What could be so wrong with that? More and more, I was convinced that the trauma of my birth had skewed my father's objectivity, and he needed to reassess his beliefs.

Maybe it would be Faelan who could be the one to show him, finally, that there might be a place where science and magick could coexist. If she stayed here, that is. Even the thought of her leaving made my stomach turn slightly. I needed more time with her. Watching her put down roots and find her way here was like watching a flower bloom under the soft brush of the sun's rays.

Amused at the poetry of my thoughts, I stopped the car outside my cottage and checked my watch. There was little time left tonight, and I needed to eat before—

A shriek rang out and I whirled, my heart pounding, as Kelpies reared up from the water.

Oban barked, running out into the yard, and I dove for him. He raced away, across the grass, hackles raised. I needed to get him inside and now.

Protect others, at all costs. Turning my back on the Kelpies, I ran.

CHAPTER SIXTEEN

Faelan

By the time I was walking home, I was lightly buzzed, happily filled up with village gossip, and was the proud owner of my first plant. Tucked in my handbag were my careful notes on how to care for Betty, as well as the name of the plant app to download to ensure I carefully tended to her needs. All in all, I was pleased with my first real "girlfriend" hangout in Loren Brae. Shona was exceedingly sweet, easy to get along with, and when we spoke about things she was passionate about, like plants and healing, her face lit up. It turns out, our interests in healing overlapped—hers with plants and teas and such, and mine for animals—and we'd spent some time comparing notes on where we could potentially help each other down the road.

I was particularly interested in one poultice she used for

dry skin, knowing it might be a more natural route for some of my itchier patients in the summer.

I crested the hill and gasped as Loren Brae spread out below me, the full moon hanging like a fat Christmas globe in the inky night sky. It looked like a postcard. Soft golden light shimmered across Loch Mirren's rippling surface and a gentle breeze brought the scents of sea and damp earth to me. The village sparkled against the dark backdrop of the hills, and the grand dame herself, MacAlpine Castle, shone bright, the village lights like diamonds scattered at her feet.

The scene pierced my heart, because for the first time I was allowing myself to fall for a place that would welcome me. Sure, Loren Brae likely had her downfalls, but for now, she was shiny and new, and *mine*. Mine to call home.

Humming, a smile on my face, I continued down the hill toward the village, cradling Betty at my side.

A prickle of awareness, just a slight buzz against the back of my neck, had me snapping my head up and out of my reverie. It was the awareness that all women had, particularly when walking alone at night, but mine was honed after years of being ostracized. I stopped, turning in a full circle to look behind me, scanning the thick bushes and undergrowth that lined the opposite side of the street.

Eyes glinted.

It was just a glimmer, a small reflection, and then it disappeared, and though I searched, I couldn't make out any movement.

Had I imagined it?

"Gloam?" I whispered, hoping my fox was silently following me home.

But why would he be silent? Wouldn't he have made

himself known? A shriek tore through the night, ripping the blissful silence to shreds, and I froze. Slowly, I turned my head toward the loch, my heart pounding violently. A dark shadow drifted across the surface, cutting through the moonlight's path reflected on the water. It was far in the distance, close to where the Stone of Truth was buried on the island, but even from here I could just make out the shape of a horse's head rearing up from the water.

Would it attack? Or was their shriek just a warning?

It was my first time hearing them, even though Sophie had told me that Loren Brae had been plagued by the beasts for a while now. The only problem? Well, I should amend that as there were many problems with this situation. I didn't have my weapon with me. Though I wasn't entirely certain what I could do with a small scalpel against the ominous beast that drifted across the dark waters. The next biggest problem I had? There was still a sizable distance between me and my flat, which meant one of two things: I could either make a break for it and risk angering the Kelpie into chase, or I could ease backward into the bushes.

The same bushes where I'd just seen eyes glimmering at me.

Neither of these options felt particularly wise, but given the fact that Betty was the only weapon I currently held, and I was uncertain of a Kelpie's speed, fading back into the dark undergrowth seemed the reasonable choice. Right, maybe not reasonable, but the one currently afforded to me.

My whole life I'd been taught to run. And as much as I wanted to stand at the side of the loch and face this beast head-on—just to prove that I could—I also wasn't stupid. What I needed was far more training before I attempted to take on a Kelpie on my own. I eased backward, keeping my eyes trained on the water, and softly stepped toward the long row of hedges that lined the street. With each step, I felt my way with my foot, praying I wouldn't trip and go sprawling across the pavement, and sweat beaded my brow. My breath came out in short bursts, and I pressed my lips together, not wanting to make any untoward sound to draw attention to myself. So far, the Kelpie continued to prowl the water near the island, and I didn't want to draw it any closer to where I was.

The back of my foot hit the curb and I stepped backward, easing each foot upward, until branches touched my back. Bending forward, I ducked, pushing my bum through the hedges, protecting Betty as I went. Just a few centimeters more and I'd be fully concealed from sight. From there, maybe I could make a break for it if I could navigate the dense undergrowth coating the hills by the light of the moon.

If the sheep could do it, surely I could as well.

If only I had Sophie's number on my phone—*why didn't I?*—so I could quietly text her.

My phone rang.

Shite. Did I summon that to happen?

The first strains of "The Lion Sleeps Tonight," a whimsical choice I'd picked so I wouldn't get annoyed if people called me off-hours, boomed into the night before I slapped a hand against my pocket, silencing it.

I held my breath, but the shadow veered, racing toward me, a dark horse thundering down across a moonlit path.

"Shite!" I turned to run, branches scraping at my face, but a low growl stopped me.

Fuck.

When I turned, there was a dog standing tall, its back to me, hackles raised, as the Kelpie loomed closer. With its shaggy coat, broad shoulders, and pointed ears, the husky could almost be mistaken for a wolf. Except wolves had long since been gone from Scotland. Worry filled me as the shadow of the Kelpie fell, impossibly large, and the dog stood its ground, its head angled high, teeth bared to the threat.

I'd made a promise to myself to protect and help animals when I'd become a veterinarian. But this oath ran deeper, to one my mum and I had always practiced. First, protect. *Then* preserve or heal, as needed. And I, a protector of animals, was hiding in the bushes when one was about to become hurt.

Indecision warred and cost me time. Before I could step out, try to help, do anything, the husky lunged into the air, teeth glinting in the moonlight as it snapped its jaws ferociously. I froze, seeing how wild and untamed this dog was, and cringed as the Kelpie reared up.

Once more the animal leaped into the air, growling furiously, and to my absolute shock, the Kelpie shrunk backward.

He was doing it. The dog was keeping it at bay. When the Kelpie turned tail and raced across the loch, back toward the island, the husky turned and shot me a furious glance over its shoulder. It's golden eyes glimmered, and I realized that this was the same beast that had been stalking me in the bushes.

Shite. Shite. Shite.

Fear rose, my throat going dry, and I swallowed once before I followed the Kelpie's suit and turned tail and ran.

I wasn't entirely sure what I was thinking, as branches bounced off my arms and scraped my face, and racing through the thick underbrush was impossible even under the bright light of the full moon. But panic is not friends with logic.

By the time I made it closer to town, I was dripping in sweat, and likely blood from scratches on my face and neck, too. Ducking through the line of hedges, I forced myself back onto the street, because there was no way I could continue stumbling along the hill and hope to make it home without a broken ankle. Panting, I turned, eyes closed, and waited for the beast to lunge for me.

Silence greeted me.

I paused at the base of the stairs to my flat, which might have been a silly choice as this was when someone was murdered in a horror movie, but I had to see. I had to know. Had the dog really been chasing me? Or had it been protecting me? And if so, where had it come from? Granted, I hadn't been here all that long, but so far I hadn't treated a husky at my practice. Which was surprising, given they were a fairly popular dog breed, particularly in Scotland's cooler climate.

All I could hear was the gentle lapping of the water on the pebbly shoreline. No panting, no growling, nothing crashing through the underbrush along the street. It could be any other night in Loren Brae, minus the usual noises of a village going about its nightly routine. Which made sense, really, since I wouldn't be likely walking to the pub or going for a leisurely stroll if I heard the Kelpies screaming in the night. Hell, no wonder the last vet had left in such a hurry. Their shriek was enough to make your insides shrivel in fear.

Movement caught my eye and I jumped, only to sigh in relief when Gloam slipped from the bushes.

"Oh, I'm so glad you're safe. Did you see what happened?"

"I saw the Kelpie rise. But I was up the hill in the forest behind the castle. Were you down here?"

"I was. I was walking the street home." I bounded up the stairs, needing to be inside my flat, convinced if I just made it inside I would be safe. Unlocking the door, I rushed inside, slamming it quickly behind Gloam, and sagged against the wall in relief. Safe. Like a child ducking under the covers, convinced that was all she needed to shield herself from the monsters. Logic might not be my strong suit at the moment, but I truly did feel better now that I was back in my flat, the warm glow from a lamp I'd picked up at a charity shop earlier that week casting a cheery welcome across my space. It had been a fruitful shopping trip, as I'd also bought a colorful rug with brilliant reds, pinks, and turquoises in it, an actual vase for flowers, and a colorful print of Scotland's hills dusted with lovely purple heather. It was just the beginning of making my place feel more like my own, but even so, I was pleased with the progress I was making.

"Why are you bringing a dead plant home?"

"Oh no." I looked down at my arms to realize I'd crushed Betty too tightly to my side and the beleaguered plant was barely standing up anymore. Guiltily, I placed it on the counter and stared at it. "Shona's going to kill me."

"Maybe it will be fine. Plants are surprisingly resilient." Gloam trotted across the flat and jumped onto the couch, turning himself in a circle for a while before he wrapped in a little ball, tucking his tail under his chin as he watched me. *"How close were you to the Kelpies?"*

"Kelpie," I amended. "Just the one. At least that's all I saw."

"How did you get it to go away?"

"I didn't." A fine trembling worked its way through my body and I realized that I was feeling shaky from the aftereffects of adrenaline. "You know what? I think I need a glass of wine."

I definitely needed a glass of wine.

Popping open the fridge, I pulled out a Sauvignon Blanc I'd opened two nights ago and poured a glass, needing something normal to do to help calm my nerves. Now that I thought about it, I couldn't be sure if the dog would really have chased me. Had that just been my overactive imagination? Or was it just straight panic because the situation was so out of any frame of reference I had experienced in the past?

"The Kelpie just left?"

"Oh, so, no. That's not entirely what happened." I recounted the events of the evening for him and when I finished, Gloam had come alert, sitting up straight on the couch.

"A dog chased the Kelpie away?" His tone held a note of suspicion.

"It did. A husky."

"I don't think that's possible."

"Really? Because it worked. Or at least it seemed to work. It was really quite the thing. For a second, I thought I'd need to stop and help it, but it fended off the Kelpie. Really quite amazing."

"Tell me what the dog looked like."

"Oh, it was a husky. I mean, it was kind of hard to see as the only light came from the moon, and you know, that whole panicking for my life thing."

Gloam made that soft yelping noise he made when he laughed at me.

"I don't know the different brands of dogs." Gloam sniffed in disdain. *"Just describe it."*

"Oh right, I guess a fox wouldn't know all the types, would they?" I smirked at Gloam calling them "dog brands." I guess I'd never really thought of it that way, because Gloam had thus far been fairly well versed on many different subjects, but it made sense he wouldn't know dog breeds by name. He likely just knew them as dogs. "Um, grayish white shaggy long-haired coat. Darker fur near the shoulders and hind quarters. Pointy ears. Longer snout, like yours."

"Wolf," Gloam said, settling back into his ball.

I blinked at him in surprise and then took a long sip of my wine. The cool liquid soothed my dry throat, and I took another deep breath.

"Wolves have not been endemic to Scotland since the seventeenth century."

"That you know of," Gloam corrected, shifting his body about. He was so damn cute, I couldn't help but reach out and scratch his ears.

"I mean, I think that anyone knows of. They have a pretty strong record of when they were last around."

"Then they're wrong." Gloam slitted his eyes. *"Who are they? How do you know* they *are right?"*

"Um, the authorities? The wildlife services who do the species count?"

"I've never been counted. How would they know if I do or don't exist?"

The fox had a point. Could it be possible that wolves had returned to Scotland and somehow nobody had reported it? Possibly. Anything was possible, really, particularly in a town where gnomes came to life and water horses threatened the locals.

"That's a fair point, lad." I raised my glass at him, a silent cheer. "Still, this wolf was massive. Surely someone would be aware of him at this point. Unless ..."

"Unless what?"

"Maybe he's a familiar. Like you are. Maybe he belongs to a magickal person I haven't met yet. It would explain the desire and ability to chase away the Kelpies, wouldn't it?"

"Perhaps." Gloam shifted, leaning his head forward as I reached out to scratch behind his ears once again. *"But then again, maybe not. I don't know all the magickals in the area."*

"Would you be able to scent it? If you knew it was a wolf?"

"I might be able to. Shall I track it tonight?" Gloam straightened, lifting his chin as though he was a soldier ready to take orders. My stomach twisted. I wouldn't get a wink of sleep if Gloam was out in those hills tonight, not with a restless Kelpie and a terrifying wolf on the loose.

A wolf.

It made sense, really, but my mind had convinced me that what I saw was a lesser threat. A wolf … in Scotland. It was like telling someone to watch out for polar bears in the desert. Therefore, I hadn't wanted to believe what I was really seeing. But now, when I closed my eyes and thought back to it, I realized that Gloam was absolutely right. It had been a wolf. Too large for a husky, with golden eyes instead of blue, and well-developed canines. And those shoulders. On his haunches, he'd been so broad. Strong. *Terrifying.*

A wolf had come to my rescue. Was he a protector of Loren Brae? But why had he looked at me with such anger? *As if I'd been in the wrong?* It was why I had run … in fear.

I'd have to ask Sophie what was happening there. Maybe someone would be able to shed some light on this.

My phone rang in my pocket, almost startling me into dropping my glass of wine, and I pulled it out to see Shona's name on the screen. Glancing guiltily at the bedraggled plant on my counter, I swiped the screen.

"Hey, I heard the Kelpies and was worried about you on the walk home."

"Was that you who called before?"

"It was. I'm assuming you got home okay?"

I stood and walked over to the plant, knowing I'd have to triage it.

"Not exactly, but I'm home and I'm fine." I paused. It was on the tip of my tongue to tell her about the wolf, particularly with hedgies and gnomes running around her garden, but I stopped. For some reason, I didn't feel ready to share about it. Maybe I needed a bit more time to process.

Maybe it was something else entirely.

"Say, Shona ... I did kind of squish Betty on the jog home. Help me out?" I laughed at her exaggerated sigh and then listened as she gave me instructions on how to resurrect Betty. By the time she'd finished, I'd downed my glass of wine and a bone-deep exhaustion was forcing me toward my bedroom. "Thanks for the help, I promise to keep you updated."

Walking across the living room, I flipped the lamp off and stood for a moment in the window, allowing my eyes to adjust to the darkness. Outside, the loch shimmered under the full moon, barely a ripple marring its smooth surface.

And up on the hill, silhouetted by the moon, the wolf stood watch.

Holding my hand out, I pressed it to the pane.

"Thank you," I whispered, relief and gratitude filling me. "I'm sorry I ran. I won't. Next time. If you show yourself to me."

"Who are you talking to?"

Gloam popped up and put his nose to the windowsill and I looked back to where the moon hung heavy over the top of the hill.

The wolf was gone.

CHAPTER SEVENTEEN

FAELAN

The ringing of my phone brought me out of a dead sleep at six in the morning, and Gloam yipped at my ear as I fumbled to answer. The fox had stayed with me last night, seeing how much the Kelpie had rattled me, and he'd been an excellent companion. In fact, it had been easier than I'd imagined to drift off into sleep, my hands threaded through the soft fur at Gloam's neck, my thoughts on the lone wolf standing on the hill, keeping guard over Loren Brae.

"Hi? Hello?" I mumbled into the phone, swiping my hair from my eyes.

"Dr. Fletcher? The vet?" a hysterically crying woman shouted into the phone.

"Aye, that's me." I straightened, already swinging my legs from underneath the comforter.

"It's my horse. Malarky. He's broken his leg. I'm sure of it," the woman sobbed into the phone, and my heart sank. A broken limb was often a death sentence for a horse.

"Right, we can't be sure of anything until I have a look at it." Flipping the bathroom light on, I peered in the mirror and winced at the scratches on my face from racing through the bushes the night before. I'd need to heal those, but there was no time at the moment. "Where are you located then? I'll be right out."

The woman rattled off an address so fast, I had to rush out into the main room of my flat and grab a pen and paper. "Slow down, love. I'm new to the area and will need a little help."

"Right, right. I'm sorry. I'm just ... he's my best friend." She hiccupped out a sob.

"I understand. I'll do my best, but I can't help if I can't find you."

This time, the woman repeated the address slowly and told me it was only a short ways outside of Loren Brae. Promising her I'd be on my way shortly, I disconnected the call and took a deep breath before going into autopilot mode. I took the world's fastest shower, dressed, threw my hair on top of my head, and brewed a to-go cup of tea. Gloam had elected to go out so he could wander, and I'd cracked the balcony door in case he'd want to return while I was gone. Opening the door, I skidded to a stop.

A small bunch of flowers wrapped in twine had been placed against my doorstep.

A smile tugged at my face, even though I wondered when Luch would have had time to drop them off if he was on nights at the hospital. Turning, I raced to fill my newly purchased vase with some water, dumped them in, and then pounded down the stairs of my flat. I prayed that this woman could keep her horse calm and lying down, otherwise, it might only do more damage to its injured leg. Hopping in my car, I switched my phone to directions, and then I allowed the automated voice to direct me down the road that hugged the rocky shores of Loch Mirren.

I couldn't help myself and glanced out to where the placid water lapped against the island in the middle of the loch, a gull swooping lazily as the sun crested the hills in the distance. Any other morning, and I'd be smiling at the pretty picture before me, but today, trepidation filled me. Had the wolf not been there to help, I wasn't certain how I would have fared against last night's Kelpie attack.

What triggered the Kelpies? From what I knew about horses, they weren't typically malicious and would usually only attack out of fear or pain. That being said, they could assert dominance if they were protecting their territory or resources. Which certainly tracked with everything Sophie had said about the Stone of Truth. But had it just been that I was walking along the loch? Was that considered too close to the stone? Or did they consider me an actual threat?

Was that why the Order existed? Those of us with power were more of a danger to the Stone than those without? It was better to have us on the side of the Stone? Mulling it over, I returned my focus to my driving.

The road wound along the loch and over the hill, directly past the turnoff for Luch's cottage, and my thoughts drifted to him. When would I see him next? Our time together this past weekend felt magickal—like a fairy tale really—and now it had been a few days of silence from him. Was he still interested in me? Had I imagined the entire thing? It had gone from so very hot to very cold so fast. Or was I just simply not used to the normal patterns of dating? I hated feeling like I didn't know what was going on, or was the fool in any situation, so navigating the ins and outs of dating was proving to be a bit unnerving for me.

He told you he wouldn't be able to text on shift.

I reminded myself of his words, that he'd be completely unavailable, and yet, still I wondered. Was that actually true? Did doctors just not text their families during night shifts? What about when they got off work and went home to rest? Was that reasonable to expect no communication?

My thoughts halted the minute I saw a man standing in the street, waving his hands in the air, and I pulled my car onto a little gravel lane. I rolled my window down, just an inch, and peered out.

"Dr. Fletcher? I'm Amy's husband. Malarky, um, our horse, is back here."

"Got it. Let me just get my bag."

Relieved that I was in the right place, I switched into doctor mode and grabbed my large first aid backpack from the back seat. Slinging it over my shoulder, I took in the man's pained expression, dirty overalls, and clenched fists.

"Can you tell me what happened?"

"She jumped a low wall with him, like so many times before, but he landed wrong."

It would be a break then, and potentially a life-altering one. Already I was thinking about how to help fix it, what I had with me in my bag for an emergency splint, as well as how I could get the couple to step away from the horse so I could, literally, work my magick.

As the man explained the accident, we followed a path with trodden down grass until we reached a woman, kneeling next to a chestnut horse lying on the ground. She had her arms around its neck and whispered furiously into its ear as she sobbed against its head.

Right, this would not do.

"Amy? I need you to step back." Horses were very sensitive, and the more she cried on him, the more I was concerned the horse would flip out. Already I could see the whites of its eyes as it tracked my arrival, and I could almost feel its fear kick up.

"Amy. You need to step back. Love, you need to let go."

"No, I can't. He's my best friend," Amy sobbed into the horse's neck.

Turning, I gripped the man's arm.

"What's your name?"

"James."

"James, you need to take Amy and get her out of here. The horse is terrified, largely because he's sensing her fear. If they're that closely connected, he won't let me treat him. Can you do that for me? It's the only way to save Malarky." I used my no-nonsense tone, the one that I brought out when I needed complete compliance, and James gave me a brisk nod, almost as if he was saluting me.

"Amy, love. The doctor needs to work. Just give her some space. Come on now. Let's step away."

"No, I can't leave him." Amy turned a devastated face to mine.

"You're scaring him and impeding his ability to get the

care he needs." I was blunt, but I had to be. Amy's mouth rounded into a little O, matching the two bright spots of pink on her cheeks. James bent, murmuring in her ear, and hauled her up and away, pulling her down the path and out of sight. Immediately I bent and put a hand to Malarky's side when he tried to rise.

"Easy, boy. I'm here to help. Let's just have a wee look at what's going on, all right? Just calm down. I'm here for you." The horse gentled under my touch, and I took a moment to swing my backpack off. Unzipping it, I dug inside for what I could use for a splint for the very obvious break in the foreleg.

My eyes fell on my scalpel, the top sheathed in a protective leather casing. The handle was exposed, and on it, a second band of diamonds glittered.

I'd somehow passed another challenge? Was it from the night before? Because I'd withstood a Kelpie? Questions reared, but I had no time to think further, as the horse shifted again, letting out a soft nicker of pain.

Pulling out a large roll of elastic bandages and a splint, I turned back to the horse and put my hands against his leg, just above the break. The horse trembled under my hands, its breath coming out in sharp huffs, and I reached for my magick to calm him. Glancing over my shoulder to make sure James kept Amy away, I allowed my magick to flow through my hands to Malarky, envisioning a soothing river of cool calm energy to lower the horse's racing heart rate.

He was young, with a lot of life left in him, and he was terrified. On some levels, animals knew when a wound could be too great, and I had a choice to make. His owners might wonder how I healed him, but he deserved a chance

—particularly when he had a home with someone who loved him so much.

"Bone and flesh, mend and weave. By my will, the pain shall leave. Hoof and heart, restore and bind, strength and healing, now intertwine."

My magick flowed in, surrounding the break in the bone, and then it began the process of knitting it back together. I wouldn't be able to heal it entirely, as it would be too obvious, but enough that the bone was strong, and would need only rehabilitation for strained ligaments. As my magick worked, I splinted the leg, soothing the horse as I wound the bandage around the splint, even though it was more for show at this point.

Once complete, I searched in my mind's eye for any other injuries, but Malarky seemed well enough. Grounding myself, I inhaled, and pulled my magick back, ready to direct the pain elsewhere—

"Malarky!"

I whirled as Amy raced forward, a sheepish James behind her, and choked as I took the horse's pain inside me. I stumbled backward, falling on my heels from the crouch I was in, as the horse rolled and stood of its own accord, keeping its injured leg slightly off the ground.

I gasped, the pain washing through me, but there was nothing to be done now, at least not in front of the couple.

I would pay, and pay dearly for this, as the size of the wound on a horse like Malarky was enough to lay me out for a day or two. James crouched next to me and hooked an arm through mine, helping me to stand.

"I'm sorry about that, I am. It was almost impossible to

keep her away." He steadied me on my feet, and I blinked at him, little spots dancing across my vision.

"It's fine."

It wasn't fine. I was dizzy beyond belief, and the darkly sticky sludge of pain worked its way through me, like hot tar oozing down a ledge. I shuddered and sucked in a breath, willing myself to composure.

"It's not a break. Hard to say if torn ligaments, but I think just an awkward landing and some seriously strained muscles. He'll need rehab, but otherwise, he should be well enough."

"Oh, thank you, Dr. Fletcher." James clapped an arm awkwardly around my shoulders even as his wife turned to me, speculation in her eyes. I'd seen that look many a time before.

"You're certain? I was sure it was broken."

"I'm certain. Shock can play out differently in many animals." I gave her a bland look, with a practiced smile, and she didn't press. "I've got to get going. Walk him slowly home, or even better, get him a lift back. There's a lovely large animal vet about an hour north of here."

"I'm familiar with them," Amy said, arms still wrapped around Malarky's neck.

"Give them a call. They'll do a more thorough assessment and get you a treatment plan." Pain sliced my gut. I needed to leave, *now*.

"What do we owe you?"

I waved it away as I bent and picked up my bag, trying to conceal the enormous pain I was in. Slinging it over my shoulder, I gave a feeble smile.

"Pop by the practice sometime this week, I'll sort it out. I really have to go. I have patients first thing."

There was no way I'd be treating any patients in this condition, but they didn't know that. With a quick wave, I forced my legs forward and down the path toward my car, feeling like I was about to fall over at any moment. When I was out of their sight, I broke into a run, needing to get to my car and home as fast as I could. There I'd be able to use some of my special teas to help rid myself of the pain.

When I reached my car, I tossed my backpack in the back seat, but when I went to open the front door, all I could do was sag weakly against the side of the car. Closing my eyes, I put my forehead against the cool metal and drew in a breath, and then another, willing myself to have the strength to get home.

"Faelan? What's wrong?"

Bloody hell.

Pasting a smile on my face, I turned as Luch's arms came to my shoulders and gaped at his bare chest.

"Um, I ..."

"Were you about to drive? Like this?" Luch's golden eyes tracked across my face, and I fluttered my lashes furiously, trying to clear the fog that was starting to cloud my vision. Or maybe it was the fact that he wasn't wearing a shirt—just a loose pair of running shorts and a baseball cap —and despite the pain, my thoughts went an entirely different direction.

"What's happened to you?" Luch's hands at my arms steadied me.

"I'm ... dizzy ..." I waved a hand in the air and heaved in

a breath. My chest felt tight, and I tried to breathe past the pain that wreathed my ribs.

"That's it. Hand over your keys." Luch took them from my hands and I gasped as he lifted me and deposited me neatly in the passenger seat, before hopping behind the wheel. "Have you eaten today? Food, water?"

"No. Emergency. Horse." Talking was painful. I closed my eyes and leaned back into the seat, not caring about anything else other than that we were moving, and I wasn't the one who had to get myself home.

"I'll figure out what you mean by that shortly." Gravel crunched under the wheels of the car and then it came to a stop. Squinting my eyes, I realized we were at Luch's cottage.

"No," I gasped, weakly. I needed my magickal tea to help me with the pain. "Home. I need ..."

"What you need is to be quiet and to let a doctor take care of you."

"No." I whipped my head back and forth, but I was too weak. I'd done one too many healings of a magickal nature lately, and my recovery from taking in pain from such a large animal would be difficult. "Home."

"Not a chance, darling." Luch scooped me out of the front seat like I weighed nothing, and I vaguely heard barking as he crossed to his cottage.

"Oban. Tell your dad he's lost his mind."

Let him help you.

"I can't. He doesn't ..." I trailed off, realizing I was talking to Oban out loud.

"I don't what?" Luch asked, and I shook my head, unable to keep talking. The pain banded my chest, down my sides, and into my legs, and my back was so tight it had seized up.

Luch fumbled at the door and then pushed inside, and I sighed in relief when he laid me on his bed. His masculine scent surrounded me, and I rubbed my cheek against his pillow, inhaling whisps of cedar and soap. I wanted to be exactly where I was and a million miles away. Another wave of pain rolled through me and I whimpered. Luch's hands were at my wrist, and I blinked up at him as he checked his watch, counting my pulse out.

"Vitals are elevated." Luch held a hand to my forehead, checked my eyes, and angled my chin. "Does it hurt to breathe?"

"Luch." He could run me through every normal diagnostic test that he wanted. Nothing would be explainable or really matter for that part. What I needed to do was rid myself of the pain I'd taken inside of me. And for that, I needed my special tea, a grounding spell, and to be connected in nature.

None of which was happening so long as I was lying in this bed.

Sighing, I tried to shove up on my elbows and gasped in shock when Luch just pressed me back down onto the bed. His hand burned at my chest, warm through my jumper, and I squeaked in protest as he raised my shirt.

"Bloody hell, Faelan. Were you riding the horse? Have you been thrown? You should have told me." A thunder cloud rolled across Luch's handsome face as he expertly stripped me, despite my protests, and gaped down at the skin he had bared. The shock in his eyes said everything I needed to know, but still I dragged my gaze down my body and winced.

Bruises in all shapes and colors covered my skin, like someone had dropped paint blobs onto paper, and they ranged in color from angry black all the way to livid green. Not my best look, to be sure, and it galled me that this was the first time Luch was seeing me almost fully naked and I was covered in injuries.

"No, it's—"

"I think we need to take you into the hospital. There's extensive trauma here. I want to get you on fluids, we'll need some pain care. We need to get some X-rays. What the hell were you doing riding alone?"

I reached out with what strength I had and grabbed Luch's wrist before he stormed from the room.

"Luch, stop."

"I will not. You're seriously injured, Faelan. You don't get a say anymore, I'm in charge."

Two paws hit the side of the bed, and I rolled slightly to look down at Oban's sweet face.

"Oban. Help me, please. Stop him." I knew Oban knew what I was. But Luch wasn't about to listen to me. He was already pulling out his phone and I knew if he called for help, an ambulance, I'd never get the real help I needed.

Oban turned and growled at Luch.

Shock caused Luch to stop and look up from his phone. Oban stepped forward, hackles raised, and growled again, long and low for good measure.

"Oban?" Luch looked confused and then cocked his ear as though he was listening.

Could he hear him?

Unsure if what I was seeing was correct, or just my imagination, I took a deep breath.

"You can't help me, Luch. At least not traditionally."

The words rasped, burning my throat, but I held up a hand when Luch started to protest.

"I'm a healer, Luch. A witch. A charm witch to be exact. It's an unfinished spell, working its way through my body. Traditional medicine will do nothing."

Luch froze and I tore my eyes away from his face and blinked up at the ceiling, fighting the tears that threatened.

This was when he would leave.

Everyone.

Always.

Left.

Me.

A soft sound, and then the bed dipped, and Luch sat. Reaching out, he squeezed my hand, and I couldn't bring myself to look at him.

"Tell me how to help you then, darling."

The unbearable sweetness of his words almost broke me, and a tear slipped down the side of my cheek and fell into the crook of my neck.

"I need a special tea. It's at my flat. And then I need to go outside. The ... I didn't get a chance to remove the pain I took inside me. It will fester unless I rid myself of it. I need to clear it from me."

"Can I make this special tea here? You might be surprised at the ingredients I have lying around."

"Unless you've harvested thistle under a full moon, I don't think so."

"It's in your kitchen cupboard?"

"You can just take me home. I can do this on my own."

"Faelan." The bed dipped again and Luch's face came into view, those golden green eyes burning in his face. "If you think for one second I'm letting you go home alone in this condition, then you don't know me at all."

Right, there was no way to fight against him, not when I was this weak. I gave him a small smile.

"Purple jar. It has runes on it."

"I'll be back in fifteen. Oban will stay with you." Luch was up and gone before I could muster a response, and I rolled my head when I felt Oban jump up next to me. I smiled at the scratch of his tongue against my cheek, licking my tears.

"Sweet friend. I didn't want to tell him. I don't know that I'll get to see you much after this."

"He may surprise you."

"I don't think so. Not after what he told me about his mum. He hates healers."

"Aye, his family does."

"There's no point in drawing this out. I can't see how he'll accept me. And I'm done, Oban. I'm done running."

The tears came harder now, and Oban stopped talking and dutifully snuggled close, letting me turn my head and cry into his fur. I wasn't sure what I cried for, but it wasn't just for the pain that ratcheted through my body. It was also likely because for a brief moment I had allowed myself to hope. To hope that finally I had the future I'd always dreamed of in my grasp, and now it would be snatched away like it had been so many times before.

The front door opened, Oban popped his head up, and steps sounded.

"I'm just going to brew it up. Like normal, yes?"

"Please." I stifled a whimper as another wave of pain worked through my body. Oban licked my cheek again and then jumped off the bed, going into the kitchen to check on Luch.

"Tea's brewing. Now it is out to nature? Is that correct?"

Luch was so brisk, matter-of-fact, and it made me cry even harder. He didn't fight me on what I'd said, didn't insist I go into the hospital, and instead was listening to what my needs were. *He's switched into doctor mode, just as I do.* This was the kind of man that women could lose their hearts over, and yet I knew I'd never have a chance to find out what could have been between us. At least not now.

Forever alone is often where we end up, Faelan of the flowers. And even then, never alone. Always connected.

Now was not a moment when I wanted to hear Eriska's words.

"Shhh, darling. You'll be fine. We'll get you sorted. Come on then, tell me what you need?"

I need you to still give me a chance.

Instead, I just nodded feebly. "Yes, please. I need to go into nature. Barefoot."

"Right." Luch picked up my jumper, but I just shook my head. When I was this injured, skyclad was the only way.

"A robe?" I asked.

"Got it." Luch went out of my sight and came back with a navy fluffy terry-cloth robe and he helped me sit up and slide my arms through it. Before I could take a step, he lifted me quite effortlessly into his arms again, went out into the kitchen, and stopped by the tea that was brewing. "Tea now or after the spell?"

"After."

I heaved in a deep breath, and then another, forcing the tears back as Luch carried me out of his back door and into the coolly misting morning rain. The tall trees around his cottage cocooned us, shadowing the morning light, and a light breeze brought the scents of damp earth to me.

"Where do you need to do this? Anywhere in particular?"

"No. Just under a tree is fine."

Luch lowered me to the ground, and I shivered as my bare feet hit the earth, connecting with the energy that rolled under the surface.

"Can you stand?"

"Aye." Turning, I handed him my robe, not caring anymore that I was standing in just my knickers, and then I crossed my arms over my stomach. "Mother Moon, now fading bright, guide this pain into the light. Nature sprites, with morning's grace, lift this ache from my body and face. Pain, be gone, in silence swept, by nature's force, you are inept."

The earth rumbled softly beneath my feet, and I dug my toes into the soft moss that covered the ground beneath the tree, and unwound my hands, reaching my arms toward the sky. Lifting my face to the trees above, I opened my palms, and two large dark streams of smoke poured from them. Meeting in the air, they swirled together, harsh black mixed with shades of gray, to form the shape of a horse. It reared in the air in front of us.

"Holy shite," Luch breathed.

"Duck," I said, realizing I'd never done this with anyone around before. I held my arms up to my face, as did Luch, and the horse shattered into a thousand dark moths that fluttered past us and into the soft morning air.

Once they'd passed, I held out my hand for the robe, the pain gone even though many bruises still mottled my body. I needed my tea and a long sleep. Then I'd be sorted. Luckily, I didn't actually have any scheduled patients this morning, so I'd just have to keep the closed sign on the clinic's door. There wasn't much to be done about that.

I didn't speak, couldn't really, as I fell into step next to Luch. What could I possibly say that would explain away the weirdness he'd just witnessed? Instead, I focused on conserving my energy and gratefully accepted the mug he handed me once we were back inside.

"What next?"

"I need to sleep." I shrugged a shoulder as I took a gulp of my special tea, the first sip already helping to restore my energy.

"What about your bruises?"

"They'll heal."

"But you sent the pain away, didn't you? Is that what you just did?"

I leveled a look at him over the rim of my mug.

"Aye."

"Then why aren't the bruises gone?"

"They're less than they were, but healing comes with a price, one that's usually worth it." I drank more of the tea, gulping until I'd drained the cup, hoping to restore enough energy so I could drive home and collapse face first into my bed.

"I have arnica cream. It will help."

"No, really. It's fine. I just need to get home and go to sleep." I paused at Luch's expression. "What?"

"You're not going home."

"What?" I swayed on my feet, the bone-deep exhaustion of healing already trying to claim me.

"Nice try, darling, but I don't let my patients check out until I know they're in the clear."

"Luch," I began, but had to reach out and grip the counter as I swayed again.

"Uh-huh. See that?" Luch picked me up again—I could get used to this—and went back into the bedroom where he pulled back his blankets and deposited me on the mattress. "I've got your car keys. Unless you're up for wrestling me for them, which, I might actually find enjoyable, I might add, you're staying put."

"But ..." I really had no argument and clearly no energy to fight him. Defeated, I turned my head into the pillow as he pulled the blanket over my shoulders.

"Rest, a ghràidh."

My love.

His lips pressing to my forehead was the last sensation I felt before exhaustion claimed me.

CHAPTER EIGHTEEN

Luch

Bloody hell, but she had terrified me.

It wasn't the magick, that I could handle, but the sight of those nasty bruises marring her gorgeous skin? It had sent a wave of panic through me that I hadn't felt since the time I saw my mum fall from her wheelchair and crack her head on the way to the floor. That had been terrifying and had stayed with me after all these years. *You can never un-hear the noise, her cries of pain.*

But knowing Faelan was in pain? Not knowing *how* she'd sustained the injuries, not knowing how critical her injuries were? It had stirred something unexpected in me. It wasn't terror I felt, but torment. As a physician, I *needed* to find the cause and treat her. As a man, I'd felt powerless and fearful.

Already Faelan occupied so many of my thoughts, but

after seeing her injured, it was like something had activated in me.

My heart had opened.

I hated seeing her weak, in pain, unable to stand on her own two feet. I'd already known that my interest in Faelan was more than just that of a man enjoying a bit of a flirtation, but today, it had rocketed my emotions far past attraction and into something more.

Something I wasn't sure I was ready to fully examine.

"I don't see a way forward."

I sat on the couch, head in my hands, while Oban lounged on his dog bed in front of the fireplace. It was too warm to have a fire today, but Oban didn't seem to mind, and he stretched out his wee paws and cocked his head at me as he let me talk it out.

"Because of what your father will say?"

"My father, my brothers, hell, probably even my mum. It feels like a betrayal to them. We've been brought up to hate healers. Hate them. Any time my mum struggled with anything, after ... It was always that 'bloody healer' to blame."

"They needed an outlet for their rage."

"They did. And it landed squarely on the healer's head. But we don't know, do we? What if it wasn't the healer's fault? What if it just was ... because ... you know."

"You're different."

"Aye, and she's not. Mum's not. She's not one of us."

"So instead of looking to himself, your father projected it on the healer."

I shifted, needing to stand and walk off my restless energy.

219

"I don't know. I wasn't there. I've certainly spent some time reading into it. What would a healer have done? You saw today what healing a horse did to Faelan. What would happen when she tried to heal a spine? There's probably a limit to what they can do before they risk putting themselves in harm's way. And is that what's required of a healer? Do they need to die for their patient? I don't recall ever learning that motto in med school." I dragged a hand through my hair as I paced, a rumble of thunder shaking the windowpanes, a storm rolling in to match my mood.

"I think it's a conversation worth having with Faelan. She might be able to shed some insight on the incident."

I paused, whirling on my wee pup. I jammed a finger in the air in his direction.

"That's ... that's a brilliant idea. I never thought about talking to an actual healer. Mainly because I've never met one. But she might be able to explain what happened. And if so, maybe my father would be open to meeting her ... if ..."

"If you become a couple?"

"If we become a couple."

"Is that what you want? I like her."

"As you've said, many a time." I resumed my pacing, my thoughts whirling. I had grown used to being out on my own, relishing the distance and space from my family, and enjoying quiet walks in the woods with wee Oban on my days off. But my time with Faelan so far hadn't felt disruptive to that. Instead, being with her was something I looked forward to, and being around her was effortless. It didn't feel like I was giving anything up—any of my carefully protected emotional balance that I needed to perform well as a doctor—instead I felt recharged after my time with Faelan.

And wasn't that a gift in itself?

"You'll have to tell her ... if you want her in your life."

I shrugged, ignoring Oban. The weight of my world, the reality of my family back home, weighed heavily on my shoulders. I'd run away to Loren Brae to find myself, to take space to breathe, and now I was more conflicted than ever. Familial responsibility hung like chains around my neck, and I couldn't help but feel like my time here was running short.

A whimpering from the bedroom shot my head up and I was across the room in seconds, pushing the door open gently.

Faelan still slept, but she whimpered again, her face contorted, and I realized she was having a bad dream. Easing the door closed behind me, I quietly crossed the room, light from a small lamp in the corner softly illuminating my path. Gently, I crawled into bed next to Faelan and pulled her into my arms.

"Shhh, darling, I've got you."

"Luch." Faelan said my name on a soft sigh, and my heart shivered and jumped off a cliff when she turned and snuggled into my arms in her sleep. Her cheek pressed softly to my chest, and I tightened my arms around her, lightly stroking her back and whispering nonsense words to soothe until her breath fell in a steady rhythm once more.

I'll hold you as long as you need.

Lightning flashed, close by, and thunder boomed quickly after. Faelan jerked awake in my arms, blinking up at me, as a torrent of rain unleashed against the window in my room.

"Hey," I said, softly, not daring to move. "How are you feeling?"

"Luch ... what are you ..." Her face was soft with sleep, her eyes still drowsy as her brain swam awake, and I waited for her to remember everything that had happened this morning.

Her body stiffened in my arms.

"It's okay, Faelan."

"No, it's not." She put her hands on my chest, moving to push away, but I held her close, refusing to let her go. We needed to talk about what had happened, and to clear the air.

"Wheehst, lass. Just listen to me." When she stopped resisting and leaned back into my chest, I relaxed and ran a hand soothingly up and down her back. "I suspected since you healed wee Oban that something was up. I just didn't know what it was. Now I do. And I have, I don't know, probably at least a few hundred questions to start with, but for now, I need you to hear that I'm not upset."

"But ... your mum?" Faelan tilted her head, her chin resting on my chest, those gorgeous gray-blue eyes scanning my face.

"Aye, my mum had an issue with a healer. Or so my dad says. I don't know, because I wasn't there. I mean, I was there, but I was a wee bairn. The healer has been an easy outlet for my family's anger, but my father never found them, nor has he been able to question any healers since. I think there's room here for a discussion so we can learn what choices were made at that time."

Faelan blinked up at me, and I could see that beautiful mind of hers whirling with thoughts.

"And your mum? What does she say?"

"She's always said it was nature's doing. She's been the only one who never held blame, which I think frustrated my father even more, to be honest."

"And you think that I could absolve all healers of your family's blame?" Faelan shifted, annoyance flashing across her face. "I'm not sure I'm up to the task. Or frankly, that I volunteered for it. I'm not some circus act, Luch. I won't perform on demand to prove to you, or anyone, that I'm on this earth to do good in this world."

Bloody hell, but I was bungling this.

"Faelan, no, please. That's not what I'm saying." I brushed a finger across her cheek. "You can tell my family to go to hell for all I care. I just meant that I've always been more open-minded about this than they have."

Faelan's eyes narrowed. "Have you? That wasn't exactly the vibe I got from you when we first met."

"Och, true enough. I was deeply suspicious of what you'd done to help Oban. But after I calmed down, I began to understand that healing was healing. And maybe science doesn't have all the answers. I like to think that it does, it's what my training's based on, but I'd be lying if I said that I didn't believe in magick. I know magick to be true in this world. But now that I've seen you heal, and seen firsthand the sacrifices you make to do so, there's no way that I could ever look at you and see evil, Faelan."

Faelan's mouth parted and a soft breath escaped.

"Truly?"

"Truly," I said. I couldn't help myself, I needed to kiss

her. Shifting, I rolled so I could capture her lips in a gentle kiss, desire flaring deep inside me.

"Luch." Faelan's mouth was desperate against mine. "I've been so worried. I didn't want to tell you. I thought you'd never be able to accept me."

"I do, Faelan. How could I not? You're incredible." I laughed when Faelan pushed me back, rolling so she could straddle me. "Hey now, go easy. You still have bruises."

"It's always like this. After." Faelan grinned down at me and reached behind herself to unhook her bra. Heat surged through me as her lovely breasts swung free, and I immediately cupped them, testing their weight in my hands.

"Like what?" Easing forward, I captured a nipple in my mouth, desperately needing my mouth on her. She was glorious, even with the bruising that still bloomed along her body, like mottled purple roses fallen against snow.

"I have *so* much energy." Faelan's eyes gleamed as she shoved me back until I was lying on my back again, my hands at her hips. "There's something about a successful healing, a long sleep, and my medicinal tea that sets me buzzing. Usually I go for a long walk to work off the energy. But I can think of other, more satisfying, ways to do that."

"Is that right?" I grinned up at her, loving this confident version of Faelan, and then moaned as she rocked against me. I was already rock hard, needing desperately to be buried inside her, but for now I was going to let her set the pace. The last thing I wanted to do was hurt her in any way.

I groaned as she shimmied down my body and took my cock in her mouth, as I hadn't been expecting that. Plus, I liked to be the one to serve, but the way she licked me was enough to have all the thoughts in my brain short-circuit. All I could do was feel.

Her breath, hot against my skin.

Her hands, gently brushing my hard length.

Her hair, tickling my thighs as she sucked me deep.

Hot, wet, languorous.

My hips bucked and my eyes flew open as I realized I was dangerously close to coming already, and I didn't want that.

Not yet.

No, I wanted to savor this first with sweet Faelan, making sure all her needs were met, watching her bloom for me like the flower she was. Gripping her shoulders, I gently eased her back, laughing at the frustrated look that crossed her face.

"Easy, love, or this will be over before you know it."

"Really?" A delighted look crossed her face and I chuckled, pulling her up my body again so I could kiss her some more. Idly I ran my hands softly down her side, enjoying her soft curves, her rounded bum, her muscular arms.

"Have I told you how incredible you are, Faelan?" I murmured against her lips, licking into her mouth, loving the feel of her breasts squished against my chest. My cock twitched between her legs, desperately wanting release, but I forced myself to slow everything down.

It was time to savor.

"Possibly, but I think it's best I hear it again."

"Incredible," I said, turning my head to nibble at her earlobe. When she shivered, I kissed the silky softness at her neck, lightly scraping my teeth over her skin. "Moody soulful eyes. Lips made for a man's."

Faelan trembled against me as I continued my lazy perusal down her body, my lips finding her breasts once more. She arched back, still straddling me, and my cock leapt to attention, already doing a happy dance. Instead, I slid it against her wet heat, and her mouth rounded as she rocked against me.

Not yet, but soon.

I turned my attention to her breasts, needing to memorize them, the feel of them in my palms. Tracing my hands over her nipples, I thumbed their stiff peaks, while licking the underside of her breast, laughing against her skin as she jerked against me.

"Is that a favorite spot then?"

"I didn't know it, but it might be." Faelan's voice held a note of awe as I spent more time licking and suckling every inch of both breasts until she was eagerly rocking against me, a thin keen of frustration coming from her lips.

"Have we found the spot then?"

"Bloody hell, Luch, but I need ... I need." Faelan dropped her forehead to mine, and I grinned against her lips as I brought one hand up between our legs. Reaching for her, I slid a flat palm against her, and she cried out into my mouth as I gently took her over the edge.

"Oh, yes, yes, yes," Faelan moaned into my mouth, her hips rocking so hard as she came that I almost followed suit.

"Bloody hell," I growled against her lips and lifted her, needing to be inside her as much as I needed my next breath. "Contraception?"

"I've got the coil," Faelan breathed against my lips. "Testing?"

"All clear."

"Me too."

That conversation out of the way, we kissed deeply as I lowered her gently onto me, my eyes almost rolling back in my head as I was enveloped by her tight, wet heat.

"Damn it, Luch. This is so good," Faelan whispered against my lips and then she arched backward, changing the angle. Her thighs gripped my side, and she piled her hair on top of her head, and helpless not to, I ran my hands up her body until I could cup her breasts.

"You're magnificent, Faelan. A fucking goddess," I moaned as she began to move, her hips rocketing forward. I could only *feel* as she rode me like she was running away from the law.

Hot waves of desire poured through me, and my vision pinpointed to only her.

This was it.

There was only Faelan.

Something feral broke inside me, and I growled again and roared as I came, bucking into her as she rocked against me, pulling her tight against me. Her teeth sunk into my shoulder, muffling her cry, but I needed it all from her. Over and over I thrust up, crying out as she met me, and when she clenched around me, throwing her head back with a silent scream, I found oblivion.

I poured myself into her, holding tight, and dropped my head to her neck, nipping gently at the skin there. I wanted to mark her, to claim her as my own, but she had enough bruises on her delicate skin already. Instead I pressed soft kisses into her skin, slick with a soft sheen of sweat, and laughed when she tugged my hair to pull my head back to look at her.

"That was ..." Faelan paused, looking for words.

"Incredible?"

"Something more than that. I'd come up with a better descriptor, but I can't think straight."

"I'll consider that a job well done then."

"Hey now, I get to pat myself on the back too. You weren't the only one doing the work here."

"Not this time, no. But the next time? Och, that'll be all me, darling."

"Next time?" Faelan blinked at me as I rolled, still inside her, and her eyes widened as she felt me harden again. "Och, recover quickly do you then?"

"It seems you have the magick touch."

At that she laughed, but then her eyes clouded briefly.

"Luch ... do you—"

"Shhh." I thrust lightly into her, and she blinked, her mouth forming a little O of surprise. "That's for another time. Just feel, Faelan. Feel what I feel."

I couldn't say it.

Not yet.

My life was now splintered, into "Before Faelan" and "After Faelan."

It was too soon, but I already knew.

This was love.

And there would be no other for me.

CHAPTER NINETEEN

Faelan

"Do you think all your challenges will be met through healing?" Sophie asked, stroking Lady Lola's back.

It had been two weeks since the morning that I'd healed Malarky and ended up in Luch's bed.

Today was our first time going on a date with another couple. I couldn't say who was more nervous—myself or Luch—and we'd very nearly canceled on Sophie and Lachlan an hour before we were meant to meet them. When Sophie had discovered that Luch and I were *actually* dating, she'd squealed and insisted we get together, and I'd agreed simply because her excitement over my happiness had warmed my heart. It was odd, really, this whole having close friends thing, and I was still getting used to the way the group of women easily dissected everyone else's personal relationships.

I was accustomed to my life being watched as if under a lens, but it was usually one of suspicion, not one of support and admiration.

We'd been invited for drinks at the castle, and we were hanging out in a games room that was easily three times the size of my flat. Lachlan and Luch played billiards, or pool—I wasn't really sure—and talked about rugby while Sophie and I hung out by a table loaded with snacks.

Which, naturally, had drawn both Lady Lola and Sir Buster to nose their way into the room. Now I was stuck, having been taken hostage by Sir Buster, as he perched on my lap and alternated between growling and giving me impatient looks because I wasn't feeding him cheese as often as he'd like.

"I don't know," I answered, truthfully, as I carefully took a bite of cheese while Sir Buster eyed me balefully. "Because I healed Mitch, didn't I? And then Malarky. Wouldn't that have been my third challenge? If it was just healing based?"

"Hmm." Sophie scrunched her nose up, leaning back into the cushions. She gave a whistle when Lachlan pocketed a ball at the table. "That's my man."

Lachlan gave her a wink over his shoulder, and she beamed.

"Isn't he the cutest?"

"In a reserved sort of way, he is," I agreed, grinning at her. Sophie and Lachlan clearly were besotted with each other and had no qualms about sharing it.

"He's not reserved when he needs to be, I'll tell you that much. But otherwise, yes. He can be a bit uptight, so I try to ruffle his feathers whenever possible." Sophie pulled her eyes away from where Lachlan leaned over the table, the denim stretching tight over his bum. Admittedly, it was a very nice bum. "Now, tell me. How's it going with Luch? You two are so cute together."

"Are we?" I flushed, unsure of how to handle such an open assessment of my relationship with Luch. It felt all too ... new and fresh and untouched. A part of me had wanted to keep our dating a secret, something just for us, untainted by the opinions of others for a while longer.

Luch told me he'd be fine either way, but he'd also been very clear that he was proud to have me on his arm, a comment that had landed us back in bed. Who even said things like that? *Proud to have me on his arm.* I grinned, remembering his words.

"Oh yeah, you're a smitten kitten." Sophie tapped a finger on her lips, and I almost squirmed in my seat.

"I don't know. I just *like* him. And I like Loren Brae. And I'm making friends, and it's just ... och, it's just things feel like they're finally falling into place, you ken?"

"I mean, you certainly balance each other well. You're both in the health professions, you care about the well-being of others or animals, so I'm sure that's something to bond over. What's he like though? I'm having a hard time getting a read on him. Munroe said he's tried a few times to invite him out for drinks, but he keeps to himself."

"Yeah, he's a bit of a homebody. The hospital's under-staffed, so long hours and a draining job will do that to you. I think he's peopled out when he gets home. He takes a lot of long walks to de-stress. I like that though. Even on days where we don't talk a lot when we walk, it's just ... nice, you ken? To walk in silence with someone. Like you're sharing space, but not taking up mental space, I guess."

"Is that something you need?"

"Mental space?" I leaned back, absentmindedly stroking Sir Buster and ignoring his growls, because I'd quickly learned as soon as I stopped petting him, he'd get annoyed with me for not giving him attention. "Aye, I do at that. Being in my profession, people need you all day long. You answer so many questions, you field a lot of high emotions, and then you go home and somehow just need to … turn it off. Just exist. And I think if I was dating someone who needed a lot from me, in the way of full mental focus after a long day? It would be tough. It's nice not having to explain that to Luch. We can be together but not drain each other."

"Plus he's a hottie." Sophie fanned herself, and Lachlan turned to her, an eyebrow raised.

"I heard that," Lachlan called.

"Just appreciating the view, love." Sophie blew him a kiss, and I was absolutely delighted to see Luch's face flush at the attention.

"As I said, I *like* him." I lowered my voice, leaning into Sophie. "And that kind of scares me. I haven't dated in a long time."

"Why?" Sophie turned to me, her face devoid of judgment.

"Always moving. People aren't that accepting of magick. Finding friends with powers? It's been …" I shook my head. "Life-changing, I would say."

"And he knows?" Sophie murmured, breaking off a piece of cheese for Lady Lola.

Sir Buster stood up on my lap, immediately taking offense.

"Stand down, little man." I reached over and gave him a small sliver of cheese to appease him. "And yes, he knows."

"And?"

"I ..." I shrugged. Luch and I had had a long talk about the healing, when I'd been ready to talk to him about it, and he'd since followed up with thoughtful questions. I kept sensing I was missing something with how he'd phrased his questions to me, but I never pushed it, since he'd told me the story about the healer and his mum's injury during childbirth. It felt like I was slowly retraining him to think differently, and we'd had a few lively discussions about the blend of magickal power with science. I had to admit, one of my favorite things about Luch was his brain. We bounced ideas back and forth, and our discussions, when we were up for them, were often lively and varied.

Luch met my eyes from across the room, as though he knew we were discussing him, and my insides warmed.

Part of the reason we didn't always talk a lot was because we were busy doing other decidedly delicious activities. After the first time he'd made love to me, so very gently and sweetly after my healing disaster, he'd gone on to show me he had another exceptionally interesting side to him.

Holy hell, but I had been right to be a touch nervous of him the first time we'd met. There was an undercurrent of energy to Luch that, when unleashed, was frankly—*wild*. Any chance he could, he was bending me over and having his way with me, leaving me panting and begging for more. Or he'd drop to his knees and savor me until my thighs were shaking and I was coming in his mouth. It was like once he'd had a taste of me, he was insatiable, and even now, just thinking about his hands on me, a warm rush of excitement went through my body. I crossed my legs and picked up my drink, needing to cool my suddenly dry throat.

"Hi. I'm Sophie, your friend?" Sophie snapped her fingers in my face, and I dragged my eyes away from where I'd been watching Luch lean over to take his shot.

"Oh my God, I'm sorry. What were you saying?"

"I know that look." Sophie laughed. "I'm very much guilty of it myself. Right, I was asking how he was, with the magick? Obviously not upset if he's here, right?"

I didn't know if his mum's story was one to share with others, so I just bit my lip and considered my words carefully.

"I'd say he's reserved in his opinion on it but open to learning. He asks a lot of questions, and I appreciate that he's trying to understand how the magick blends with science."

"That's fair."

"Ladies." We both gaped up at Luch, not having heard his approach, and Luch held out his hand to me. Sir Buster immediately leapt from my lap. "I'm on early tomorrow."

I knew the expression on Luch's face, and my cheeks heated.

"That's right, I forgot. How silly of me."

"Uh-huh." Sophie laughed and got up, putting Lady Lola on the ground. The dogs immediately gave chase to each other, racing around the room, and Lachlan came over to wrap his arm around Sophie's waist.

"I'm glad we did this. See you at Sunday dinner one of these weeks?"

"Definitely. If I'm not on nights," Luch said. We quickly said our goodbyes and Sophie winked at me as Luch almost dragged me out of the castle. Before we'd even made it halfway home he had my back pressed to a tree, my arms over my head, and was kissing the delicate skin of my neck.

"You were thinking about this, weren't you?" Luch's breath was hot against my skin, and desire ran warm and liquid through me.

"It's hard not to." I smiled and turned my face to his kiss. "You look cute playing pool."

"Just cute?" Luch asked, affronted.

"Devastatingly handsome," I amended, arching myself forward so my body brushed against his.

"It's hard for me to focus on others when you're in the room. I just want to scoop you up and whisk you away." Luch trailed kisses across my cheek and nibbled at the delicate lobe of my ear. "Mine. All mine."

Heat flashed at his words. I'd never thought I'd be someone who responded to a man's possessiveness, but from Luch? It was intoxicating. I wasn't sure if it was because he was a doctor, and could maintain a singular focus with such precision, but when he switched over to "it's go time" mode, I'd never felt so seen or enjoyed in my life. We could be having a simple conversation about a book we read, relaxing after a long day, and the instant Luch shifted into his desire for me, I knew I'd be his entire focus until he'd made sure I'd found my pleasure, over and over, before he'd take his.

His careful attention made me feel … treasured.

Important.

Cared for.

Respected.

I hadn't even known that I needed or wanted that from a man, but being with Luch was such a far cry from being with the, well, *boy* that my last boyfriend had been, that I really had no comparison.

A dog howled, a small sound in the night, but Luch whipped his head up, his attention diverted. He dropped my arms and I straightened, surprised.

"Is everything—"

"Shhh," Luch said, his ear tilted to the night sky.

That was odd. It took a lot to break Luch's focus, even though it was probably for the best. It wasn't like the man could ravish me against a tree in the garden of MacAlpine Castle. Surely, they had cameras around here? Flushing, I stepped away from the tree and back out onto the pavement. I could only imagine what that would look like if Archie reviewed the camera footage.

The waters of Loch Mirren remained calm, but I no longer trusted them, not after the night where I'd seen the Kelpies in real life. Since then, I skirted the loch, often taking the long way back to my flat to avoid walking along the shores. Unless Luch was with me, of course.

He always made me feel safe.

"Sorry, it must be nothing." Luch shook his head and then took my hand, and I breathed a sigh of relief. The last thing I wanted was to have such a nice night end with a battle on the Loch Mirren shores.

"That's quite all right. I mean, it's good to be cautious,

isn't it?" I'd told Luch about my encounter with the Kelpies, and ever since then, he either dropped me off at my place, or he walked with me if I went anywhere at night. I appreciated the protectiveness, even though it didn't make sense in the long run.

What we needed to do, as an Order, was to ban the Kelpies from Loren Brae.

I still hadn't told Luch about the Order of Caledonia, as he was still coming to grips with the idea of me being a healer.

One step at a time.

Day by day, we'd ease into this relationship, and maybe, if Luch was really as solid as I was beginning to feel he was, we'd navigate this unusual town together.

CHAPTER TWENTY

Faelan

It had been almost four weeks since that fateful day of healing Malarky, and Luch and I were officially a couple.

Dating.

We'd leaned into that perfect blissful time in a relationship where we could barely keep our hands off each other, the other person had zero flaws, and every date was a new discovery. I loved every moment of it. I relished the feeling of being cocooned in a little ball of bliss.

Yet, *still*, I couldn't help but feel uneasy.

Never before had all parts of my life fallen into perfect place before. I had new friends, I had joined a magickal Order that accepted *who* I was, and I had a man who seemed proud of me and understood what I did for a living.

It felt ... wrong. I knew that was horrible to think, but

I'd grown so used to my life imploding that having a time where there were no real problems didn't sit well with me. A part of me felt like I was always looking over my shoulder, waiting for the next attack.

"Earth to Faelan."

"Och, sorry." I snapped back to attention. I was at Willow's shop and trying on an outfit she insisted I would "slay" in. I wasn't sure I really felt like slaying anything, but I did have a date at Grasshopper this week with Luch, and I wouldn't mind something new to wear.

Willow, a bubbly American who radiated sunshine, was also a member of the Order of Caledonia. While Sophie had been doing good about hosting a "family" night every Sunday at the castle, Willow had initiated a weekly girls' night for all of the members to hang out away from the men in their lives. This week's focus, apparently, was my abysmal wardrobe, and even though I'd told Willow that I had to keep it pretty simple as at any time I could be covered in vomit or feces, she insisted I still deserved a few frivolous things that would make me feel beautiful.

"She's a terrorist, Faelan. Just let her have her way." Orla, the pint-sized builder working on the Common Gin construction project, grinned at me from where she sat on the floor in overalls, her back to the couch.

"Now, as I was saying, we don't have a lot of time before your next date, but if you wanted to feel sexy what would you normally wear?"

"Um." Honestly, it had been ages since I'd put much thought into dressing up. Instead, I purchased serviceable clothes that could pack easily in a duffle when I moved on. "I guess a skirt or a dress? But I don't own any."

239

"A girl after my own heart." Orla raised her glass to me. Kaia, a goldsmith, snickered and held up her glass too.

"Same here," Kaia said. Murdoch, her crow, bobbed his head in agreement behind her.

Honestly, if anyone peered through the window at that moment, they'd probably be highly confused. We had a veritable menagerie around us. Apparently, once our magickal familiars had caught wind of our girls' nights, they'd decided to join. So along with seven women crowded into Willow's fitting studio, we also had a cat, two gnomes, a crow, a broonie, and a fox. I was told Orla's goldfish didn't travel well and her dog was happy at home with Finlay, and Eugene and Edith were enjoying their blissful time as new parents. And though the castle dogs weren't Sophie's familiars, Sir Buster and Lady Lola lounged on one side of the room, casting baleful eyes at the cat, Calvin, that prowled the rug, taunting them.

The gnomes had taken themselves to a corner, canoodling on a cushion on the floor, and Gnorman was currently feeding Gnora a grape. But it was the shy broonie that fascinated me. He had big eyes, rarely showed himself, and apparently enjoyed mischief. Brice was his name, and he was incredibly endearing—when you caught glimpses of him. Usually I'd just see a blur of movement and some soft chitter-chattering before something appeared before me.

Like just now, when my glass of champagne was miraculously topped up.

"He's so fast." I looked at Lia in shock and she laughed, tucking one of her wild curls behind her ear. Owner of Grasshopper restaurant, Lia spent most of her time tucked away in the kitchen and was rarely about. These girls' nights were her saving grace, she'd told us on more than one occasion, making her feel human again.

"He really is. And when he's not up to trouble, he's wildly helpful." Lia blinked down at her now full glass as soft chattering filled the air. For a moment, Brice glimmered into view and then he was gone again.

"Honestly? I can't believe I've spent my whole life being harassed for my magick when if I'd just landed here first, I'd have found kindred souls." I shook my head in awe. It had been a fact that I'd been marveling over, quite a bit, of late. How many countless hours of worry and fear would we have avoided if we could have just found this place to begin with? And how did I eventually find my way here, all on my own?

"I've been thinking about that, actually. Since we first learned about you. It's taken me some time, but I think I've found some more information." Lia held up a leather book.

"What is that?" I asked, curiosity mixing with unease in my gut.

"Ladies, come on. Let me at least get started on some outfit ideas." Willow stomped a screaming pink high heel.

"Go fitted," I said, not turning to look at her. "I never wear fitted. Skirt, top, dress. And a bold color. Something totally out of the norm for me."

"Sparkles?" Willow whispered, hopefully.

"Too far."

"Damn it. Fine. Let me think." Willow bent her head to her iPad and I focused on Lia.

"Your mum? Her name was Eriska, right?"

Hope bloomed. I wasn't sure why, but even just hearing her name brought her laughter back to me. It was as though she was hovering over my shoulder, joining us for this connection of women and friendship, and I swallowed, my throat going dry.

"Aye. Eriska Fletcher." I took a shaky sip of my champagne and dug my hand into the fur at Gloam's neck. He sat, curled next to my leg, one eye cracked open to keep an eye on the dogs. Frankly, I was proud of him for even staying in the room with them, but he'd told me that Sir Buster was all bark, and Lady Lola only cared about snacks and naps. "Her maiden name."

"You took your mother's last name?" Lia peered at me over the top of the book.

"No father to speak of." I shrugged. It didn't sting anymore, not really. Even though I'd dealt with outrage from other people in my life growing up, I'd never questioned if I was loved. Eriska had loved enough for two parents, hell, her optimism and enthusiasm for life could have filled the world with love.

"No interest in finding out?" Orla asked and then winced. She put a hand in the air. "To be clear, I am the last person to ever push someone into a reunion. You do you, girl."

"It's just a door that I'm happy to remain closed. He died not long after Eriska had moved us on, and I'm not confident that anything good would come of tracking down his family and trying to force something unneeded. I think people always have these romantic stories in their heads that bringing family back together will always end well, and I just haven't seen that to be the case." I shrugged, hoping I wasn't being too pragmatic for the girls.

"I'll admit, I do find it a touch sad. But I come from

such a different space. I have the best parents in the world and a large family that is constantly in each other's business. But then I look at Munroe and the difficulty he's had with his family, and I can understand why he's enforced boundaries. I don't think there is a 'one-sized fits all' solution to these situations. It's especially nuanced. And if you aren't lying awake, night after night, yearning for that connection, then why seek it out?" Lia smiled gently.

"It is sad. But then so is a lot of life. There's also a lot of love to be found elsewhere, and to be given. I always try to remember that when I'm working with animals. I hope they feel my love and positive energy when I help them."

"They do." Gloam lifted his head and put his chin on my thigh and I scratched at his favorite spot behind his ears.

Talk of love made me wonder about Luch. The only other person I'd felt so connected to was my mum. And now, these amazing women. But there were times when Luch looked at me and I swore he loved me. Each time, I'd thought it was too soon. Was it? How long did it take for two people to fall in love? *What does that feel like?* If I didn't know the answer to that, did that mean I wasn't in love with him? I did know that I didn't want things to change. I felt happy. Content. *Settled.*

But that alone made me nervous. Like waiting for the axe to fall. I wasn't used to calm waters, I was a ship built for weathering storms.

"Right, so what I can find in here really has to do more with your great, great, grandmother than it does anything with your father. I was just asking to make sure I had the last names correct. Because I do have a Flora Fletcher who was also a healer."

243

My mouth dropped open and I let out a small squeal.

"No way. Do you really? Och, I don't know much about Flora. Just her name and she worked with her hands as well. But my mum didn't have much in the way of records. We moved too much."

"Yes, it's quite clear." Lia brandished the book and I stood and crossed the room. Sophie slid over on the couch to make room, and I dropped down between them both.

I leaned down and looked at the faded writing on the page. The script was precise and elegant, in the way of old-fashioned cursive, and just seeing her name written down lit me up. It was as though she hadn't entirely been erased from history, that she still mattered, and I reached out to brush a finger lightly across her name.

"There she is."

"It says she was also a healer, and that she was almost persecuted for being a witch when she helped to heal a child under suspicious circumstances. Instead of the family being grateful, they accused her of witchcraft," Lia read out loud and the entire room made noises of disgust.

"Typical. Here someone save's your freaking kid's life, but instead of being grateful they attack." Shona huffed out an annoyed breath.

"But," Lia continued, holding a finger in the air, "it looks like Lachlan's kin stepped in and did something to stop it. Flora went on to live a long and healthy life at the castle."

"That's my man," Sophie said, proudly. "The Order must have found her and taken her in."

Tears pricked my eyes and I held a hand to my chest.

"Roots," I breathed. I hadn't realized just how much it

mattered to me, to feel connected somewhere, to know of those who came before me. "I have actual roots."

"Oh, you do. You really do. You're home now, Faelan." Before I knew it, I had five women surrounding me, all giving me a hug, while trying not to spill the champagne I held. The dogs jumped up, and Sir Buster, sensing an opening, made his move on Gloam. Dashing across the room, he bared his teeth in a show of bravery, when Calvin simply walked up and swatted him across the nose.

Sir Buster shrieked and raced back to his corner and we all laughed, even though I was still wiping tears from my eyes.

"Willow?" Lia asked, and I realized she'd been the only one not to hug me. Instead, she drew furiously on her iPad, but her eyes stared out the window, not seeing anything.

"I think she's having a vision," Sophie whispered, coming to her side, but not touching her. "Willow? Are you okay?"

Willow heaved in a massive breath and then seemed to snap back into reality, her slack expression changing to one of confusion, before she blinked down at the pad in her hands. Looking back up, her eyes sought mine. Her gift was one of foresight, and she'd told me sometimes the visions came through when she was sketching.

"Oh no," I whispered, fear clenching my gut. Gingerly, I stood and walked across the room to her. She tilted the iPad to face me. "It's bad, isn't it?"

"I don't know. I couldn't quite grasp it all." Willow looked down at the drawing she'd made. On it, a Kelpie loomed from the water and swooped low over a wolf that bared its teeth to the beast.

Relief filled me.

"Oh, that already happened. Everything's fine."

"Wait, what? This happened? Why didn't you say anything?" Sophie looked from the drawing to me, concern on her face.

"What does it show?" Kaia asked.

"Um, it was almost a month ago? I'm sorry. I meant to bring it up and then I didn't want you to think I wasn't capable of defending myself, and I don't know ..." I shrugged, embarrassed to be caught out like this. Had I committed a sin? Would they be angry with me?

"This was why you were asking me about how else to fight them, weren't you?" Sophie murmured, squeezing my shoulder. "It's fine, you know. It's rare that anybody can hold their own against a Kelpie, Faelan. You're not expected to know what to do."

"Hell, one of them tossed me halfway across the loch," Kaia offered.

"One almost drowned me," Shona added.

"Well, shite. I'm sorry I didn't say anything. I didn't want you to think I was failing you so soon into joining the Order."

"It's okay." I looked down as Orla came over and squeezed my hand, looking up at me with sympathy on her face. "I get why you didn't say anything. When you're so used to hiding, it's scary to open up, isn't it?"

"Aye." Warmth filled me. I appreciated their easy under-standing and acceptance of me.

"I don't know." Willow bit her lower lip, worry in her eyes. "I've never had a vision about the past, Faelan. It's always about the future. This felt ... I don't know. Close. Soon. It's not great."

"Is that a wolf or a dog?" Sophie studied the drawing.

"Wolf," Willow and I spoke at the same time.

"That's so strange. We haven't had wolves here in hundreds of years," Shona murmured.

"This calls for more champagne," Lia said and crossed the room and opened the door. Just as she stepped through the door, the huge ghost coo leapt through the wall.

We all screamed, but none so loud as Lia, who threw her hands up and crossed her legs.

"Damn it, Clyde!" Lia shrieked, and then bounced around, her legs crossed, trying desperately hard not to laugh.

"Oh no, did he do it again?" Sophie asked.

"Do what again?"

"One time! *One* time he made me pee my pants," Lia said, giggling. "Though I'm not going to lie ... maybe just a little bit this time?"

"Ewwww." We all laughed as Lia turned tail and ran down the hallway, cursing Clyde the entire time.

CHAPTER TWENTY-ONE

FAELAN

Willow hadn't been lying when she'd said she'd make me a sexy outfit. My mouth dropped open in front of the mirror when I put it on.

"Told ya." Willow snapped the gum in her mouth and crossed her arms, looking pleased as could be.

She'd taken me at my word and had chosen a bold purple for the dress that hugged my body like a second skin. The neck scooped lightly, but in a demure manner, and long sleeves ended just before my wrists. The skirt hit mid-calf and the back had a zipper that ran all the way from the high back to the hem. That was the sexy part, aside from it being fitted, but the suggestion that someone could unzip the dress and have it fall from my body in one motion was decidedly enticing.

"This ... this is a dress. It's gorgeous, Willow."

"Wear your hair up, but messy like, with some tendrils coming down. Big earrings. No necklace," Willow advised, folding the garment bag over her arm and heading toward the door of my flat. "He's going to swallow his tongue when he sees you."

"You think? Gosh, I just. Wow." I patted my hands down the dress and beamed at her. "I feel like a very modern Cinderella or something."

"And my work here is done."

Before I could ask her what I owed her, Willow raced from my flat telling me she had her own hot date. I hadn't worked up the nerve to ask her again about her vision, but since I was fairly certain it had already happened, it hadn't much bothered me.

The women's easy acceptance of me, and my silence regarding the run-in with the Kelpie that night, had almost brought me to tears several times in the last few days. Now I just had to tell Luch about the magick at the castle. I hadn't brought it up, not yet, as I still hadn't told him about the Order of Caledonia. I planned to do it tonight, over dinner, because it was time I stopped hiding any secrets of what I was from him.

I still had one challenge to pass.

This puzzled me, because I'd been certain I'd see another band of diamonds ringing the handle after I'd healed Malarky, but there had been no change. That made it even more confusing what the Stone wanted from me. Was putting myself through severe pain to heal a young horse not enough? What more did it need? Since that day, I'd been careful to not use my magick, only very lightly if needed, and luckily I hadn't been faced with anything too serious that required me to do so.

It had actually been fairly quiet. Or maybe it was just that I was enjoying my bubble of bliss. But I hadn't been waking up at the witching hour, there had been no more Kelpies shrieking in the night, and no majorly traumatic catastrophes at work. In fact, I'd gotten into a good routine —*as much as one can when dealing with animals*—and I was close to being ready to hire someone to help me at the clinic, which would be a huge win for me and my practice.

I'd even purchased colorful cushions for my couch, ridiculous little things with beaded tassels, and I didn't let myself think about having to pack them up. Luch had brought me several more vases, and bundles of flowers continued to show up at my doorstep. I always had a fresh bunch in the waiting room in my clinic, and several around the photo of Eriska on the windowsill. I loved having the flowers crowd the frame, as though we really were still sitting among the flowers together, stealing a moment of laughter on a sunny day. Sentimental, I walked over and picked up the picture, smiling down at it.

"Och, I wish you could see me now, Mum. I've finally got it all."

Even as I said it, a shiver ran down my back, and I nestled the frame back among the flowers. My gaze went out to the waters of Loch Mirren, placid on a calm day, no breeze to rough the surface. It was meant to storm later, and I couldn't help note how serene everything looked. Living this close to the loch had taught me the water constantly changed, its moods as mercurial as the Scottish weather.

But now? I got the sense it was waiting.

A knock at the door shook me from my thoughts, and I raced across the room, and flung the door open, even though I still had to do my hair and makeup.

"Pretend you didn't see this!" I gasped to Luch, whirling to run away from him. His hands were around my waist in seconds, his mouth at my neck.

"And why am I pretending I don't see this delicious snack right in front of me?" Luch growled at my neck, and I giggled, struggling to get away.

"Because I still have to do my hair and makeup. I want to properly present myself for a reaction."

"I'll give you a reaction."

Cool air hit my backside as Luch made use of the zip, and I gasped as his hands streaked down my sides, pulling my underwear to the floor.

"Luch. If you mess up this dress I swear Willow will kill you ..." I ended on a moan as he dropped to his knees behind me, widening my legs, his mouth finding me. I bent over the table, with zero shame, and bared myself to his tongue.

"It's a stunning dress, Faelan, one I'll admire even more knowing how I bent you over and took you in it." I grinned against the tabletop as I heard him unzip his trousers and then he slid deep inside me, his hands at my waist.

"Oh. My." I bit back a scream as he took me, hard and fast, and exploded around him, pleasure rushing through me in hard sharp waves.

"There she is. My gorgeous woman. All mine." Luch's breath was hot at my ear, and I moaned as he slid even deeper. It was always like this between us. Not the way he was taking me right now, but always this sharp, hot need. It was like we were meant for each other, our bodies recognizing each other, and he loved to say over and over how he claimed me as his. Normally, the overbearing nature of someone "claiming" me would have annoyed me, but for some reason I just ate it right up when it came to Luch.

Maybe it was because it was so unlike his gentle nature in every other aspect of his life. He was kind with animals, understanding with his patients, and endlessly patient with his family. So if he needed a space to be demanding and a little rough around the edges, I loved that he could have that with me.

I loved a lot about him actually.

Just the thought of that made me clench hard around him, and he laughed at my ear.

"Keep that up, darling, and we'll never make it to dinner."

"At this rate we'll be late," I grumbled as I straightened and slipped the dress carefully off and hung it over the back of the chair. Turning, I held up my hands when Luch's eyes heated at the sight of the sexy bra I wore. "Nope. I need a quick shower now and have to do hair and makeup. You do not get to touch again."

"That's just fine, love. I'll just bide my time thinking about all the decadent things I'll be doing to you in that bra later."

Heat flashed through my body and I held a finger of warning up to him.

"Wheesht! I mean it. I have to get ready."

Dashing into the bathroom, I raced through a quick shower, piled my hair on my head as instructed by Willow, and rubbed some smokey shadow across my eyes. After slicking on the only lip gloss I had, I donned a simple pair of silver hoop earrings, and then I slid my feet into a pair of strappy flat sandals. Even Willow wouldn't be able to convince me to wear heels. Walking back out into the main room, I grabbed the dress, giggled as I dodged Luch's lunge, and ran back into the bedroom.

"No! Stop! I get to make an entrance." I was whining, I knew that, but he needed to be patient. *This dress is too gorgeous* not *to wear on a date.* Naturally, his chuckle was hearty as it came through the door.

"Fine, but if we don't leave in three minutes, I'm breaking down this door."

"Damn it." How the hell was I supposed to zip up this dress from bottom to top? Turning, I sighed into the mirror.

"What's the problem?" Luch's voice rumbled from behind the door.

"Can you come zip this up and then pretend you didn't see me so you can make a fuss when I walk out?"

"Anything for you." The words held a weight to them, landing in my chest and burning themselves into my heart, and I pressed my lips together as he came through the door, holding a hand in front of his eyes. I wondered if he had any idea what such a sentiment meant to someone like me.

"Right, I'm turned around. Zip me up." I laughed as he nipped my bum as he knelt down, finding the zipper, and then zipped the dress all the way up, ending with a kiss at the neck. "Now go away."

"As the lady wishes." I waited to hear the door click closed and then turned. Stopping, I checked myself over in the mirror. It was a great dress. It showcased all of my assets in the best way possible but was both demure and sexy in its own right. The perfect dress, really, and I couldn't wait to tell Willow how much Luch had loved it.

Though I'd be leaving a few bits out when I did.

Laughing softly, I grabbed my purse and stepped out, throwing my hands in the air.

"Ta-da."

"Och, my heart." Luch held his hands to his chest, marvel on his face. "Your beauty rivals that of a freshly bloomed rose, damp with dew, sparkling in the early morning light."

"Well, now, isn't that fancy? I'll take it." I laughed as Luch came over, his hands at my waist, his kiss soft against my lips.

"You look incredible. I'll be the luckiest man at the restaurant tonight."

"I'm so excited. I've gone to family nights, but I've never eaten *as a guest* at Grasshopper before. I can't wait to see Lia in all her glory."

"You're really making great friends with them all, aren't you?"

"I am."

I paused at the bottom of the stairs, the snap of the cold night air sending a shiver across my skin. Autumn was well on its way, and every morning I could see it in the crystals starting to frost the grass.

"I thought I'd drive us up. I wasn't sure if you'd be in heels or not," Luch said, opening the car door for me. One ripple marred the perfect surface of the water.

But it was all it took to mess up the perfection.

Was that the same as me keeping the secrets of the

Order from Luch? Worry clawed at my stomach as I stepped inside the car. MacAlpine Castle came into view as we crested the hill and I sighed, enjoying seeing the building lit up at night. Luch drove around the side and parked in the lot, and I admired the twinkle lights lining the pathway to the side entrance for Grasshopper. Lia's restaurant operated out of the old castle kitchen, and they'd transformed what used to be a ballroom into the restaurant space.

"Wait." Luch shot me an annoyed glance when I went to open the door and I bit back a laugh as he raced around the car and then opened the door with a dramatic sweep of his hand. I beamed up at him.

"Why, thank you, good sir." I took his hand, that little spark of energy zipping between us, and stood. "Have I told you how handsome you look tonight?"

"Why, no, we've been too busy admiring you." Luch flexed his arms beneath his coat, and I laughed, hooking my arm through his. He wore a dark suit coat thrown over a simple white button-down, with dark jeans cuffed at the ankles, and thick soled leather boots. Honestly, I felt a little like I was a princess, being swept away to her castle, as we walked up the path toward the front door. Music drifted out, along with the steady hum of restaurant noises, voices and cutlery clinking.

Luch lifted his head, sniffing loudly, and I glanced up at him with a smile.

"Smells good, huh? She's an incredible cook ..." I trailed off at the absolute fury on Luch's face. "What ... what's wrong?"

"Those bastards," Luch seethed, stomping inside the restaurant, leaving me at the door in confusion.

"Luch?" I asked, almost afraid to step inside. I'd never seen him like this before. Annoyed? Yes. Frustrated? Yes. But the stone-cold rage on his face transformed him into a man I didn't know. If I stepped through that door, would I learn something that I didn't want to know about Luch? Uncertainty had me hesitating for a moment, but then I took a deep breath, channeled the goddess that Willow had designed this dress for, and strode inside.

Luch stood next to a group of five men, arguing furiously—yet in hushed voices. It was impossible to ignore that they were engrossed in a very serious discussion. The next thing that was impossible to ignore was the fact that these men were clearly his brothers and his father. They were almost carbon copies of each other, all with dark hair, chiseled faces, and broad shoulders. More than one woman cast an appreciative glance their way, and I could hardly blame them. It was only one man, his hair having gone slightly gray, that I zeroed in on. He didn't argue. Instead, he stood, his chin lifted high, his eyes scanning the room. It was almost as if he had no interest in partaking in the discussion, because he'd already assumed the outcome would go in his favor. When his eyes landed on me, I stiffened.

It felt like someone had thrown a glass of cold water in my face.

Luch's father reached out and lightly touched the shoulder of one of the brothers and nodded toward me. I didn't flinch when the entire group turned to look at me, but I wanted to. Luch's face was locked up, his expression hidden, though his eyes burned. But his family? As far as they were concerned I might as well have been a cockroach in their food by the way they looked at me.

Luch strode forward and wrapped an arm around my waist. Leaning in, he pressed a kiss to my cheek, his lips hovering near my ear.

"I'm sorry. They ambushed me."

I tilted my head, meeting his eyes.

"Do you want me to go?" I hated asking it, but if he needed me to leave, I would. I couldn't help but wonder if Luch had told them about me. It would be unfair of him, to share my secret with his family without giving me a chance to explain more deeply about healers, and indecision warred. Judging from the looks they were giving us, I was already persona non gratis.

"Kind of, yeah." Luch gripped my arm when I jolted, surprised by his response. "They're ... they're really difficult, Faelan. I don't want to expose you to them."

"Have you told them about—"

"About what?" I looked up to see his father at our side. The man had appeared instantly, with barely a sound, and the fine hairs on the back of my neck rose as he looked down at me, disdain clear in his features.

"About our date tonight?" I answered smoothly, refusing to cow before this man. I'd had my fair share of experience standing up to difficult people before, and I called on every ounce of my experience to meet Luch's father's eyes directly. I smiled. "I'm Dr. Faelan Fletcher, and you are?"

"This is my father, Richard Carmichael." I noticed Luch didn't address him as a doctor, and when a muscle ticked in his father's jaw, I realized he'd done so on purpose.

"A doctor? Isn't that nice. What is your specialty?"

And just like that, we were down to business.

"Animals." I smiled politely when Richard's gaze flicked to Luch's face. "I'm a veterinarian."

"Is that right?" Something flashed in his face and then smoothed out. "You must be the reason we haven't heard much from Luch lately. We took it upon ourselves to come down here and make sure he was doing well."

"Dad, I'm fine. As you well know because I talk to you often."

Richard completely ignored Luch, instead turning to gesture to the four men hovering behind him.

"His brothers. Lupin, Mark, Andrew, and Ian."

Each man nodded briefly at me, but none of them spoke when introduced. I swear they looked like they were bodyguards, ready to crack their knuckles and beat someone up. *What the hell is going on?* Luch said they'd ambushed him, but given Luch was a grown man, why did these men look as though they were protecting him? I now doubted Luch had told them about *what* I was, so why on earth were they almost champing at the bit?

"Carmichael?" the hostess called, breaking the tension, and Luch once more turned to me.

"We have a date. So we'll just be enjoying ourselves without you," Luch said.

"I've taken care to adjust the reservation. We'll all be sitting together." Richard turned and followed the hostess into the hall and I couldn't do anything else other than fall into line. I could only imagine how this must look, me trailing after this line of hulking men. Movement flashed in the corner of my eye, and I flicked my eyes to the corner of the room to see Brice hovering in the corner. I raised a finger, acknowledging him, and then pointed to the kitchen.

I hoped he'd get my message that I needed help.

I wasn't sure what that help was.

But whatever was about to go down wouldn't be good.

We all politely listened as the waiter read off the specials for the evening, but I was too distracted to take in anything he was saying. The tension at the table was so thick, I was surprised icicles didn't form from the ceiling. Around us, the restaurant flowed, and snatches of laughter and snippets of conversations drifted to me.

"Faelan?" Luch nudged me and I realized the waiter was looking at me, his pen raised on his pad.

"Oh, I'm sorry. A Sauvignon Blanc, please." I looked at Luch. "Has anyone ordered food?"

"We didn't open our menus yet." Luch gave me a pained look, and I realized that I was revealing how distracted I was. Forcing myself to focus, I unfolded my napkin and smoothed it in my lap and looked at the silent men sitting across from me. Was I meant to carry the conversation here? Uncertain of my footing, I waited.

"Ms. Fletcher—" Richard tapped a finger on the table.

"Doctor." I didn't care if I was being rude.

Richard raised an eyebrow at me but then continued. "We feel you're the reason that Luch isn't coming home."

"Dad, this is ludicrous. I'm an adult with my own life. You can't come here, with whatever this is—"

"An intervention," Richard supplied and Luch sat back in his chair, aghast.

"An intervention? You've all lost your minds. You can't

possibly think that this is the way to get me to leave Loren Brae."

"What is the way then? Tell us. Because it's been over a year now and nothing's changed."

"Maybe because I don't want it to change? I have a right to my own life, don't I?"

My gaze bounced between the two of them, trying to understand the undercurrent of whatever was going on here. There was so much that wasn't being said, and yet every word seemed to matter. The waiter returned with a tray of drinks and asked for orders. I ordered the aubergine lasagna, having never even opened the menu, and dearly hoped the food would arrive quickly. Everyone at the table waited until the waiter left.

"Ms. Fletcher—"

"Doctor," I said again, taking a sip of my wine, enjoying throwing this man off his stride.

"We think it would be best if you remove yourself from Luch's life."

I laughed, stunned that we were even having this conversation. Luch was an adult man, successful in his career, and lived a healthy and happy life. What could possibly be behind such a ridiculous display of authoritarianism?

"Richard," I said, widening my smile as annoyance flashed in his eyes that I didn't refer to him as a doctor. "I'm not sure what 'royal family-type' move you're attempting to pull here, but I will be very clear. I do not take orders from you. Or anyone, for that matter."

"Dad—"

"We're prepared to make you a deal."

Luch exploded, slamming his fist onto the table, and the entire restaurant went silent. I froze as every man at the table, including Luch, rose.

Every instinct in my body told me to run. It was the same thing I'd felt the first time I'd met Luch, but a hundred times stronger now that we were around his family.

A blur of motion flashed across my eyes, and I gasped as a red wine glass went flying toward Richard.

Brice.

My mouth rounded, and I gasped, but not before Richard pivoted, preternaturally fast, and avoided the spill of wine. He turned, seemed to track Brice, and my pulse kicked up.

Had he seen the broonie?

"Sir, we're going to have to ask you to leave."

I turned to see Lia standing there, Munroe at her side looking elegant in a suit, and two waiters behind them.

"Me?" Richard pointed a finger at his chest. "Luch's the one creating a scene."

"That's not true," I said, before anyone else could speak, refusing to believe that this man had actually fathered Luch. How could he throw his son under the bus like that? "These men interrupted our date and forced us to dine with them. They were not invited, nor welcomed."

Light that match and burn those bridges, baby! But I couldn't bring myself to care one bit about this incredibly cold and rude family. They'd just offered to buy me off so I'd stay away from their son and brother. I couldn't fathom a world in which my mother would ever have considered something of that nature. It was astounding that someone like Luch had managed to find his way in a world where he was raised around this group of people.

"Understood. If you'd please leave my restaurant," Lia said, turning to the others, subtly stepping next to me in a show of support.

Richard looked around the restaurant, realizing he had an audience, and turned on his heel and strode out. Luch's brothers all followed suit, shooting nasty looks at me over their shoulders as they did, and in moments they were gone. Or at least I hoped they were gone. I wasn't sure I wanted to meet them in a dark car park later.

"Luch. Faelan. My kitchen." Lia's tone brooked no disagreement, nor did Munroe's stern expression behind her.

My eyes met Luch's.

"I need to go speak to them," Luch's voice rasped, and my heart fell. He was choosing his family, because of course he was. They were family. Even if they were cold, robotic, and without any empathy whatsoever.

Without another word, I followed Lia into the kitchen, leaving my heart behind with Luch. In all the ways I had imagined potentially meeting his family, it had never been like this. I'd known they were difficult, but that descriptor seemed like an understatement compared to what I'd just witnessed.

I kept my head high as I sailed past the other patrons and followed Lia into the kitchen, and into controlled chaos. A sous chef worked at the stove, waiters zipped past with plates, and others stood at a long table chopping and prepping. Scents of garlic and basil hung heavy in the air.

"I'm taking fifteen," Lia called out, untying her apron.

"Yes, Chef," the kitchen responded. Lia stopped at a mini fridge, pulled out a bottle of already open wine, and held it in the air. I nodded. Quickly she filled glasses, Munroe taking one and offering it to me, and then nodded toward an arched doorway that was partially cracked open to the night. Following her outside to what must be a table for the employees to take quick breaks, I dropped down into a chair and heaved out a sigh.

"Brice came and warned me. What the hell happened?" Lia went right to the point, glancing over her shoulder at her kitchen. I winced. My drama was taking her from a very busy night.

"Tough looking group," Munroe observed, leaning back to absentmindedly rub a hand over Lia's shoulder. She leaned into him, and he dug deeper, working out whatever knots she had there. I'd met Munroe a few times at the weekly dinners now, and though I was told he had an obscene amount of money, he'd always been kind and seemed down-to-earth to me.

"Luch's father and brothers. They came here to order him to come home and offer me money to stay away from him."

Lia shot Munroe a knowing look. "Sounds like the ice queen."

I raised an eyebrow in question.

"My mum. She's ... tricky."

"Tricky is an understatement. In fact, she'd probably fit in just fine with Luch's family. It's unbelievable, isn't it? That such great people could come from ... that?"

"I don't know Luch all that well, but from the times our paths have crossed he seems class. Honestly, I'm surprised he went after them and didn't stay with you," Munroe observed, and I took a deep gulp of the wine. There was a chill to the night air and I crossed my arms over my chest. Maybe it was just a chill in my bones from the run-in. I couldn't be sure.

"I needed to make sure they were leaving."

I started and turned to see Luch walking up, his shoulders slumped, hands in his pockets.

"Luch."

"Do you want us to—"

"No, you can stay." I threw a glance at Lia. I didn't like whatever had just happened with Luch, and I wasn't sure I could trust him now. But Lia? I trusted her. "I might need backup."

"Happy to help. I own many knives." Lia gave Luch a scary grin, and he sighed, wrenching a hand through his hair while Munroe bit back a chuckle.

"I, obviously, didn't know they'd be here tonight." Luch didn't sit, instead he paced in front of the table, his face impossible to read.

"That's a relief," I said, somewhat mollified. I watched him pace. Five steps forward, five steps back.

"I ... I don't know how to explain why they are the way that they are." Luch pressed his lips together before continuing. "At least, I can't."

"Not a great excuse, buddy. You're not giving Faelan much to go on," Lia said and I could have applauded her.

"I am both a part of my family and at the same time I want nothing to do with what they want for me. Their blood runs in my veins, but that's where the similarities stop. They can't ... won't ... accept that." Luch continued his pacing, mulling over his words, and my heart felt like it was bleeding out with every step he took. "Something broke in them, my father particularly, the day I was born. I've been living with the guilt of it my whole life."

At that, Lia looked at me in question, but I just gave a subtle shake of my head. I didn't want to interrupt Luch.

"It turned him cold. Colder than he was, I'm told. The only soft spot I've ever seen in him is for my mum. His inability to help her has soured something inside of him. He's looking for an outlet—someone to blame. And if it isn't me, for being born, then it's for the healer that stood in his place because he didn't make it from his surgery in time to help."

At that, Lia's mouth rounded, and again, I shook my head.

"I've lived my whole life with the guilt of being born."

"Does your mum feel the same way?" Munroe asked, and Luch stopped, surprised at the question. It was almost as if he'd forgotten Lia and Munroe were even there.

"No, she doesn't. She's bottled sunshine. You'd never know she was in a wheelchair or had any difficulties in her life if you didn't see her. She's never made me feel like I was a burden."

"Well that's something, isn't it?" Lia asked, quickly glancing at her watch.

"It is. But not when I have the rest of them to deal with. You saw for yourself how they are. They're relentless."

"But why?" I burst out, frustrated, and stood. "*Why*, Luch? Why do you need to go home? This was beyond anything a normal family would request. What aren't you telling me?"

At that, Lia and Munroe both stood as well.

"I think this is the time we exit. Good luck." Lia squeezed my arm, and Munroe nodded to us both. They ducked inside, closing the kitchen door behind them, leaving Luch and me standing in the light of the almost full moon.

My heart pounded in my chest. I needed answers, because I knew, knew in my very soul that there was something going on here that he wasn't telling me. And, while, yes, I still had some things to share with him about the Order of Caledonia, it still didn't change what he knew of who I was as a person.

Yet I felt like whatever he was holding back would change my view of him forever.

"Just tell me. Please," I whispered. I didn't want to beg, but I couldn't go on—not if there were massive secrets between us.

"I can't." Luch looked at me, his eyes burning. "I ... I can't, Faelan. I'm sorry."

"Of course. Family stuff. And I'm not family, am I?" Hurt whiplashed through me, and I picked up my handbag from the table.

"It's not ... I can't." Frustrated, Luch fell into stride beside me. Heat radiated from him, and I wanted nothing more than to cuddle into him in the cool night air. Instead, I clenched my arms around my body, stepping farther away from him as I pounded down the path toward my flat. "Faelan. Please, just listen. It's not my place. I just can't share, okay?"

"And I'm supposed to just accept that? I'm supposed to accept that you have some massive family secret that brought your entire family here to try and buy me off to stay away from you? And then what? What happens if I do accept that? Where do we go from here?"

"I ... I don't know." Luch's face was miserable. "Back to our happy bubble? I don't want to lose you, Faelan."

"But the happy bubble isn't real." My voice rose, and I continued down the path, glad I had stuck with my instincts to wear flats, my feet slapping the pavement angrily as I walked. "I loved it, too, Luch. But it's not real, is it? It never was. It never can be. Not when there are all these secrets."

"I just ..." Luch stopped me, his hands at my shoulders, and turned me to him. "Can you give me time? Can I ask that of you? A favor?"

Wary, I looked up at him.

"Do you understand that?"

"We think it would be best if you remove yourself from Luch's life." Those words. I'd heard them so many times before.

"We think it would be best if you leave town. Permanently."

"You are not welcome here, and you need to leave."

"Remove yourself from this town or I'll light the bonfire myself."

They had stung. But his father's spiteful, detestable offer ...

"We're prepared to make you a deal."

"I've spent my life being run from one town to the next, forever the outcast. Can you even imagine how that felt, to me, to be assaulted like that tonight? By your own family?" I held a hand to my chest, and my eyes stung with unshed tears. "I don't need them to accept me, but for them to offer me money? How could you have told them about me, Luch? There's no way they would have acted like that if I was just a normal person. Is there?"

Luch's lips thinned, and my heart cracked.

"You did, didn't you? You told them about me ..." Betrayal sliced through me. I'd expected too much of him, it seemed, when it came to keeping my secrets.

"I swear I didn't, Faelan. But when you'd first arrived, I might have had a conversation with my father about my suspicions about the new vet in town. But that was it, I swear to you. I've never even told them I was dating anyone."

Now I was conflicted. Should I be annoyed he'd kept me a secret or frustrated that he was keeping secrets from me? Everything swirled around in my brain and when my tears almost spilled over, I decided.

What I needed to do was go home alone and breathe.

I needed Gloam.

I needed my cozy, wee flat.

And I needed to be alone.

It was what I was used to—not relying on anyone—and until I could work through the multifaceted and unsettling feelings from a situation where I didn't have all the information, there wasn't much else I could do.

"I'm going home. Alone." I held up a hand when Luch went to speak. "I have no idea how I feel about any of this, other than hurt. And I'm not even sure of all the reasons I'm hurt, because I don't have all the facts. But what I do know is that I didn't like whatever that was. And until you get the situation with your family sorted out, I'm not sure what future we *can* have together, because the one thing I won't compromise on is my safety. And tonight? Your family made me feel unsafe. As did you."

The words fell like a physical blow across Luch, his face crumpling, and he ducked his head.

"I'm sorry, Faelan. Truly. I would never, ever, want you to feel unprotected in my presence." Luch took a step back, and my heart cracked even more. "I will give you the space you ask for, and I hope you'll give me the time I've asked for. I ... you mean a lot to me, Faelan, and I'm not ready to let you go."

"You might not have a say in that." Turning, I began to walk.

"Faelan?"

"Aye?" I turned to stare at him. My entire body trembled with the effort it took not to cry.

"I'm ... I'll be working nights this week. Just so you know. If you don't hear from me, it's not because of this."

Through the years, I'd had enough practice hiding my feelings and pulling my armor around my emotions. It was almost second nature to smooth my features out and pretend indifference as I shrugged and turned, hoping Willow's dress with the sexy backside was making him question his entire existence as I walked away.

CHAPTER TWENTY-TWO

Faelan

Lia had called an emergency girls' night after what she'd seen the night before, and after a day of work where I'd basically operated on autopilot, I found myself tucked on a loveseat inside Bonnie Books, Agnes's bookstore, which was right around the corner from my practice. I'd been meaning to visit for a while, but I hadn't exactly had any free time to read of late, not with Luch in my life, and opening my own practice.

But now, it seemed, my nights would be freed up, so a good book might be just what I needed.

"Och, that's delightful." Agnes nodded to one of the books I'd picked up from a pile to be reshelved on the table next to me. "Vampires. Hot vampires. Lots of angst."

"Is that right?" Sophie asked, intrigued, and I passed the book to her.

"Hot vampire sex is not what I need right now."

"No, what you need is hot make-up sex with your man," Sophie said, and I sighed, crossing my arms over my chest and dropping my chin into my palm.

"There's nothing to make up. What's to be done about it?" I asked.

The group of women sprawled on the couches and floor, everyone picking through books of interest, all studiously ignoring the reason why we'd been called to meet tonight. But now that Sophie had breached the subject, everyone snapped to attention.

"So. Tell us. Go on ... just get it out," Shona insisted. "You'll feel better for it."

"I—"

A knock at the door had Agnes hopping up. She wore cottage socks, leggings, a silky sleep tank with lace at the edges, and a fuzzy cardigan that hung loose from her shoulders. She'd dressed for a coorie in, and like me, she lived above her work.

"That's the food." Agnes swung the door open to Graham, whose mouth dropped open when he took in the sight of Agnes's silk top. "Hi, Graham."

"Um."

"Eloquent as always, Graham."

Graham snapped his eyes away from her shirt and held up the two brown bags in his hands.

"It's just that words leave me when I'm confronted with such beauty." Graham's cheeky grin slipped back into place as he looked over Agnes's shoulder to the women in the room. "And all in one place. A luckier lad, I do not know.

I'm just grateful I didn't send our kitchen help on delivery tonight."

"Och, wipe that grin off your face. It's not like we're having a pajama party, Graham." Agnes rolled her eyes and took one of the bags from him, crossing the room to put it on the table.

"But if you were ..."—Graham's grin widened—"could you tell me what you'd be doing? In great detail, of course."

"Of course." Agnes dropped her voice, all sultry like, and prowled back across the room. Graham's jaw went slack as she took the other bag with one hand. "First, we'd all change into something much more comfortable ..."

"Uh-huh, go on."

"And then ..." Agnes trailed a hand up his chest. Graham's eyes widened. "We'd kick all the boys out because it's our clubhouse."

With that, she shoved him back and slammed the door in his face.

We all hooted in laughter as Agnes held the bag of food in the air like a champion.

"When are you going to stop toying with that man?" Sophie demanded.

"I am not toying with him," Agnes exclaimed.

A knock at the window had us all turning. Graham pressed his face to the pane, his mouth pulled down in a dramatic frown, and he ran a finger down his cheek as though he was crying.

We all howled, and Lia threw a cushion at the window. With that, Graham held up his hands in defeat and crossed the street to the pub.

"Right. We've got snacks, we've got wine, what we

don't have is the story. Talk." Agnes could have been a drill sergeant as she unpacked food and delivered orders. I noticed she was studiously avoiding looking at the window where Graham had been, and as much as I wanted to grill her on the history with that relationship, I didn't feel like I knew her well enough to do so.

Plus, we were here to talk about me.

That, in itself, made me both cringe and smile. *I have people.* Despite the pain I felt about Luch—*what the hell can't he tell me?*—I also felt immense comfort. There were wonderful friends in my corner who had left their comfy homes to be with me tonight. *To discuss my woes.* Like I said, cringe-worthy *and* smile-worthy.

I'd honestly never been in the position with a group, an actual group, of friends who were all invested in listening to me talk about my life. Friends had been few and far between in my life, so this was completely outside my normal operating procedure.

Maybe I just need to start there.

Tucking my feet underneath me, I pulled a cushion onto my lap and hugged it, needing comfort.

"I've never really had a group of friends before. I don't really know how to start this," I said, and Orla's face softened. She raised a hand.

"Same, girl. Same. It gets easier. They'll just batter you over the head with friendship until you accept it. Might as well crack on with it now, as you're a part of us forever."

"I wouldn't say batter." Shona smiled. "What's a much gentler type of assault?"

"Is assault ever gentle?" I wondered.

"Either way, you're ours now. Might as well accept it."

Willow beamed at me. "And let me be the first to say that I am pissed that my dress was ruined on an argument. Or at least that's what I've been told."

"I mean, it wasn't entirely ruined." My cheeks pinkened and Willow hooted in laughter.

"All right then, you go, girl."

"Ahem." I cleared my throat. "Right, so, basically, long story short—I've been on the run my whole life. Coming to Loren Brae and finding you all? It's ... a relief, really. I can finally make a home. Have friends. Not be looking over my shoulder constantly with the worry that I'll be run from town. Date. Actually date."

"You're planting roots," Shona said, nodding.

"Exactly. And at first I wasn't ready to tell Luch about what I was. But he found out anyway, though he'd told me he'd had his suspicions." I filled them in on everything, from the morning of Oban's healing, all the way to when I'd met Luch's family last night. Agnes paused me once to force some food down my throat, but by the time I'd finished talking the room had gone silent.

"What in the world?" Sophie wondered.

I took a deep slug of my Irn Bru. I didn't want to drink tonight, worried that alcohol would make me do something impulsive like track Luch down at work and beg him to explain what he was hiding from me.

"How much time are you going to give him?" Kaia asked.

"I don't know. I guess as much time as he needs? I mean, does it matter? I'd like an explanation, at some point. But whatever his family secret is, it seems he's just not ready to share it."

"It was enough to send him running," Orla mused.

"Do you think he's magick?" Shona wondered and I froze.

It wasn't the first time the idea had occurred to me, but at the same time, how could he keep something like that from me when I'd shown him my own secret?

"Honestly? I hope not. I really hope not. Because if he is … don't you see the position that puts me in? I've shared my past and almost all the parts of myself with him and he's not done the same for me. So where would that leave us?"

"Maybe he can't, though. Like he's taken an oath or something?" Sophie suggested.

"Or maybe he's not ready to put it all on the line." I looked up in surprise at Agnes's words, a bitter note in her voice, and found her staring out the window at the pub.

"Um, I don't know. That's the thing. I just don't know. So what do I do? Wait it out or just move on?"

"I think you need to give it a few days. See if he comes back to you, offers an explanation. Give him a little time. You obviously care about him, Faelan," Shona said.

I love him. But maybe … that won't matter.

I stifled a yawn as I stood.

"I appreciate the advice, ladies, but I'm absolutely beat. I barely slept last night and had back-to-back patients all day."

"I'll walk you back up the road," Sophie said, rising as well. "I'm headed that way."

"Do you want a lift?" Shona asked. "I drove in because I didn't want to walk back alone in the dark."

"Nah, it's close enough. I like the walk. I know I own the castle and all, but it still gets me, every time, when I walk up that hill and the castle is all lit up against the dark sky." Sophie held a hand to her heart.

"I get that. I felt that last night, walking to the restaurant. Makes you feel like a princess."

"It really does," Sophie gushed and tugged at the hem of her UCLA jumper. "If a princess wears leggings and sweatshirts, that is."

"Hey, it's your castle. Your rules." I laughed, feeling a touch lighter than I had all day. Turning to the room, I held out my hands. "Honestly? This helped. It didn't solve anything, but it helped. Friendship matters and I want you to know that I won't take any of you for granted."

"Och, you're going to get me going." Willow waved a hand in front of her eyes, and then after a hearty round of hugs, Sophie and I were out in the cool night air. We fell into step, walking down Main Street toward the loch.

"I'm happy here," I said, surprising myself. "I mean, just look at this place."

"I know. It's just a postcard, isn't it?" Sophie agreed.

The moon hung, bright and full, a fat bulb in the sky, illuminating a silvery path across the loch. Lights twinkled in the windows of the houses, and up on the hill, MacAlpine Castle stood, a beacon in the night. It was a quiet evening, not unusual for a small town night, but as we rounded the corner where Main Street T-d off with the loch, apprehension flared through me. Something felt ... off.

A low growl sounded and Sophie grabbed my arm.

"Did you hear that?" Sophie whispered.

"Aye." I scanned the bushes that lined the road, searching. We waited, but when nothing more came, we looked at each other.

"My flat's not far. Should we go for it?" I asked, fear creeping in.

"What if running makes it chase us?" Sophie hissed.

A howl broke the night, and Sophie shrieked, leaping into the air and grabbing my arm.

"Oh my God. Look!" Sophie pointed and there, just up the hill, I could make out a pack of wolves, their heads thrown back as they bellowed to the moon.

It was their distraction that proved to be our mistake.

One we might pay for dearly.

Another shriek split the night sky, and this time we both whirled to face the loch.

But it was too fast.

We had no time to react.

In seconds the Kelpies were bearing down on us, thundering up the shoreline, their eyes blazing red, their mouths opened in a scream.

"Fuck," Sophie said, but before we could do anything, another howl ripped across the loch and a wolf peeled off from the pack, thundering down the road to meet the Kelpies.

The water horses reared, finding a new perceived threat, and changed direction, meeting the wolf head-on in the street.

"No," I breathed, terror racing through me. "He helped me. That night. He helped. We can't let him—"

The wolf snarled and leapt onto the back of one horse, claws raking down its kelp-slicked hide. The creature screamed—an unearthly, watery shriek that rattled the windows behind us—and twisted, trying to buck him off. The other Kelpies swarmed, hooves pounding the tarmac like war drums.

The wolf was a blur of muscle and instinct. He moved with terrifying precision, lunging low to tear at tendons, springing up to latch his jaws onto throats that should've been made of flesh but looked more like shifting seaweed and bone.

Sophie grabbed my hand. "We have to help him."

"I don't know how!" I cried, heart pounding, watching as he clawed his way across the flank of one Kelpie, blood—black as ink—spurting from the gash. The beast screamed, staggering, and the wolf launched from its back to meet the next head-on.

There were three of them. Maybe more. It was hard to see under the light of the moon and with the blur of motion. Each one a monstrous blend of horse and nightmare, their bodies dripping with lakeweed and rot, their mouths full of jagged, mismatched teeth.

The wolf didn't hesitate. He threw himself into their midst, biting and tearing, fur flying as they reared and slammed hooves down with the force of boulders. A hoof caught his side and sent him flying. He landed hard, rolling across the ground in a blur of fur and dirt before he staggered to his feet again, breath heaving, blood soaking his flank.

"No!" I screamed, but he charged again.

One Kelpie tried to retreat into the loch. He chased it, snarling, forcing it back, but the others converged—two at once slamming into him. There was a crunching snap—a sound I'll never forget. And then a scream—his this time—

cut short as one Kelpie bit down on his hind leg and *pulled*.

The rip of flesh was sickening.

He collapsed, howling in agony, dragging himself forward with only his forelegs, blood pooling beneath him in a thick, dark smear. He turned his head, snarling through the pain, baring his teeth even as one Kelpie lifted a hoof—

Sophie stepped forward.

"No more," she said, voice shaking with something deeper than fear. Her hands lifted, fingers splayed wide. "Stop, at once. You weren't summoned, and I banish you back to the deep."

The wind shifted. The loch behind us churned, and the air itself seemed to tighten as she spoke.

"Return to the water," she cried, louder now, voice ringing like a bell. "Return to the depths that bore you!"

The Kelpies faltered. One screamed, a high, distorted wail as it whipped its head toward her. But Sophie stood firm, her whole body trembling with something ancient and electric.

Other voices rose at our backs.

The Order.

They were here now, circling us, voices raised to the Kelpies.

"Back to the depths. *Now.*"

And they went.

Not all at once—but like the tide pulling back. They shrieked, they thrashed, but their forms began to unravel, seawater spilling from their eyes and mouths as their shapes twisted, collapsed, and finally scattered like smoke across the surface of the loch.

Silence fell.

Holy fuck. Oh God, that was terrifying. The Kelpies—

"What—"

"Faelan—"

I turned, heart clenching, as the wolf lay trembling in the road. His body convulsed once, then again—and then began to *shift*.

A gasp.

Bones cracked and lengthened, fur melted away, limbs rearranged. He arched off the ground with a final cry and then collapsed, naked and bloodied, onto the stones.

A man.

I ran.

I didn't think. I didn't breathe. I just ran to him, skidding to my knees in the pool of blood that spread beneath his side.

"Sophie, help!" I cried, pressing my hands to his wound. Bloody hell, but this was serious. His thigh had been ripped open, the flesh torn to the bone. He was barely conscious, his skin cold and clammy, blood smeared across his face like war paint.

He looked up at me.

Tawny-green eyes. Midnight-black hair. His expression was of agony and terror.

Luch.

He's ...

"Oh, Luch," I whispered. *How did I not know?*

The wolf. The one who had saved me the other time. *Of course.* Luch's lashes fluttered against his cheeks, but his eyes remained closed.

"Luch … no," I gasped out, fear and confusion making me freeze.

He tried to speak, but only blood came.

"Don't you dare," I said, choking on a sob. "You saved me. Again. Don't you *dare* die on me now."

Sophie dropped beside us, eyes wide with terror. "What do we do?"

"I don't know," I said, pressing harder, tears blurring my vision. "But I'm not losing him."

And under the full moon, I whispered the only thing I could think of—the only truth I knew, "Oban needs you. *I* need you. Don't you dare leave us."

The other wolves drew near, whimpering, and when they saw Luch, they turned to me with a growl, trying to push me back. Fear made me bold, and I stood up, pulling my scalpel from the sheath in my coat pocket.

The wolves bared their teeth, their growls growing louder.

"Stop them. Please, Sophie. *Help me*. Make them stay back. We'll lose him." I knew, instinctively, that this was Luch's family, and they would do everything in their power to stop me from healing Luch, simply because they didn't trust healers.

"You heard the ladies. Let's go to work, lads." A group of men stepped forward, the husbands and boyfriends of *my* friends, Lachlan at their head, and formed a wall between me and the pack of wolves.

Dropping back to my knees, I bent my face, pressing my lips to Luch's forehead.

"You don't get to leave me. I won't allow it."

And then I reached for my magick.

CHAPTER TWENTY-THREE

FAELAN

"Tell us what you need, Faelan. We're here." Lia's voice at my side had me blinking back tears. I'd never had someone with me as I'd healed before, aside from my mother, and it brought to a head long-buried feelings of longing for familiarity—for family.

"Aye, Faelan. We're with you. We've got healing tonics, poultices, anything you need." Shona squeezed in on the other side of me.

A tonic wouldn't help this.

I wasn't sure that *I* could help this.

Closing my eyes, I dragged in a shaky breath and put my hands back on Luch's prone body.

There was just so much damage.

Too much.

"Do we need to call for an ambulance?" Lia whispered, worry lacing her voice.

"I don't know that they can help. I have to go ... inside myself now." I couldn't talk to them and maintain a connection with Luch. The men shouted, the growls intensifying, and I went deeper inside myself, ignoring the clamor around me. If I couldn't focus, I'd be useless to Luch.

He's just a patient.

Do what you would for any patient.

"I'm here, Faelan. Use me." Gloam's words reached me, and instantly I understood what he was telling me. How many nights I'd sat with him by the window, overlooking the loch, picking his brain about how the animal magickal world worked.

He was a connection to the animal world, as well as the mystical one, and he was offering himself as a conduit to increase my powers of healing.

Blindly, I reached out, and Gloam slipped beneath one hand, his soft fur sliding between my fingers, as I kept my other hand on Luch. Reaching into my very core, I unlocked my healing, allowing it to flow through me. Gloam's presence, enabling me to be connected both to the earth and the animal kingdom, intensified my strength. Power rippled from the ground up, through Gloam, and into me. We were all connected, a circle of energy, and I poured everything I had into Luch.

Even then, I could barely see his soul. It hovered at the edges of darkness, the last line of sunlight on a dying day, and I gasped, terrified to see him so far gone already. Pushing deeper,

I reached for his light, twining my own through his, weaving as fast as I could. Tender gold threads mixed with silver, our souls entwining, and I pulled gently, dragging him away from the abyss that loomed, ready to welcome him home.

Not yet.

He had more time here.

We had more time here.

Desperate, I held on to his soul and splintered my thoughts, almost as though I was keeping one eye on his soul that inched toward the veil, and the other scanning his body, looking to where I could make a fast repair. I worked steadily, healing what I could as I raced through his body searching for the worst of it.

There was just *so* much.

It was hard to decide where to begin, so I just fixed as I went. Knitting broken bones, weaving blood vessels back together, tightening ligaments and tendons that had been stretched. Sweat dripped down my brow, and beneath my back, and my hands trembled as I held on to Gloam and Luch, desperate to heal.

But it was his femoral artery that scared me the most.

Healing I could do.

But loss of blood was an entirely different thing. I could repair, but I couldn't replicate blood. He'd need a transfusion, and soon, and I wasn't even sure where to begin explaining the need for one if the doctors wouldn't be able to see where the blood loss had come from.

It was a catch-22.

If I healed his wounds, I'd give him a fighting chance, but then traditional medicine would have to take over.

And then there would be questions.

Too many questions.

The closest hospital was the one where Luch worked and there was no way they wouldn't do a full inquest into what was happening here. Living without scrutiny in Loren Brae was one thing, but there would be a formal review if Luch went into emergency services with the need for a blood transfusion and very little evidence of trauma.

And yet.

There was no way around it. He'd have a fighting chance if he could get the help he needed, outside of what I could give.

Even if it meant I'd have to leave.

Decided, I turned toward Lia.

"He needs blood. Call 999."

"On it." Lia pulled away, and I continued my work, bending my power to my will, determined to give Luch a chance even as my energy waned.

"You must pull back. It's too much," Gloam cautioned, his tiny body shuddering beneath my touch. He was but a conduit, but even so, this was both an incredible gift and a huge tax upon his strength.

Sirens sounded in the distance, breaking through my concentration, and I heaved in another deep breath, forcing myself to focus, to heal like I'd never healed before, slowly inching Luch's soul away from the darkness that threatened to claim it. It was like holding on to the sun, trying to stop the day from dying, and I was determined to keep him away from the edge.

"You have to stop. The ambulance draws near. You must redirect this pain, Faelan." Gloam's words were a shout in my head, an order, and I knew he was right.

If I didn't redirect the pain, I'd take it into me, and it wasn't likely I'd survive such a blow. When a healer took pain from a patient inside them, it was lessened, like coffee passing through a filter, but it was still dangerous. It was why it was necessary that all healers redirected the pain to an appropriate place, or they'd bear their own wounds from it. Like when I had bruises on my body from healing Oban, even though his injuries had been far more serious than what I'd taken on from healing him.

But this? I'd be putting my own life in danger if I didn't pull out now and finish performing my duties as I'd been taught. As had been passed down through the ages. I understood what Gloam was urging me to do, even if I didn't agree with it. My heart wanted me to heal Luch up until the last possible second, when the ambulance arrived, but my head understood the danger.

"Hold on, Luch. Just a bit longer. Help is on the way." I began my closing ritual, tears leaking from my eyes, hating that I had to leave him like this.

Two things happened at once.

The ambulance barreled around the corner, its siren cutting off in a sharp squawk just as one of the wolves burst past the men, teeth bared, a vicious growl in its throat.

It leapt for me, and I shrieked, pulling back, breaking connection with Luch and Gloam.

Darkness claimed me.

CHAPTER TWENTY-FOUR

LUCH

"I said get out of my way. This one's mine."

I blinked, my vision blurry, a ceiling whipping past. I was moving, I knew that much, and I recognized the voice.

"Lynn?" I rasped, confused. Was I at work?

"Don't worry, Dr. Carmichael. I've got you. Nobody will take care of you like your own."

"What ..." I couldn't understand what was happening.

"He really needs a doctor," another voice growled, arguing with Lynn.

"This is our hospital and we take care of our own. I kindly ask you to step back or we'll make you step back."

"But he's my son."

My dad was here?

It all came flashing back, in an instant, and I struggled, trying to sit up.

"You just lie right there, darling. I've got you." Lynn's hand pressed me back, holding me easily on the stretcher.

"Faelan." I could barely speak, couldn't move, nothing was working. My thoughts were a jumbled mess, my vision still blurry, and I couldn't work out what was going on.

"We've got her too, Dr. Carmichael. Is this your lady friend? I knew you were dating someone, didn't I? I told the others, that there was no way you were single. Even Jacob said you'd seemed happier lately. I called it." Lynn's voice was cheerful, even though her steps were hurried and the stretcher moved fast. If Lynn was moving this fast, then this was serious, more serious than she was letting on with her chatter. Her bedside manner was impeccable, and Lynn excelled at distracting and comforting the patients from the severity of the pain they were in.

Which was exactly what she was trying to do now as they wheeled me into one of the private rooms.

The door slammed and Lynn's face came into focus as she bent over me.

"It's just us. I took a private room when I saw who it was. Tell me quick what's really going on here." Lynn darted a glance over her shoulder. The A&E was notorious for being busy and it was rare to have a private space, even in a more rural area like Loren Brae.

"I ..." My voice rasped as Lynn took my vitals.

"Your heartbeat is abnormally fast. Your temperature is high, but you're not breaking a sweat. You have injuries and bruises that would suggest a far greater trauma than what

I'm seeing, and yet all we're told is you need a blood transfusion. Something's going on, and I'll do my damnedest to protect you, but I need to know what I'm dealing with to help you."

"It's ..." I froze, unable to find the words. How could I tell her? My entire world would be compromised.

Lynn's clear blue eyes assessed me.

"It's something magickal, isn't it?"

My eyebrows went up and my mouth moved but nothing came out.

"Listen, Dr. C. I've lived my entire life just ten minutes outside Loren Brae. You wouldn't be the first, or the last person, I've had to treat that has come to me under unusual circumstances. You think I've ever said a word of it? You know I love gossip as much as the next, but never would I break a patient's confidentiality. But you have to tell me how to help you."

"My father." My voice was but a rasp, and I could barely lift a finger to point toward the door. "His blood."

"Och." Lynn glanced to the door and back to me. "That's ... that's not really standard practice, Dr. C. Patient-to-patient transfusions hold a multitude of risks, as I'm sure you know."

"I promise. It has to be him." Talking was becoming increasingly difficult. It felt like I had a boulder on my chest, and Lynn's face blurred into two talking heads.

"Stay with me, Dr. C. If you insist, I'll grab him." Lynn squeezed my arm, and the door opened and closed. I stared up at the ceiling, wondering why hospitals never made the ceilings more interesting. For the amount of time patients had to lie in bed and stare upward, it would be nice if they could look at something other than boring white ceiling tiles.

"I told you he was my son." My father's smug tone came through the door as Lynn returned.

"Be that as it may, unless he requests you, family stays in the waiting room during triage." Lynn came back to my side and squeezed my arm.

"He asked for me?" A curious note hung in my father's voice.

"He did. Said it could only be you to give blood. He's insisted, though as a doctor, he well knows the risks of a patient-to-patient transfusion." Lynn said the last part much more loudly than the first, admonishing me, and my lips quirked in a grin.

"He's right." My father's face blurred past my vision and a chair scraped across the floor. "In this instance, he needs it from me."

"You're certain?" Lynn was asking me, but my father spoke.

"I'm a cardiac surgeon, I well understand the risks. I agree with my son's assessment and am available for the transfusion." He laid his arm on the bed next to mine.

Lynn tutted her frustration but did as she was told. I barely felt the prick of the IV, and I took a deep breath, hoping the weight on my chest would ease as my father's blood entered my veins.

Wulvers were notoriously good healers.

But even so, a trauma of this nature would require help. Our blood was different from humans and a transfusion from a regular person would do little for me. In fact, it could very well harm me.

It was just one of many reasons that my father wanted me to come home.

Add it to the list.

I closed my eyes, willing my father's blood to be speedy in its healing, as the last few moments before the attack played through my mind.

Faelan's disappointment in me and my family.

My father and my brothers prowling Loren Brae under the full moon instead of returning home.

Finding my father growling at Faelan and Sophie, scaring them.

Irritation flooded me.

He'd gone past overbearing to almost unforgivable at this point, and if I had the strength, I'd tell him to get the fuck out of my hospital room. He'd had no right to pull the little stunt he had at dinner the other night. I'd told him and ordered the lot of them to leave Loren Brae.

Instead, they'd stayed and run the woods in their wolf form, forcing me to defend my territory against them.

Even though they were family.

When a lone wolf splits from the pack, there was usually a good reason for it. In most cases it was because there were too many Alphas, and the one who breaks away leaves to start his own pack elsewhere. I suppose if I had done so, with my father's chosen bride in attendance, he might have let me go more peacefully.

Instead, I'd left, refusing to allow him to force his choice of a wife upon me.

Continuing our Wulver bloodline, and following the old ways, had become something that he'd fixated on after my mother's injury.

The Wulver clans were small, spread out among the Shetland, Orkney, and outer Hebridean islands. To avoid inbreeding, each year at summer equinox, the clans met and had a small festival to introduce eligible partners to those in neighboring clans. Tradition was held dear, as our way of life was deeply hidden from the outside world. It was rare for a Wulver to break away, to start fresh somewhere, and when it happened, all efforts were made to recover the wayward wolf. Even force, if necessary. It was considered a security measure, as one small privacy leak could threaten entire clans, and it was easier to keep members in line if they were kept near.

Beyond being a security risk, I'd threatened our bloodline, according to my father, who so studiously ignored his own lapse when it came to that.

Our mother was not of the Wulvers.

And despite having borne four other sons, her subsequent paralysis after my birth had convinced my father that it was because he'd chosen a wife outside of the clans. A normal human.

Nobody could tell him differently.

Soon my brothers had taken up the belief, following his directive to find wives with suitable bloodlines, as well as sharing in his distrust against all healers. My father had become a zealot in favor of traditional Wulver ways.

Ultimately, it was what had led me to leave. Not only did the islands have more than enough skilled doctors for such remote areas, but I'd needed space to try and pick out my own path, outside of my father's controlling voice.

I closed my eyes, resigned.

This incident would only make him spiral, and he'd be relentless until I gave up and came home.

Maybe it didn't matter.

After this instance, I might have to leave anyway.

None of that mattered, not now. What mattered was willing myself back to health so I could check on Faelan. I knew she was in here, but I didn't know why. Had she been hurt in the attack? Had I not fended off the Kelpies well enough?

"Son ..." My father surprised me by reaching over to squeeze my hand. "You scared me. I wasn't certain you'd make it."

"I shouldn't have." The pressure on my chest was beginning to ease, as strength returned to me, and I took in a deeper breath. My leg throbbed, where the Kelpie's teeth had ripped through tendon and bones, and I wiggled my toes experimentally.

All seemed to be in working order.

Which was impossible ... unless ...

"Did Faelan heal me?" I asked, my voice becoming stronger. I rolled my head on the pillow to see my father's stony expression. "Well, did she?"

"Aye, she did. No matter how I tried to stop her. By the time I got through the barrier to you ... she just dropped to the ground."

My heart stopped.

It just stopped.

Panic gripped me.

If she took the pain in, that meant ...

I struggled to sit up. I had to go to her, to see if she was still alive. Nobody would be able to help her, as they wouldn't know what to do. My injuries from the Kelpie would just eat her alive.

"Hey, now. Just rest, boy. There will be time enough to check on the lass."

"No, you don't understand." Fury had me jerking away from my father's touch at my shoulder, and the IV line went taut between us.

"Careful, Luch." My father held up the arm with the IV. "You'll rip this out."

Bloody hell, but I couldn't do that either. I needed every drop of this blood.

"She needs my help. If she took the pain in, she could die."

"It happens, son. We see it all the time."

My teeth bared at his careless cruelty. This wasn't some random patient that we'd lost due to an accident. This was someone who had given herself to save my life. Did he not see what she had done to help me? His own son he professed to love so much?

"Without her, I'd be dead. At the very least, you owe her the respect of understanding what she's sacrificed."

"Is it a sacrifice? I don't know. All I saw was her hands on you."

"Look at me!" This time it came out as a shout. The blood was working fast, and my energy was returning. I drew myself to a sitting position and ripped the sheet off my leg. A jagged red scar, a slash of red paint on a white canvas, marred my inner thigh. But that was all it was—a scar. I pointed to it. "This. This is what she's done for me. You saw it. You were there. He'd ripped my leg almost completely from my body. Tore my artery. I shouldn't be sitting here right now. And it's not you I have to thank, it's her."

"Luch—"

The door opened and my mum wheeled in, a stern expression on her face.

"Boys, I can hear you yelling all the way down the hallway."

"Mum." Tears threatened. I didn't want her to see me like this. Leslie Carmichael was made of strong stuff, but she always hated when one of her boys was in pain.

"My sweet boy." Mum wheeled herself closer, easing the door closed behind her. "Och, it hurts my heart to see you in the hospital bed like this."

"He'll be just fine, soon enough." My father sniffed, and gave me a look, warning me against bringing up anything that he'd said.

My mum was pint-sized, pretty as a picture, and knew a bullshitter when she saw it.

"What's happened here? Nobody will give it to me straight." Mum raised a steely look to me, and as much as I always tried to shield her from any pain, I didn't have it in me to hide what had happened.

"I've fallen in love."

"Bloody hell." My father threw up his hands, the IV tugging between us.

"Oh, Luch. That's wonderful." My mother wheeled closer and reached out a hand to take mine. "And I dearly would love to hear more, but can we first talk about what landed you in this hospital bed?"

"Leslie, how did you even get here? You were supposed to stay home."

"Surely you didn't think I'd hang back while you went to harass my sweet baby boy, did you?" My mother's voice was like ice. "Anne drove me down and thank goodness for it, or the lot of you would try to hide this from me as well. Go on, Luch. Tell me. Ignore your father, he's clearly being an arse."

My father sat back, properly chastised.

"She's a healer, Mum, and an amazing one at that. She healed Oban, and she helps others, too. But, she healed me after a Kelpie attack and I'm terrified that it's too much for her. That she won't be able to come back from it."

"A Kelpie attack?" Mum brought her hands to her mouth, her face in shock. "Oh my God, Luch. That's awful."

"And your husband only made it worse. Instead of letting her help me, he tried to stop her."

"I didn't know if—" Dad jumped up and brandished the arm not connected to the IV in the air.

"If what?" My mum stared him down.

"If she'd screw it up. If she'd hurt him. Like the healer hurt you. So I tried to stop her."

"And in doing so, you interrupted the vital part of the process where she takes the pain from the patient and directs it elsewhere. If she can't do that, she takes it inside her, but at great cost to her own safety. Injuries of this nature? It might be too much." My voice cracked, and I wished I could rip the IV out and storm down the hallway to find her. I couldn't though, not yet. I'd barely make it a step off the bed before collapsing to the floor.

Come on, blood, work faster.

My mother took in my face, and ignoring my father entirely, wheeled herself to the door and cracked it open.

"What's your girl's name?" Mum asked over her shoulder.

"Faelan Fletcher."

"Lynn, darling?" Lynn appeared in the doorway. "I'll need an update on your patient, Faelan Fletcher. Immediately. Otherwise you're about to have a very stubborn patient to deal with."

"Och, doctors, I swear they make the worst patients." Lynn made a tsking noise and I could hear the smile in her voice.

"Oh, I well know it." The two women shared a smile.

"I've already checked. She's in intensive. Vitals are stable, at the moment, but she's not responsive."

"I need to go to her." My heart clenched. "Lynn, they don't know what she needs. It's not what ..."

"Shh, lad." Lynn eased inside the room and closed it tightly behind her. "You'll just be telling me what she needs and we'll sort it out. She's got unusual contusions and bruises all over her body. Blunt-force trauma almost, yet no bones are broken. No internal bleeding. Nobody can make head or tail of it."

It would only get worse, the longer she held the pain in. But how could she release it, if she wasn't coherent? We needed to wake her, somehow.

"She needs a special tea, to start. It's at her house. Can we call for help? Someone who can go?"

"Of course, though I'm not sure how we'll get tea into her." Lynn tapped a finger on her lip.

"I'll drip it into her mouth. Anything. But she needs us."

Lynn came over and put a hand to my wrist, checking my pulse against her watch.

"Color's returning to your skin. You're looking a lot better, Dr. Carmichael. Care to enlighten me on anything?" Lynn looked up from her watch.

"Best not. If it's all the same to you."

"No problem by me. Either way, I've got your back. I doubt I'll be able to keep you in this bed much longer, correct?"

"Correct." I gave Lynn a small smile. She knew me well.

"I'll make you a deal. If you stay here another twenty minutes, I'll chat with that nice Sophie in the waiting room about getting the tea for Faelan. Does that suit?"

"Sophie's here? Aye, of course. She'll know what to do."

"Then, and only then, can you go to her. But I can't have you falling over and hitting your head, understood? Whatever this"—Lynn waved her hand at the IV between my father and me—"is doing ... well, it's working wonders. A few more minutes won't hurt, and it will put you in a better position to help your woman. Understood?"

"Understood. I'll be good," I promised.

"And I'll make sure he follows orders," Mum followed up.

"In that case, I'll be off. Twenty more minutes. And try and drink some water if you can." With a shake of a finger in the air at me, Lynn left.

"I like her," my mother said, wheeling her chair back to my side.

"She's both terrifying and incredibly comforting. Runs the entire hospital. Knows everything about everyone."

"You're lucky to have her." Mum squeezed my hand and then leveled a look across the bed at my father. "Haud your wheesht, Richard Carmichael, and settle yourself. It's time you follow *my* orders."

"I will not—"

"Och, you will." Mum drew herself up in her chair and gave him a look that had his shoulders hunching over. Nobody had the ability to cow my father, other than my tiny mum. She was his sun, and he fought every cloud he could from shrouding her glory. "Because this will be the last time I say it. You've ignored me for years now, but I want you to hear me very clearly. Are you both listening?"

"Aye," my father and I said in unison.

"If you ever, and I mean, *ever*, bring up the birth and my subsequent injury again, with the intent to place any sort of blame on the healer, on my non-Wulver bloodline, on anything other than the fact that accidents just happen —I will leave you."

My father gave a sharp intake of breath.

"Leslie, no."

"Never, in all my years, have I threatened this, so I hope you understand how deadly serious I am. There is nobody to blame for what happened to me, Richard. Your son is not to blame. The healer is not to blame. Even you, for choosing a wife outside of the magickal bloodline, are not to blame. There is no blame when accidents happen. I know you hated seeing me like this, but bloody hell,

Richard. I've led, and continue to lead, a beautiful life. How could you begrudge me the use of my legs when it's never really slowed me down? I'm happy. And I love my life. It's you who always seeks revenge, not me. And revenge for what? The healer didn't know what was wrong with me. She'd already gone by the time paralysis had set in. Maybe if she'd been there she might have been able to help. Nobody knows. But what I do know is that our son, our smart, handsome, strong boy has grown into a man who has fallen in love with a healer. And her life hangs in the balance because you were blinded by your own unfounded beliefs. Never have I been more ashamed of you."

My father flinched next to me, and I did the same, even though her wrath was not directed at me.

"And you should be ashamed of yourself. A Wulver's job is to protect, not harm. You have a responsibility to the poor lass, Richard. Now, I'm going to find this nice Sophie, and see if she can tell me more about what's going on. I'm so angry that I can't even be in here right now. But I'm glad you're on the mend, Luch. As soon as you can, go to your woman. Love is an incredible gift. It can heal most wounds. And even make you forgive seemingly impossible hurts."

"Leslie ..." My father's voice was ragged, and I turned, surprised to see such intense pain on his face.

"Not now, Richard. I can't." Mum wheeled herself out, and my father hung his head.

Silence filled the room.

This was such an unusual side of my father—one where he was properly hurting from his own actions—and I had no clue how to proceed or even what to say. I was so used to his Alpha commanding presence, that seeing him like this—

a downcast *man*—shook me to my core. Finally, my father sighed, shook his head, and looked up at me.

"She's right, you know. Always is, your mother. Good head on her shoulders. Love is a gift, and if this Faelan's the one for you, then I'm sorry I tried to get in the way. I was blinded by my own shite. Your mother has the right of it. I'm sorry, Luch."

It felt like that boulder dropped back on my chest. Never in all my years had my father admitted he was wrong to me. It made me look at him in a different light.

Taking in a deep breath, I reached out and squeezed his hand.

"It seems we all do stupid things sometimes. Me included."

"What did you do that was dumb?" My father looked to me.

"I let Faelan walk away."

"Och, even I know better than that. Never let the right one walk away. Or in your mother's case, wheel away." My father checked the watch on his wrist. "And in fifteen minutes, I'm going after the love of my life. I hope you'll do the same. Is there anything I can help with?"

"No, I don't think so."

"We'll stay on. Just in case."

"Thanks ... I appreciate that."

We sat back in silence, our eyes on the clock, two vastly different men with fearful and contrite hearts. My father's shocked me. To have changed his position so ... genuinely?

"Love is a gift, and if this Faelan's the one for you, then I'm sorry I tried to get in the way."

To have recanted every vile word he'd said ...

But in that moment, as much as I wanted to process his words and consider what they meant for my future, all I could concentrate on was the need to get to my woman. The woman who so sacrificially healed me, despite the consequences. The woman I loved more than life itself.

I needed her to know what she meant to me, maybe had meant to me from the moment I'd laid eyes on her, and had not had the guts to tell her yet.

CHAPTER TWENTY-FIVE

FAELAN

"The prettiest of all flowers, my sweet Faelan."

"Mum!" I ran across the field to where Eriska stood, her loose dress blowing in the wind. It was a sunny day, rare for Scotland this far into autumn, and my mum's arms were filled with wildflowers.

She was just as I remembered her, a sunshine smile, friendly eyes, but now with hair going slightly gray rioting around her head.

It was then that I understood I must be dreaming.

My mother never aged in my memories.

Yet when I dreamt of her, I somehow aged her up, as though I still needed to keep the same gap of years between us. It was how I kept her living, I supposed, not just through memories but through what I thought she would look in the now.

But her hug felt real.

And I knew, in the deepest corners of my heart, that her love still was real.

Love never went away.

It just *was*. Once there, love just existed. The threads of it entwined in the fabric of the universe, contributing to a greater tapestry of all that is and ever was.

"My love. My heart. Faelan of the flowers. What brings you here? Why do you walk so closely to me?" Eriska's brow creased, and only then did I really take a look around at where we were. Usually when I dreamt of her it was in the fields by our favorite picnic spot. But this ... this was different. Yes, there were flowers, but we were no longer in the field. We stood on the edge of the field, and I realized it was on the edge of a cliff that dropped sharply into nothingness. When I peered over, all I could see was inky night sky, a sea of stars shimmering like sand being tossed in waves, and I gasped.

"Where are we?"

"Oh, my child." The corner of my mum's eyes creased in concern. "I think you know."

I did know. I'd seen it enough times when I was healing a critical patient, hadn't I?

"It's the veil, isn't it? Something's happened." I wracked my brain, but for some reason, standing in this in-between space, I couldn't recall what had led me here. I couldn't remember much of anything, actually, other than the people I loved and the places I'd been.

"Something has happened." Eriska tilted her head, her hands squeezing my shoulders, a look of sympathy on her face. "But I'm certain it's far before your time, my child. I'd read you. This is ... unusual."

"You read me? My death?" My head snapped back as I looked at her in shock.

"Of course. I wanted to know what kind of time you had. I needed to impart as many lessons in you as I could before I left you."

My mother, despite her flightiness and eternal optimism, had always had a deeply pragmatic streak. Her brow furrowed as she looked me up and down.

"You're wounded."

"Everything hurts." Even now, in this space of in-between, I could feel the pain that wracked my physical body.

"Was it a healing? Did you not divert?" Worry filled her face and her hands tightened on my shoulders.

"I ... I," I tried to remember what had happened. All I knew was it was horrific. Something atrocious had happened. "I don't know. It was bad."

"Oh Faelan, my love, you need to go back. It isn't your time yet." Eriska nudged me away from the cliff's edge, turning me back toward the field of flowers. "Come, walk with me for a while."

If it meant that I could have more time with her, I would. With one glance back at the sea of stars, lapping gently against the base of the cliff, I walked alongside my mother.

"Tell me of this man. You're in love, I can feel it."

"Can you?" I angled my head to look at her. I knew, had known, her presence was near, but I hadn't known how much she could see or feel about my life. Or if I was all just imagining it in my head to bring myself comfort.

"I can. I don't get to visit as often as I'd like, but I did see him once. He's a doctor, no?"

"He is. A good one at that." My stomach twisted, and memories slammed back into me so hard, that I tripped and my mother caught me, righting me. "He's ... Wulver. Oh my God. He's a Wulver."

"A ... no." Eriska brought a hand to her mouth in shock. "That's, well, that's incredible, isn't it, honey? I mean, we always thought they were the stuff of legends. But they exist, do they? Fascinating, really."

"Fascinating?" I hiccupped a sob. "Fascinating is all you can say? What about the fact that the man I love turned into a werewolf before my eyes and didn't think to bring it up? Like, oh, hey, by the way, I get a little furry around the full moon?"

"I could see where that might be a difficult conversation to have with someone." My mum kept her arm hooked through mine. "Maybe he just needed time?"

"Well, he ran out of it, didn't he? A Kelpie attacked. He protected me, in Wulver form. And I didn't divert."

"Oh, oh no." Eriska whirled, her hands to my face. "Darling, we need to fix this."

"Did you know?" I asked, ignoring her point about fixing this. "About the Order? That I had a connection in Loren Brae?"

"Of course." Eriska beamed at me. "Why do you think I made sure you saw the advertisement for the practice for sale?"

"That was you?" I thought back to the number of times the ad for the vet practice had crossed my path.

"Aye, it was. Your great, great, grandmother was a healer there. One of the few places we stayed for a long time. I always wanted to get back there, but life led me elsewhere."

"You didn't tell me, though. Not much about it. That would have helped." Frustration twisted low in my gut. All those years of feeling alone …

"Everything comes in its own time, my sweet girl. And now? *Now* is the time for healing."

"How? I'm here," I said, annoyance lacing my voice. I was frustrated. Angry with Luch for hiding from me, and at myself for losing my focus during an intense healing session.

"Well, here is a good place to be." Eriska smiled at me, her eyes full of love. "I know I was never one for many gifts, as I didn't have much to give, but let me give you this, my love."

"What?"

"Come, sit with me, one last time."

"Last time? Won't I see you again?" I asked, confused, as I dropped to the ground with her, nestling among the tall wildflowers, their petals fluttering gently around us in the breeze.

"You will, here and there, in your dreams, and I'll always live in your memory. But like this? This is special. So let me give you a gift."

"Wait, maybe I don't want it. Maybe I want to stay here with you." Tears filled my eyes, and stubbornness took over. Life with my mum had been far from perfect, but at least I'd known I was loved.

"You can't, my darling child. The only truth in life is that nothing ever stays the same. All we can do is linger in moments, celebrating them for what they are, and learn to move forward with grace."

"I don't know what moving forward looks like. Not from here. Not with him." I gestured to myself, harsh bruises standing out on my arms.

"That's what makes it even scarier. But just because you can't see the way doesn't mean you shouldn't take the first step. So let's do it, here and now, together."

"But what if it's not the right choice? What if he's not the right choice?" I scrambled to keep asking her questions, to linger here in this moment with her.

"Do you love him?"

"I do." The truth of it sat there, hanging in the air between us, and Eriska's smile widened.

"Then you'll figure it out. Love always finds a way, Faelan of the flowers. And how exciting! My baby girl has finally found love. With a most unusual and exciting partner. You'll never have a dull moment, the two of you. I think you need to give this a chance."

"He hurt me," I whispered, blinking back tears as the image of my mother began to blur, the dream state I was in starting to slip away.

"And he likely will again. Loving someone doesn't mean they'll never hurt you. We're all human after all." Eriska laughed and shook her head. "Well, mostly human."

"I ..."

"Wheesht, Faelan, our time fades. Let me help." Eriska squeezed my hands. "Look at me."

I did, my love for her on my face, and she smiled. "Repeat after me."

I nodded.

"WHAT I TOOK, I took in care,
    But pain not mine, I cannot bear.
    By root and river, flame and mist,
    I break the hold of pain's dark fist.

THROUGH SKIN AND SOUL, I set it free,
    Return it now to earth and sea.
    With love I heal, with love I part,
    Let light reclaim my weary heart.

AS MOONLIGHT FADES and sunbeams rise,
    I call the peace behind all skies.
    Sprites of Wind and Mothers of Stone,
    Guide this hurt to be dethroned."

AT THE FINAL WORD, the wind picked up, and a tornado of flower petals swirled around me and when I blinked my eyes open, white ceiling tiles greeted me. The steady beep of a heart monitor told me where I was, and I shifted, turning my head to see a woman in a wheelchair by my bed.

"Ah, there she is. Welcome back, Faelan. We haven't met yet, but I'm Leslie, Luch's mum."

"Is he?" I couldn't bring myself to say the words.

"He's just fine and chomping at the bit to speak with you. I only sent him away because he hasn't eaten in a day now."

"A day?" I croaked. My throat was dry, and I had a powerful thirst.

"You've been out for two now, since the accident." Leslie wheeled forward and picked up a cup with a straw and leaned toward me. Turning my head, I took the straw and sucked, my eyebrows winging up as I realized the concoction was an iced version of my special healing tea.

"Iced tea?"

"Any type of your tea we could get into you, we tried. Luch insisted. He's quite rabid for you, I'll admit." A melancholy smile crossed her face. "And I'm happy for it, even though I know it means he won't be coming home."

"He won't?" I shifted, testing my limbs, surprised to feel the pain had disappeared.

Eriska. She'd done this.

Sending up a silent "thank you" to her, I scooted up the bed so I could sit up and take a proper look at Luch's mum. She was a tiny thing, but pretty as could be, with kind eyes and a warm smile.

"I know a man in love when I see one. And if he's anything like his father, he'll never leave your side."

"He did though. He walked away. The other night."

"So I hear. And I think he knows he screwed up. What can I say, Faelan? I can do my best, but they're still men. Bound to screw up once in a while." Leslie laughed. "I hope you can bring yourself to forgive him."

"I don't want to hold on to grudges." I remembered

Eriska's words about moving forward with grace. "I healed him because I couldn't imagine a future without him. It would seem silly to hold on to something so small in the face of that."

"Sure, and it's a relief to be hearing you say that," Luch said from where he stood in the doorway, and my eyes whipped to his. My heartbeat escalated. "Though you'll still be getting a proper apology from me."

"Luch," I whispered, relief filling me. He was alive. And healthy. He wore a loose pair of scrubs and there was color in his skin. I wanted to run into his arms and cuddle against his chest.

"And before he does that, I also owe you an apology." To my shock, Luch's dad pushed him lightly aside and strode to the bed. He glanced at the monitors beside me, reading them, and then gave me a quick nod. "Vitals look good."

"Thanks," I said, looking at the man who almost killed me.

"It has come to my attention that I'm a stubborn arse, and have a blind spot for certain things, which has led me to cause serious issues for those I love. I'm sorry I insulted you, by offering to pay you off."

"You what?" Leslie exclaimed.

"And I'm sorry that I didn't trust you to heal Luch. You saved my boy, and for that I owe you a debt. Anything you need—ever—and I will give it to you."

"Thank you," I said, understanding how difficult apologizing was for a man like Richard.

"Now, I'm going to take my beautiful wife out of here and let her scold me for a while."

"It'll be more than a scolding, Richard Carmichael. What were you thinking? Pay the poor girl off?" Leslie was already berating Richard as he held the door for her, and he hung his head as he followed her out.

"You're right, darling."

"How ... how are you?" Luch came to stand by me, raising and then lowering his hands awkwardly as though he didn't know what to do or say.

"I'm hurt," I said, and Luch snapped to attention.

"What do you need? Should I call Lynn? Where does it hurt?"

"Here." I tapped my heart.

"Oh." Luch's face fell. "My father's the heart surgeon."

"I think I know what will help."

"What's that?" Luch's eyes were wary, his face heavy with sadness.

"A hug." I patted the bed next to me.

"Can I? Are you sure?"

"I'm sure." I scooted so that Luch could crawl in, and he lifted me easily, maneuvering me until I was cradled against his chest, and when I heard his steady heartbeat beneath my ear, the tears came.

"Och, don't. I'll never forgive myself if you cry, Faelan."

"Happy tears," I gulped out. "I promise."

"I haven't slept. Two days you've been out, and nothing was bringing you back. I tried the tea. Everyone was here. Sophie, Lia, Shona ... the whole lot of them. Did you know they're all magick too? We had every type of healer and healing things we could find in here. And nothing helped."

"It all helped. I just needed one last healer. My mum."

"You saw her?" Luch sucked in a breath, and I tilted my head to look up at him.

"Aye. I was on the edge, between the worlds, and she brought me back."

"That's … terrifying. Just to think how close you were. I almost lost you." Luch's voice rumbled in his chest and his arms tightened around me. "Before I could even tell you what I was. It was all a mess in my head. I should have trusted you with my secret, Faelan. You gave me yours, I should have told you mine. I'm sorry, I am, for not showing you my world sooner."

"I understand. I don't like it. But I understand."

"Do you?" Luch shifted so he could pull me more tightly against him, and the heartbeat monitor registered an increase in my beats. We both laughed softly.

"I do. Because if I'm being truthful with myself? I'm not sure when I would have told you about healing. Not with what you'd told me about your mum, and especially due to your clear dislike for healers. If I hadn't been tossed into telling you, I might never have said anything. Or waited a good long time before I did."

"You're giving me a lot of grace, Faelan. But I'll take it. I don't ever want to lose you again or give you reason to think you can't trust me."

"Is that it? The last of the secrets?"

"Well, I have two more."

"Two more?" I twisted and pushed myself up on his chest, glaring down at him.

"Aye. The first is … well, I can hear Oban talk to me. In my head."

"Och, that's nothing. I can hear him, and most of the other animals too."

"What? You never told me that!" Luch's mouth dropped open, and I laughed, surprising myself.

"I guess I hadn't. Huh, we do have a few secrets, don't we?"

"I guess we do."

"So what's the second one?" I was already getting sleepy again, the emotional toll of seeing my mum, waking up, and seeing Luch again already making its mark on me.

"The second one is that I love you. I love you so very much, Faelan of the flowers, and I will through all time. Of that much I know. We feel it, you know, us Wulvers." Luch tapped his chest. "We're bound now. I'll always protect you and walk by your side, if you'll have me."

"I will," I said, and smiled against his lips when he came in for a kiss. "And I love you, Dr. Carmichael. And while I dearly love seeing you all sexy in your scrubs, I just don't have the energy for anything else right now."

Luch's laugh rang out across the room.

"Only you would suggest we could get dirty while you have a waiting room full of your friends desperately waiting to see you again."

"I do?" I'd never had friends, or family, who'd wait in the emergency room for me before.

That's when it clicked into place for me.

I'd done it. I'd found a home, friends, and now with Luch? A family.

"You sure do, darling. A lot of people that care deeply about you. Myself included."

"They can wait ... just a little longer, right? I can't seem to work up much energy to do anything more." Already my eyes were fluttering closed, and I snuggled closer into Luch's chest. "Just a little bit more. Just like this."

"Anything for you, my love. Sweet Faelan of the flowers, together we'll walk the fields, mine forever."

Those were the last words before I drifted into a peaceful and pain-free sleep, knowing in my heart of hearts, that I'd finally grown roots and was ready to bloom.

EPILOGUE

Faelan

"Ugh, dogs." Gloam looked at me and peeled off from where we walked toward the castle for a Highland Games event that Lachlan and Graham were hosting for tourists. I'd been told that Sophie had bested Lachlan in a swords match before they'd fallen in love, and I'd been promised a replay of that moment if I came.

Maybe I was also coming because Sophie wanted more photos of hot men in kilts for the castle's marketing campaign, and there was promise of Luch in a kilt tossing a caber about.

It had been over a month since the accident, and Luch had allowed me to watch him change under the full moon. It had been unnerving, even thrilling to watch, as flesh shifted to fur, and body changed to animal. Yet the eyes remained the same, that tawny green gold that I loved so much, and luckily, I found I could still communicate when he was in this form. It was just like talking to Gloam, actually, and I'd gone on a long walk with Luch under the moon, with Gloam keeping his distance while Luch was in wolf form, and it had felt comfortable. Normal, even. Well, normal for me, at least. But my normal didn't have to look like anyone else's normal, did it?

The practice was booming, and I'd been lucky to hire Zara to help me with admin work. She was great with the clients, a whiz at technology, and used her own special computer systems to help her with filing, reading reports, and making calls. Even better, her support dog Mitch came to work with her every day, and we got to educate the community about working dogs and how to treat them when people saw them out in public. At first, Zara hadn't even wanted to get paid for her work, since she'd been so grateful that I'd helped save Mitch, and I was coming to learn she had her own powers. She hadn't shared her magick with me, yet, but I was certain in her own time she'd open up if she felt comfortable. In the meantime, I'd told her about my healing abilities, and she'd taken it in stride.

That was the other thing—though I would always be cautious with whom I told about my abilities, I now had learned a powerful lesson.

It didn't matter anymore who really knew that I could heal with magick.

On a larger scale, it probably did. Like if someone told someone who wanted to, I don't know, maybe make a movie of me or something like that, then yes, it would matter. But to tell a few trusted friends who lived in Loren Brae? I no longer had an issue with that. Because I'd come to realize that I was the one in the power. I owned my own business, I was a full member of the Order of Caledonia, and these women, and their men, had my back. Unquestionably. Nobody could run me out of town anymore.

And if they tried, they'd have to get through an exceptionally scary, extremely strong, wolf.

There was a reason they referred to security as being a blanket, and I now tugged that around my shoulders, the warmth of acceptance from family and friends adding a spring to my step as I neared the castle.

I even walked by the loch on my own now.

After I'd left the hospital and returned home, I'd discovered my scalpel had a third band glittering on its handles. It must have been healing Luch that had sealed the deal, and now I suspected the Kelpies would leave me alone. Or at least, I hoped. Things had been quiet since the attack, and I hoped it would stay that way as we found the other members of the Order.

Sophie was just a touch on edge, as she didn't have a line on the next person yet, and I'd promised to help her pull some threads on leads she'd had on my day off.

But not today.

Today was for ogling hot men in kilts.

Which, really, should be a national holiday as far as I was concerned.

The hedges rustled and I raised a finger.

"Don't even think about it, Clyde."

Clyde shoved his head out, and if a highland coo could pout, he did.

"Listen, if you want to surprise people you can't rustle the branches. I'm sure you'll do better next time."

Clyde threw his head back and bellowed, and I jumped, laughing at myself, before I rounded the final curve to MacAlpine Castle. The expansive garden was filled with people, and several were not wearing shirts.

"Faelan!" Lia waved me over to where the women of the Order all clustered in a group with a whole pack of dogs at their feet, all of them sitting obediently for Hilda who brandished cheese.

"Well, now, the view isn't too bad, is it?" I asked Agnes, who I'd caught staring at Graham. Admittedly, it would be hard to take my eyes off him if I wasn't besotted with another man. Tattoos snaked up his muscular arms, and a dragon writhed down his side, the tail curling low at his washboard abs.

"What? What view?" Agnes snapped to attention and turned to me, a pretty pink flush at her cheeks.

"Ladies." I beamed at Graham as he approached, swinging a sturdy-looking wooden sword in his hands. He stood, all muscles and masculinity, heated eyes on Agnes who looked everywhere but at him. "How's it going then?"

"Och, just fine, Graham. Lovely to see you out from behind the bar. That's a nice tattoo, isn't it then? Is that a dragon from …" I leaned closer to look at it more carefully.

"Falkor," Agnes said, a catch in her voice. "From *The Neverending Story*."

"A symbol of resilience." Graham looked at me, but I had a feeling his words were for Agnes. "Of hope and understanding one's own worth."

"It's a great tattoo," I said, filling the silence that fell after his words. "The artist is brilliant too."

"Who is brilliant?" An arm swung around my shoulders and I turned to smile up at Luch. My mouth dropped open. "Are you making time with my woman, Graham?"

"Obviously." Graham grinned and winked at me, but I was too busy gawking at Luch to be charmed.

The man wore a kilt and a sturdy pair of boots, and seeing him like that made me want to drag him into the trees and ...

Luch brushed a finger down my cheek, his eyes heating at my look.

"No time for that, darling. I'm up next."

"Are you?" I said, woefully, and Luch laughed. Grabbing me close, he dipped me for a heady kiss, and everyone around us cheered.

"Hold it, hold it, yes, that's it, perfect." When I came up for air, I found a delighted Sophie with a camera in hand. "Now Agnes and Graham. Och, go on, don't give me that look. Just get together and look normal. It's for my socials."

"Since when are you an influencer—" Agnes's words were cut off when Graham stalked closer, wrapped an arm around her waist and dipped her low, before claiming her mouth in a steamy kiss.

Her hand came up to his chest and ... lingered ... instead of pushing him away.

Everyone cheered, just as they had when Luch had kissed me, and when Graham pulled Agnes back up, he held her close for a moment, whispering something in her ear.

When he pulled back, her face was crimson, and he had a steely look of determination in his eyes.

"All right, mate, let's do this," Graham said, and then he stomped off to the field. I gaped as Luch followed, and they both stopped by a set of cabers, each heavier than the last.

Luch squatted and the women drew around me as he lifted the huge trunk, balancing it in his arms.

"I'd let him carry my tree any day," Hilda sighed, and we all hooted with laughter.

"Back off, woman, this one's mine."

It warmed me to say it, and I almost did a wee dance in place, so gleeful was I that I'd finally found a place I belonged. *And the incredibly handsome, strong man, who loved me to bits didn't hurt either.*

"That's fine then. So long as none of you take a shine to mine." We all turned as Archie strode across the garden, shirtless in a kilt, and despite his years, he was equally as handsome as the rest of the men out there.

"I mean, we'd be hard pressed not to, but none of us want to fight you for him," Sophie said. "I heard you're mean as a cat backed into a corner in a fight."

"And don't you be forgetting it, lass," Hilda said, blowing Archie a kiss across the field.

To our complete delight, he caught it and pressed his palms to his lips.

"Let me tell you, ladies, he may be all bark, but sometimes, he's just the right amount of bite."

"Gross, Hilda!" We whirled to find Lachlan, shirtless, with an appalled look on his face.

"Och, I've had to hear enough out of you two, haven't I?"

We all laughed again as Sophie dragged Lachlan away, her shoulders shaking with laughter, and I crossed my arms over my chest, truly content.

Who would have thought that buying Loren Brae's vet practice would have been the best thing that I'd ever done for myself? Eriska was right. The only constant in life was change, so all I could do was linger in the moment and soak up every ounce of joy that I could.

When Luch finally dropped the caber, I shot my arms up and cheered.

"That's my man! Love you, baby."

"Love, is it?" Agnes leaned into my ear.

"Oh yeah. It is. A thousand times over."

"That's nice to hear, Faelan. You deserve happiness."

I turned to look at her and then back out at Graham.

"And so do you."

"You know what, maybe I do, Faelan. Maybe I just do."

HAVE you fallen in love with how sweet Luch is? Download this sweet surprise birthday bonus scene!

Join my mailing list and download the free bonus scene here - triciaomalley.com/free

Fancy a wee drink and some grub in your favorite Loren Brae pub? The Tipsy Thistle has its own line of merchandise! Shop here - triciaomalley.myshopify.com

SNEAK PEEK - WILD SCOTTISH MAGIC

The tension is ramping up in Loren Brae. Will the newest member of the Order of Caledonia be ready to join? Be sure to order today.

LIORA

"The Heartbreak Witch?" Zara screeched through the phone at me, and I collapsed back against my scratchy hotel pillow. Covering my face with one of my hands, even though Zara couldn't see me, I tried to push back the panic that was wrapping its ropes around my chest.

"I know, Z. I knooooow." Humiliation washed over me, my skin flushing with the heat of it.

"How did this even happen? You're viral? On *witchtok* of all things?" My older sister, Zara, was almost blind, far better at magic than me, and had Her Life Together. With capital letters, like that. She'd just taken a job at the local vet's office in small town Loren Brae—a town I'd briefly lived in and run away from—but Zara had insisted on moving back there despite my reputation. In her words, she was there to "un-sully" our name.

I'd left Loren Brae after a particularly chaotic magickal disaster, determined to never look back, and now I feared I had no choice but to return.

"Everyone is talking about you," Zara hissed, and I winced.

"I … I know. Or so I heard before I logged off of witch-tok. And every other social media app that I have."

"I thought you weren't going to do readings anymore." Zara's voice held more sympathy than censure, and that somehow stung even worse.

She knew, more than anyone else, how much I hated with every ounce of my being that I couldn't seem to make my magick work. Not like hers, at least.

Maybe the internet was right—it was time for me to hang up my hat, so to speak—and finally admit the one truth that I'd been avoiding for a very long time.

I was an absolute shite astrologer.

Even thinking it made my gut churn in pain, because somehow, somewhere, along the way I'd become convinced that astrology was where my magick was meant to manifest. I loved it. And it loved me, I was certain of it, but something hadn't quite clicked yet for me. At least to make accurate predictions, that is.

I'd spent endless hours poring over charts, reading astrology books, researching astrocartography and other iterations of astrology, and still … somehow I managed to land myself in hot water.

"But she was so excited, and she was offering so much money," I said, groaning as I tugged at my mousy brown hair. "Rent was due. I swear, Z, I've been working really hard. I know astrology inside and out. It's not my fault that the prediction came out the way that it did."

"You ..." Zara took a deep breath before continuing. "You told the girlfriend of one of the most popular rugby players in the world that he wasn't her soulmate and she was destined for unhappiness."

"I would never!" I sat up, outraged. "That's an exaggeration. I swear people don't listen when I tell them what I see."

"Liora." This time it was a sigh of resignation, and my shoulders hunched. "Astrology is meant to be used to look for personal traits or forecast good times in the year ahead to make a move or start a new job. You know, to look at when the planets are favorable to take action. You can't predict a love match from astrology."

"I mean, you can see if someone is a good match or not based on their birth chart," I mumbled.

Zara sighed, again, and I pinched my nose. A horn sounded outside, and shouts carried through the grimy window of the only hotel I could afford to stay at after I hadn't been able to make rent and my roommates had ousted me from our tiny flat in Glasgow.

"Even so, it doesn't determine love. You know that, Liora. People can be horrific matches but still decide to work it out. To figure out a way to love. It's not on you to predict the outcome of a love match for someone. When will you learn? I thought after ..." Zara trailed off.

My stomach roiled. I knew what she was referring to.

The entire reason I'd left Loren Brae and had thought I'd never look back.

I'd been young. Convinced I knew the way of things.

And I'd given an impassioned reading, certain I was in the right of it, and had ruined a relationship with the blame landing squarely on my shoulders. It had been the talk of Loren Brae for months.

"In fairness, it's not my fault she ran back to her boyfriend and told him he wasn't her soulmate," I said, pulling my thoughts away from memories past. "I never said that."

"What, exactly, did you tell this WAG?" Zara asked, referring to the term for wives and girlfriends of sports stars in the UK.

"I told her, that based on her chart, it looked like she might be destined for more than one great love in her life."

Zara gasped. "Liora, you didn't."

"It was true though."

"But you can't say that to someone who is head over heels for her boyfriend. They've had a big row now. Broken up over this."

"Well, in theory, wouldn't that make me right?" I pulled my stubbornness around me like a cloak. I hadn't been wrong in my reading. "If they were so much in love and perfect for each other, an astrology reading shouldn't have been able to tear them apart, right?"

"Be that as it may ... it's landed you in hot water, again, and without a place to live from what I can gather?"

I glanced to the pile of luggage in the corner of the room. It wasn't much, but it was mine.

Tears welled.

"Aye," I said, defeat filling me.

"Come home, Liora. We'll sort it out. It might do you

some good to take a break from this and focus on what you really want out of life."

I gulped back a sob. It wouldn't do to cry to Zara. She'd always had such a clear vision of who she was and what she wanted out of life, while I'd clung to astrology because it was what I loved. But it appeared that it didn't love me back. Maybe it was time to admit defeat, and set my sights on becoming employable in a different profession.

"I can't—"

"You can. I'm delighted to be back in Loren Brae. And you will be too. Things have changed, Liora. It's a good place to land, at least for a little while. Come back. Mitch misses you." I grinned as Mitch, her guide dog, barked in the background when he heard his name.

"I …" I looked around the tiny hotel room, largely taken up by my luggage, and sighed. "Okay, Z. I'll take some time off. I'll come back to Loren Brae."

Be the first to enjoy this delightful addition to the Enchanted Highlands series. Order Wild Scottish Magic today!

AFTERWORD

I always love being back in Loren Brae, and this story was loads of fun to write as it wasn't a typical "shifter" style novel, but I still wanted to incorporate some of the interesting myths that Scotland is famous for. I so enjoyed reading about the Wulver myth and how it was seen as a kindred protector, instead of a terrifying alpha shifter.

A huge thanks to Zein and her guide dog, Mitch, for reviewing the scenes with a guide dog to make sure I had an accurate depiction of the commands used. Zein is a huge advocate for guide dog awareness in Scotland, as many people are not aware how dangerous it can be to interrupt a working dog that is helping a visually impaired or blind person navigate. Just a note–it's best to always be respectful of a working dog (or any animal, really!)–as the owner will let you know when the correct time to approach is.

Thank you to the Scotsman and his family for tirelessly answering all of my very random and specific questions about very random and specific language usage in Scotland. You all really help my books to shine!

As you're reading this, we've started our next chapter in life – The Scotsman and I are off to travel the world as "slowmads" for a few years. Be sure to follow along on my newsletter or socials as we explore. I guarantee there will be much inspiration to be found from our travels!

Sparkle on,

Tricia O'Malley

Looking for the perfect magical read to cozy up with? You'll fall in love with this Charmed meets Outlander mash-up, where Sloane MacGregor and her sisters return to Briarhaven to break a curse, only to find love waiting for them instead.

Love's a Witch
AVAILABLE NOW

USA

UK

ALSO BY TRICIA O'MALLEY

THE ISLE OF DESTINY SERIES

Stone Song

Sword Song

Spear Song

Sphere Song

———

A completed series in Kindle Unlimited.

Available in audio, e-book & paperback!

"Love this series. I will read this multiple times. Keeps you on the edge of your seat. It has action, excitement and romance all in one series."

- Amazon Review

THE ENCHANTED HIGHLANDS

Wild Scottish Knight

Wild Scottish Love

A Kilt for Christmas

Wild Scottish Rose

Wild Scottish Beauty

Wild Scottish Fortune

Wild Scottish Gold

Wild Scottish Charm

Wild Scottish Magic

"I love everything Tricia O'Malley has ever written and Wild Scottish Knight is no exception. The new setting for this magical journey is Scotland, the home of her new husband and soulmate. Tricia's love for her husband's country shows in every word she writes. I have always wanted to visit Scotland but have never had the time and money. Having read Wild Scottish Knight I feel I have begun to to experience Scotland in a way few see it."

-Amazon Review

Available in audio, e-book, hardback, paperback and Kindle Unlimited.

THE SIREN ISLAND SERIES

Good Girl

Up to No Good

A Good Chance

Good Moon Rising

Too Good to Be True

A Good Soul

In Good Time

A completed series in Kindle Unlimited.

Available in audio, e-book & paperback!

"Love her books and was excited for a totally new and different one! Once again, she did NOT disappoint! Magical in multiple ways and on multiple levels. Her writing style, while similar to that of Nora Roberts, kicks it up a notch!! I want to visit that island, stay in the B&B and meet the gals who run it! The characters are THAT real!!!" - Amazon Review

THE ALTHEA ROSE SERIES

One Tequila

Tequila for Two

Tequila Will Kill Ya (Novella)

Three Tequilas

Tequila Shots & Valentine Knots (Novella)

Tequila Four

A Fifth of Tequila

A Sixer of Tequila

Seven Deadly Tequilas

Eight Ways to Tequila

Tequila for Christmas (Novella)

———

"Not my usual genre but couldn't resist the Florida Keys setting. I was hooked from the first page. A fun read with just the right amount of crazy! Will definitely follow this series."- Amazon Review

A completed series in Kindle Unlimited.

Available in audio, e-book & paperback!

THE MYSTIC COVE SERIES

Wild Irish Heart

Wild Irish Eyes

Wild Irish Soul

Wild Irish Rebel

Wild Irish Roots: Margaret & Sean

Wild Irish Witch

Wild Irish Grace

Wild Irish Dreamer

Wild Irish Christmas (Novella)

Wild Irish Sage

Wild Irish Renegade

Wild Irish Moon

"I have read thousands of books and a fair percentage have been romances. Until I read Wild Irish Heart, I never had a book actually make me believe in love."- Amazon Review

A completed series in Kindle Unlimited.

Available in audio, e-book & paperback!

STAND ALONE NOVELS

Love's a Witch

She's got runaway magic. He's got a town to protect. Too bad fate has other plans.

Highland Hearts Holiday Bookshop

As Christmas looms, and lonely hearts beg for love, I'm tossed into the world of magic and romance, aided by a meddling book club who seems more interested in romance than reading.

Ms. Bitch

"Ms. Bitch is sunshine in a book! An uplifting story of fighting your way through heartbreak and making your own version of happily-ever-after."

~Ann Charles, USA Today Bestselling Author

Starting Over Scottish

Grumpy. Meet Sunshine.

She's American. He's Scottish. She's looking for a fresh start. He's returning to rediscover his roots.

One Way Ticket

A funny and captivating beach read where booking a one-way ticket to paradise means starting over, letting go, and taking a chance on love...one more time

10 out of 10 - The BookLife Prize

CONTACT ME

I hope my books have added a little magick into your life. If you have a moment to add some to my day, you can help by telling your friends and leaving a review. Word-of-mouth is the most powerful way to share my stories. Thank you.

Love books? What about fun giveaways? Nope? Okay, can I entice you with underwater photos and cute dogs? Let's stay friends! Sign up for my newsletter and contact me at my website.

www.triciaomalley.com

Or find me on Facebook and Instagram.
@triciaomalleyauthor